Secret Words

BOOKS BY
JONATHAN STRONG

Tike and Five Stories
Ourselves
Elsewhere
Companion Pieces

Secret Words

a novel by

JONATHAN STRONG

For Betsy
Hope to see you soon!
Love, Jonathan

Z
ZOLAND BOOKS
Cambridge, Massachusetts

First edition published in 1992 by
Zoland Books, Inc.,
384 Huron Avenue, Cambridge, MA 02138

Library of Congress Catalog Card Number
91-66473

ISBN 0-944072-19-4

First edition
Printed in the United States of America

Text design by Boskydel Studio

Library of Congress Cataloging-in-Publication Data

Strong, Jonathan.
 Secret words : a novel / by Jonathan Strong. —1st ed.
 p. cm.
 ISBN 0-944072-19-4 : $18.95
 I. Title.
PS3569.T698S4 1992
813'.54—dc20   91-66473
                                                      CIP

for my sister

Secret Words

Stinted Common

I

Mothers don't hurt children, then who does? When I'm at work it makes me wonder. They're dragging them in and they're all crying, mothers too. I talk to them in a calm way, I tell them to have a seat. There's not enough seats in the place but someone will get up and someone will take that seat and then someone else will come in and someone else will go. I keep a calm smile on for all of them. Being overweight helps to be a receptionist because these mothers like coming up to you not feeling you're in high heels and makeup making them feel worn out and slow by comparison. But these mothers will hit their kid right before my eyes if the kid is making too much noise in the waiting room and doesn't sit down or because her two kids are fighting each other.

My nephew Stephen gets hit and we know about that, his father taking it out on him every night even now he's about graduating high school. So many times it's the fathers hurting the children but I know it's not just that.

There's something going on that I don't understand. Yesterday when a mother I never saw before comes in streaming tears down her cheeks, long black hair, she reaches over my hand on the appointment book and squeezes and squeezes. Let me see somebody, let me see somebody, she's saying. I know we're full up for a couple weeks, not even a ten-minute slot since they cut our third counselor with the new budget. I don't know what to do but with somebody squeezing you it makes you feel it more so I say have a seat by me, there was one, and since all the kids in the room were yelling no one heard me talking to her. I pretended we had a slot and waited to see if maybe somebody didn't show which certainly does happen.

I took her information but instead of just the numbers I start asking things I shouldn't and the tears keep streaming. She lives in the same project my sister does. She has one kid, she's married to this man who doesn't know what's going on. She's seeing somebody else and she can't help it. It was all in her way of telling me it. I get this way, she says, I have to see him, I can't stop, I even lock in my own kid so's I can go out to him. What kinda mother's that! Her hand is squeezing my other hand now and her whole arm from her fingers is twitching like it has something in it and only her shoulder and her wrist are stopping it from flying away. Her other arm down by her side also is twitching and she's holding the chair leg to try to stop it. And it's partly from her crying or something inside her stomach almost that makes her whole front gulp in and out under her loose dress. I dream about him all the time, she's saying, and I'm going to say his name out loud in the night to my husband, I know I'm going to. Her voice is like a sharp whisper I can hear through all the kids yelling. You don't have anything to give me, do you! she says almost angry at me, not crying at all suddenly. I feel her nails on that squeezing hand and she whispers leaning close in my face: You wouldn't know how it is wanting a man like that. She tosses my hand back on the appointment book and walks to the door with her long hair swinging on her back, yelling how no one can ever help her here or anywhere.

That Mrs. Velis looks over at me with Jack on her shoulder and says, How do you put up with these types coming in here, Barbara? And I'm thinking Jack only gets his treatment in private. I seen it in Mrs. Velis's folder and it's got me wondering again. Then I went and wrote it with a marker on the corner of the bus stop shelter waiting after work. I didn't know I was writing it almost: Mothers don't hurt children, then who does? I wrote it small with my mind just drifting when no one else was waiting there. It was from having the marker in my pocket instead of remembering to put it back in my desk drawer.

My brother-in-law does things to Stephen still though you wouldn't know to look at Stephen with his blow-dry haircut and designers and even though he's skinny he's tall now. Ever since I'm working at the Center my sister Catherine figures she can tell me about it now but before I'd just hear it through Ma who didn't have much of an idea, only her suspicions. But my sister won't come to the Center herself, as many times as I ask her to. William her husband comes home after stopping off for a beer but he's not one of those abusers who gets drunk to do it, he just has enough to take the edge off him. Then he's relaxed. He thinks it's funny giving Stephen a few cuffs when he comes in late from school. William doesn't get really mad at him, says Catherine always, that's what makes it harder though, she doesn't know when to make him stop. He pounds the kid on the arm to see how much he'll take. He calls Stephen everything you can think of but it's like a fun contest thinking up the worst thing to call your kid. Catherine sometimes sends Stephen over to Ma's so he can get some homework done. He likes sitting in the living room with me and flipping through Pa's magazines but it's hard getting Stephen to talk even when it's not about why he's come over.

When I think about him and my brother-in-law William or about Mrs. Velis and her Jack or that woman who was squeezing my hand, what I'm afraid of is if I could do those sort of things to anyone myself.

II

What that woman whispered at me isn't true though probably Ma would believe it about me. But maybe I just think about being with a man in different ways, I think about it like a fantasy and it's not going to be that sort of man I actually ever am with probably. Maybe I think about the very handsome types even more because I know I won't even come near them, where someone like Catherine goes for a William who's good looking enough but not particularly.

Then there's that Paul Felice who lives downstairs from me in front and he's someone I don't know what I think about. He's polite in the dark front hall getting the mail. He's chubby and what's more, which is the thing, he's black. He's from Saint something in the West Indies. The stamps on his mail have little Queen Elizabeths on them. When I was moving in he helped carry a few boxes though my brothers didn't think we needed any extra help. It wasn't easy my moving out of home ten years later than I should've first done it and my brothers coming to help me and me meeting this first person in my own new building, this chubby black man. He's obviously the educated type with a sort of English accent so you'd think he'd rather be living in a different area like nearer to some college.

My brothers Peter and Gregory would never act unfriendly to a black man. Gregory's even friends with that black family on his street and their kids play. But then my oldest brother Peter was kidding me last night at Ma's: So how's your black boyfriend, Barbara? Pa didn't even look up but Ma says, What's he talking about? I know he could be yours for the asking, says Peter. Barbara wouldn't want any black boyfriend and you know it, Ma says to me as much as Peter. And this Paul's not handsome in my eyes at all but I can just hear his voice, all the words he takes saying the simplest thing. Yesterday morning going to work I wrote on the corner of the shelter of my bus stop but on purpose one of his sentences which he said on my way out the door: It's not likely to be a terribly pleasant day I fear.

III

It takes getting used to. First being at the doughnut shop for years ever since I started working nights there in high school then my first job as receptionist was for two years at the Stinted Common Animal Clinic but that didn't give me an idea what this Center would be like. People with their dogs in a waiting room are on their best behavior. They want you to think they're kind to animals and they've got their dog under control which they certainly don't always. You never see them yell in the waiting room, they keep it under their breath. So the Center was different but I liked it. Ma was glad for me even if it gave me the money to move out from home finally. She knows that's better too.

I don't miss them at home because it's not far and I see them as much as I want. But seeing Peter and his kids, just to drop in on them in the house next door, I don't do that as easy now. His are the kids I like best. Catherine's only got Stephen and he's not sociable anyways and Gregory's kids are growing up in a different kind of neighborhood. But with Peter's kids it's like seeing again how the street was when we four were growing up ourselves.

Yesterday when I was going over for a meal to Ma's that old crab Marjorie in the other half of Ma's house peeks out her door and tells me: Pick your head up. She's been telling me how I'm slumping ever since I was in school. I have other things to think about, I tell her. Her side of the steps are light brown and ours are dark brown which makes me think how all these years Ma and Pa never did get together with Marjorie on anything. There's that careful line down the steps measured off by Marjorie exactly, I bet. When Peter's girls and their friends go sit on Ma's steps, because they're wider than Peter's, Marjorie comes out and tells them to toss their cigarette butts only on Ma's side. We'll put our butts where we want, Ursula says to her once and it went around the kids as being the best comeback of the week. They love telling each other what each of them says and does. It brings things back for me listening to them yapping.

Ma was on the phone to Catherine when I came in last night, the same old thing. He shouldn't still be with you at home, says Ma. Then: Well that's your William, she says, so you just tell Stephen to get a bus over tonight, tell him Barbara's here. Ma hardly looks at me, just waves. And then what when he graduates? she's saying into the phone leaning in the kitchen doorway.

I sit down in the living room near Pa reading in his recliner. Later I hear Peter's two oldest coming up their steps and I peek out the curtain and there they are, Ursula and Celia and some of their friends, tossing popsicle wrappers out on the sidewalk. He is not! Celia's saying and some other girl, not Ursula, comes back with: All you got to do is look at him, Celia!

The back door bangs and there's little Julia asking Ma for cookies. I suppose you smelled something, says Ma. There's another sheet in the oven too so take the cool ones, Ma tells her. Bring me one, Julia, Pa says. Julia brings a plate in but I'm myself off snacks. Let me see what you brought, says Pa, hmmm, this one looks like a lumpy old toad. Julia's already gathering in crumbs around her mouth. And this one, says Pa, looks like, and he tweaks her, your nose! Julia squirms away and runs for the kitchen. Pa's good at playing with her still but it stops always when they get older. He doesn't play with teen-agers.

Then she comes charging back in and flops in front of me on the furry rug and sprawls her arms back messing my skirt. I can see the skin on my fat legs bunching up so I flatten out the plaid. Can I squeeze the part behind your knees? says Julia, the thing I can't stand for her to do. I'll terrorize you, I say being as mean as I can. So she goes limp with her head back on my lap and stares at the ceiling. That's when I find myself thinking about something else as if this eleven-year-old niece of mine was floating some-how there across my lap, as if I was floating myself: Steps, stairs, Paul is downstairs, Paul is downstairs, him and his stares. It comes to me like a song.

Later I'm helping Ma in the kitchen and Julia pops out the back door and swings herself around the post at the bottom of the railing. I watch out the window while the light fades fast. Her brother Lucius is back behind Peter's house bouncing a ball off their back wall. Ma blinks each time it goes whop. I go up on tiptoe with my tummy into the counter edge and watch him out the side window. Lucius hasn't got much to do. What's he going to do when summer comes besides baseball? The older girls will work and there's the two little ones but in the middle Lucius is just the wrong age for most things.

I hear Peter's van. The girls and their friends on the front steps keep yapping but I hear Celia say Hi Dad when he's halfway down between the houses. I see him crouching up to the corner to jump out at Lucius. Dad, you want me to take a heart attack? Lucius yells. Whip me that ball, fella, says Peter but Lucius keeps bouncing his ball off the back wall a couple times more till he's got Peter off guard then he whips it at him. I miss watching all this at my new apartment.

Stephen'll be here soon and then you can relax, I hear Ma say to Pa who hasn't come out from his magazine since he ate the cookies. Most of their talking they do from different rooms. They don't usually look at each other or even hear each other, just her clanking things in the kitchen and him sneezing in his recliner, but they can feel each other.

When Stephen's there he taps so lightly Ma and Pa wouldn't have heard so I go. I see fluffy black hair in the little window in the door and know it's him from the way his head bends forward. Here for supper? I say. He just nods coming in. Ma, it's Stephen, I say. Hi Gramp, says Stephen. My boy, Pa says. Lots of homework as usual, says Stephen finding a magazine. I set the table for Ma and watch him out the corner of my eye sitting on the edge of the sofa turning pages. There's a color picture of the Pope with his hawk eye and there's what's-her-name Mrs. Thatcher with her pearls and he turns the page and there's Sylvester Stallone suddenly.

Take your bag up to Barbara's old room, Stephen, and wash up, says Ma. Is he spending the night? I whisper to her. She looks at me like something's really serious and not to ask any more.

I V

For a week Stephen's been spending all his nights. I'm going back over for meals more than I should really. If I stayed around my own new place I might invite that Paul Felice for supper or maybe just in for a snack. Paul's always carrying an old briefcase and he wears an old overcoat he probably got at the Goodwill when he came up from the West Indies and saw how cold it got here. He'll even wear it on a nice spring day.

There's plenty of blacks coming to the Center now but not as many as over the East Center since they're moving in that neighborhood more, according to Mrs. Velis. The blacks here around Autumn Hill and in the project mostly speak French or come from Cape Verde. I tell Ma she has to look at it the way it was when Nonna came here in the first place. Pa says her English was only a few words and his father didn't speak any, just sang his opera songs doing his gardening. They had the same troubles and the Irish hated them so what's the difference? I even tell her they're Catholics, these blacks around here. But the ones down in East aren't Catholics, she says, they're Abyssinians, they been over here longer than any of us and look at

them still! Well look at Gregory, I say, making friends with
those black neighbors of his, the Bartlettes. But that's out
the western end, she says, what do you expect with the
college types moving in there now.

Gregory himself didn't go to one of the big-name colleges. He went over to the old Boston State that's folded. In
high school he was hoping he'd get a scholarship at least to
one of the bigger-name ones around the Boston area,
maybe not Tufts or Harvard but somewhere. He didn't
though. Back in high school Gregory looked sharp, sort of
a slick dresser even sometimes with Italian-style shirts.
He got over his fat stage earlier but we were both the two
fatties when we were little kids. Peter played too much
sports to be fat and Catherine was the skinny one from the
start. They get fatter as they get younger was Pa's way of
explaining us four.

Since I'm off snacks now it's not snacking keeps my
weight up, it's how I keep myself always calm, I think.
Paul said something in the front hall yesterday when I was
walking out and didn't have anything I could think to say
to him: You seem like a rather meditative person, I'm
rather that way myself, he says. I have to keep writing
down those sentences that come out of his big lips. I look
at his lips every time and they seem kissable somehow to
me. Who'd ever think when all I go for on TV is the Clint
Eastwood type? Something keeps moving inside my stomach when I see Paul in the hall. I'm rather that way myself
keeps going in my head.

And the blacks at the Center make me look at them
more close now. When Mrs. Figueroa comes up to the desk
I look at her skin. She's probably half-Spanish and it's hard
to tell how black she is but Mrs. Guimond from Haiti's as
black as they get. They like talking to me the same way

Mrs. Velis or Annie Randall does about clothes and kids. I read in one of Pa's magazines this article he showed me saying overweight people inspire confidence, you're not afraid they're going to beat you out so you can relax around them. All Pa's reading does is give him little ideas like this to tell you about but it's what he likes to do being retired.

Yesterday was baseball night for Peter's boys. I had an early supper over there with them all in their little kitchen. They were already at the table, the three girls on the wall seat and Peter keeping the boys separate on the chairs. My sister-in-law Camilla's dishing up spaghetti from the end seat so I squeeze on the corner between her and Quintus, her youngest, with his baseball cap on all ready to go. I wish everything in her kitchen wasn't so pink, it doesn't go so good with the food.

Lucius, pass your plate, says Camilla. Whenever I go there I have to stop and realize what it's like to have five children. They're always slow to get going except Quintus is trying to drag us away as soon as his last spaghetti slips into his lips. He says his coach never believes him it's not his fault he's always late. So he's out the back door leaving it open and I hear him running in the street yelling to his friends and one of them on a bike yells, Beat you there, Quinny! with a zooming-by voice, he must be pedaling hard to the park. Quintus is yelling back to get us moving.

I wasn't going, I was staying to help Camilla clean up but first I stand out on the front step and watch Quintus trying to get in the locked van. The old man on the second floor across the street is laughing out his window at how furious Quintus acts. Then Celia comes out with her dad's keys and Quintus grabs them to open the rear. He jumps in and jumps right out again then runs past me back in the house. Then Ursula comes out and says, We two ain't going, we're going up the store. And there's Stephen on Ma's front steps coming out to see what's going on. Hey Stephen you fag, what you doing over here still? says Celia. Still visiting, says Stephen. Your dad kick you out? Celia calls back laughing and Ursula and her slope on up the street looking out for their friends.

When Peter comes out with Lucius and Julia and yells for his keys there's no Quintus but he comes from around back with his baseball glove he was looking for and tosses the keys to his dad. So it's just the boys and Julia in the van and when they drive off the van's blowing black puffs out its exhaust all the way up the street. Now Stephen's sitting on the top step next door at Ma's with his knees up and his head down on them. He's got his hands up and around behind his neck making him look headless to me. Behind the white window shade I see Pa's reading light making a glow now. The front of the house is all in the shadow with the houses across the street still sunny. Want to come see my new apartment later after I help Camilla clean up? I say but Stephen says he's got lots of homework. It's Friday, I tell him. He says he'll come tomorrow instead, he just wants to go up to bed early.

V

I went out and got some snacks to have in for him. Then I was working on the linoleum tiles with this pry tool I borrowed from Peter. Whoever had this place before had a cat who misbehaved one too many times so I told the landlord Mr. DiNapoli I was pulling up those smelly tiles. He didn't care but he wouldn't do it himself of course. It's just in the kitchen area on one side of my living room and the first tiles came up fine. Peter's getting me a square of new linoleum from where he works at Common Lumber that'll fit. But then I get in the second row and they start sticking and I'm prying away. They break off in the middle and there's some lumpy dried-up glue I can't get off the floor. I put on my slacks for this one, down on my knees, and you can smell it and I'm sweating and swearing because Stephen's going to get there and I wanted it nice for him to see. Typical Barbara, I'm saying. It's things like this that get me down on myself and that's just when he rings.

You have to go down to let him in because the older people in the building don't want you letting in someone you don't know. Stephen walked over with his backpack on and his homework in it. He takes the stairs up as slow as I do and I'm warning him about the floor mess. It isn't the first thing he sees because it's behind the door when you open it so I show him over to the all-new bathroom which is what convinced me to take the apartment. It's better than Grandma's even, he says. Well I'm a soaker, I say, that tub's my second home. But I told him I don't really go for the soft toilet seat having a soft enough seat of my own. That gets him to smile. Teenagers don't ever smile much, you usually get a smirk out of them is all. Back in high school when I was selling doughnuts the manager always would say, Barbara, you got to smile. He even awarded a bonus to the employee who he thought was the friendliest each week. Catherine doesn't want her Stephen working but I think he should. Even when Pa said I didn't have to work anymore so I could take more time for school I said I wanted to keep doing it. I got to like talking to people over the counter. I got that friendly bonus lots of times.

Stephen and me were having a Coke and onion-and-garlic chips sitting on my window seat that is the other special feature that sold me on the apartment. The old cushion smelled like a cat too so I got Peter to get me a square of foam and I got some cherry-red corduroy and sewed it up and bought a couple of throw pillows to lean back on. That and the tub are my relaxing places. When I was moving in I worried about it being a bay window hanging over the street but then Peter told me I may be overweight but not as much as that and didn't I know about construction? These beams go all the way back into the building, he says, it's just a tip of them that's sticking out, and the building would have to flip its lid if it was going to tip me out. Then he gets me from behind in one of his holds till Gregory calls him off me.

Stephen said he'd help me with the tiles so that's what he spends his visit over here doing, prying with that tool, and I'm using sandpaper on the glue spots. I got linoleum picked out, one of the Spanish patterns, Peter's bringing it by after Sunday hours.

What kind of people come in that Autumn Hill Center? says Stephen while he's prying away yesterday with his skinny hairy wrists. All sorts, you should see some of them, I tell him. It's just for mothers, right? he wants to know. Fathers come in, kids come in, it's mothers mostly though that have the actual appointment, I tell him, but those counselors also have family meetings and you get old people too without any family around. It's supposably a drop-in center but now it caught on so you do have to have appointments but you don't have to be on any plan, I say, it has state funding like those school board programs or the Stinted Common Wilderness Summer. Then Stephen says, Hey you know that school board president Joan Ippolito? She comes around school, he says, what a joke, she's got to be a dyke, Barbara. But you know who her uncle is, I say. Yeah but I hear they're taking him to court, says Stephen. Since when does that stop those guys? I say. Her uncle and George her brother own half the rentals in Stinted Common, I told Stephen and I had him going on a whole conversation like he usually never does. You know I saw it on a wall the day she came to give that speech, he says, Ippolito's a Lesbian someone wrote, all the kids were saying it in the halls. Well they say that to the wrong guy and they get their heads blown off, I tell him.

We got up the tiles and Stephen did some homework on the window seat while I took a good soak and then we walked back down Milk Street to Ma's. You going to keep staying over there for a while? I ask him. What I'd like, he says, is a place like yours. All the homework you do, Stephen, you'll probably get one someday, I say.

VI

I feel luxurious. I don't have what Camilla and my other sister-in-law Gwen do, namely their kids plus one of my brothers to put up with, but it's better than my sister Catherine stuck in that run-down project with her William coming home to her. Mrs. Guimond who lives in that project too was telling me yesterday how there's nothing she can do at all in her life, she thinks, but then I look in her face and I don't see someone who wouldn't try. That's what I tell Peter when he jumps on me for defending these people like the ones from Haiti. She says where she comes from there's people living actually in cardboard boxes and she points across the room at the big box with the this-side-up arrows that the Center's new fridge came in. See that, she says, that's some man's house where I come from. I say I don't believe it. She says she's trying to explain how it was for her there and why doesn't she feel happy up here, she's got nice clothes she makes herself, she's got two rooms for her and her kids. But they beat on her kids in school and what started her coming first to the Center was when she was first in the project and she got cut up in the face by some teenagers. The police took care of her but after the hospital they brought her by the Center when she still had stitches on her cheeks. I still look for those scars on her black skin. I keep coming back here, she says, because I'm scared all the time.

But on my window seat I feel like I'm in a clean smooth box hanging over all that stuff down there. My building's safe, it's mostly elderly and it's on the corner across from the All-Night and the taxi lot's there so someone's always looking out. Peter and Gregory were careful before I moved in. They hung out at the store a whole Saturday evening to get a feel for the street here. And Peter comes by from work bringing me things like the linoleum that he cut down to fit perfectly.

I wish you didn't tell Ma about that guy Paul downstairs, I told him though. You call him Paul? says Peter. I don't call him, that's the name on his letters, I told him. He's from down there somewhere, isn't he? says Peter like he's pointing off to some island far away. I tell him I looked in Pa's almanac last week but there were so many small islands and I couldn't see which name went to which. Then Peter says, So you're already planning your Caribbean honeymoon, Barbara, and he starts going boojy-boojy-boojy and we get into one of our brother-sister wrestling matches. Peter wants me to get married so bad but I'm wondering what he'd really think if it was to someone like Paul.

It gives me more time to think, living in my own place. At home there's always helping to do around the house or just sitting around yapping. I never had all this much time before. It makes me dreamy lying in the tub or looking out the bay window and I sit there at the bus stop or at the bus stop from work, even when there's people waiting all around me, and my mind goes and words come to me I don't even think of. So at work one of the counselors Alice McKeever asked me once if I'm feeling depressed lately. It's funny that's how I look to her. After a couple of months receptionists sometimes have that problem here, she says, I mean counselors are trained what to expect but you were used to dogs and cats, Barbara, not what you get from these people. So we find it's good to talk it out, she says. Really, Barbara, she says, we should have a talk someday on your lunch hour. I suppose it all could be getting me down, I tell her and then I start to thinking maybe it is.

Your name's Paul? I asked him in a polite way in the front hall last night coming home when the one bulb in the chandelier was on so we couldn't see each other too well. It is and didn't I hear your brothers calling you Barbara? he says with his head turned up at me from putting in his key. It seems awfully chilly for April, he says. I started feeling scared of him for a moment in the hall but I remember each word he said. I suppose spring does finally arrive, doesn't it? He always puts in doesn't it or isn't it. Oh yes, I tell him, it does, but we don't go on from there.

VII

I was helping Camilla with the dishes on another baseball night and she's still trying to get me to buy tickets off her for this benefit she's on the committee of. But wouldn't you like to see the old Atherton Theater again, how they're fixing it up? she says. I keep passing her plates to dry. Remember Peter and me going in high school to make out and you and your girlfriend would be spying on us from the balcony? she says. Camilla, you do this pot, I say, it wasn't me left all this mess to cake up in here. She says she didn't get around to it last night and left it soaking.

So how about it? she says. Peter told her to give me a break on two tickets for the price of one. Camilla doesn't give up. It's because her cousin Gina's husband Dom, the one from Italy, started a committee with people like George Ippolito and his uncle's crowd organizing Italian Opera Night at the Atherton and bringing over Dom's sister who's a singer back there. I thought they were turning the Atherton into bowling alleys, I say. I told you before, Camilla says, those people didn't keep up on their taxes, City Hall took it over. But George was in on that bowling alley thing too and I'm not benefiting any George Ippolito, I tell her. But they're making it an auditorium for the public, says Camilla, for events, the mayor's on the committee, it's nonprofit. You're just in it because of Gina and Dom, I say, I can't see you and Peter sitting through some opera concert. He's on the renovation committee and I'm on the benefit committee, says Camilla. She just never gets aggravated. I love being difficult with her and watching her keep on talking away drying her dishes seriously looking out for spots.

But Camilla, you don't like that kind of music though, I say and dump in the knives and forks in the sticky water rattling on each other. I watched Pavarotti on TV, she says. Yeah but not Dom's sister at the Atherton. Dom says she's very successful back there, Camilla says, she's been on

Rome radio and everything. Then she goes on about how in Italy every town has their opera and how here in Stinted Common being full of Italians it's the perfect place to bring over all these singers Dom knows to perform and how he's trying to get something going like that. So what if George Ippolito's putting up some of the money, or old man Ippolito even, says Camilla. Maybe downtown in Boston they put on the big-name opera, she says, but Dom says this'll be real Italian opera for Italian-Americans who live here. Over in Italy everybody knows those songs, she says. I tell her how I watched Pavarotti on TV too and all I saw was him pawing some lady with three chins and I could see actual spit flying on TV. I couldn't watch much of that, I told her, just give me Clint Eastwood. Oh you and Clint! says Camilla flicking her dish towel at me, about as much of a rise as I ever get out of her.

Since it's uphill to my new apartment I prefer taking the bus back if Peter isn't there to drive me. I was sitting at the bus stop near Ma's and thinking how it's the Autumn Hill Center they should be having a benefit for, not some Italian Opera Night at the Atherton, but then I'm thinking how much Peter's been helping me and how Camilla always drags him along on things for her family and I could do something for Peter once, then suddenly I thought of Paul. I could ask him to the benefit with me. Then I felt my marker there at the bottom of my coat pocket and out it comes. This shelter near Ma's I never wrote in the corner of yet. I find a little spot and out come words. I feel luxurious, I write first. Then I stop thinking totally and when I look at what I wrote it says: All the time scared. So now while I'm waiting for the bus I'm thinking of Mrs. Guimond's face and I'm thinking of Paul's.

VIII

Yesterday I had lunch at the sandwich shop with Alice McKeever and I tried to explain to her about my family and that I'm not depressed like she thinks. I told her about growing up with my brothers and Catherine and the way it was on our street with all the kids growing up together, how Ma and Pa lived in our half of the house first with Pa's parents and when the kids were born eventually my grandparents moved to an apartment before my grandfather died. I being youngest never had them living with us that I can remember but my grandfather still came over to take care of the garden because their apartment didn't have one and Pa didn't go in for it himself. I remember the stakes for tomatoes and the grapes hanging off the trellis and Nonno singing out behind the house which is now all paved. He died by the time I would really remember him well but my grandmother over in the Home still talks about him always as if he was alive, I told Alice. She outlives her roommates always. Pa goes to see her every day but she doesn't really know me now, she gets confused easy.

You interested in this? I asked Alice. She was eating her tuna and I was talking on and on and she just nods. I don't think I'm depressed, I tell her, because I love to be near my family and actually there's a man I'm getting interested in sort of lately so maybe I look dreamy to you because of that. Alice is smiling at me. That's nice, she says and then she says, I just don't want you feeling too responsible for these people that come in here because you do so well with them and Bill and I don't want you feeling disappointed when things don't seem to get much better for them. I tell her I know it's hard to change your life. Alice puts her hand across the red tabletop and touches my hand. It even gets me down, she says, I know exactly what to expect and it gets me down still.

I asked her did they ever think of having a benefit for the Center. We sure could use one, says Alice, ever since they cut Lou Ann I don't know what's going to go next, they give us that fridge but they cut Lou Ann! I ask who is it cuts things and she says the governor's office, they have to keep trimming, but then somebody over there decides every Center in the state should get a fridge. Somebody's uncle probably sells fridges, I say, but anyways about the benefit, my brother Peter, the one I told you about with the five kids, he's on the renovation committee making that old theater the Atherton into a place for public events like benefits. I don't think people around here have money for benefits, says Alice. Where she grew up in the suburbs there was always a bunch of wealthy people raising money for this or that but not in Stinted Common, she says. She moved here when she was going to graduate school. She figured it was convenient to buses out to her classes and also over to where she was interning then in Boston but she hardly leaves town ever now, she says. Last time she was in Boston was to the State House testifying about the cuts. Lot of good I did, she says making one more touch on the back of my hand.

Here's Alice McKeever, I'm thinking, and she and Bill Potts the other counselor aren't much older than me. Alice was just thirty. She's divorced so she's by herself now and her apartment's probably like mine though it's up Sugar Hill which is nicer. Alice is too thin and she dresses very plain in order to look sober and neutral at the Center, she says. I'm the one that comes in with my plaids and my scarves and bright blouses, cherry and apricot and like that. I must've got used to colors from the sunshine yellow uniforms selling doughnuts because before that in high school Ma would only let me wear a white blouse with a nice pin on it.

Who's there on the steps when we get back to the Center but Ursula and Celia. You're supposed to be up at school, I say. Don't tell our mom, says Celia, we decided to take a walk. This is Alice my boss, I say, and these little class cutters are two of my nieces. So why'd you come over here? I ask them. Celia, who's the loud one that takes after Peter, gets on her knees and is saying, Barbara, Barbara, I'm pregnant, I'm pregnant! Ursula's just laughing. Alice goes on up to her next appointment and with Bill covering the desk I have to get in there too. Can't we come up? says Ursula. I tell them I can't stop them, it's a public place, but I got a phone and I can call up Mr. Bagley's office so maybe they better get moving back over the hill to school. Come on, Barbara, what if we really got problems? says Celia. And we need to see that Alice about it, says Ursula. These girls love kidding around. It's incest, it's incest, Barbara, I can't talk to anyone about it, I'm so mortified! says Celia falling on the sidewalk grabbing her knees. I'm just standing with my hand on my hip looking aggravated. Yeah see, Quintus he's this sex maniac, Ursula says all serious. Yeah I know he's only ten but he's always, excuse my language, Celia says but that's all she can say she's laughing so hard.

And there comes Mrs. Figueroa for an appointment. She steps around Celia who rolls into her legs. I blow up at them: Celia, get up and get back to school, Ursula too, I'm going in and calling on you. Don't be such a flaming bitch, Barbara, they're saying. Mrs. Figueroa doesn't even look at us, she just goes in. It's our lunch period, says Ursula, and we can go out for lunch if we got permission, so there. I'm not telling, just get out of here, I yell at them. Hey Celia, let's go up the store and get some Raisinets, Ursula says walking off all miffed. But I want to see in Barbara's office, Celia says, I never seen it. You know what you'd see in there? I say. You'd see a lot of disadvantaged people in the waiting room and I'm sitting at a desk telling them to wait. You should be embarrassed, I say. Was that one, says Celia, that Puerto Rican or whoever she was?

Now I'm ready to boil over at these two. Get out of here, I say tight in my throat. I have a right to know, Celia says. You don't have a right to know, I say, you don't have a right to know, get out of here. Don't get so exercised, Barbara, says Celia. Ursula's turning back and looking impatient on the corner. We're going, we're going, Celia says. She's definitely going through her big bitch stage.

When I turn around to go up I have this feeling of what if it was Stephen instead to come there on his lunch period with his backpack saying how he's got to come talk to someone about his father. Walking up the stairs I pretend he's there with me almost crying. I can even feel the shakes that would be in him and I'm helping him up the stairs. I'll get Bill Potts to see you, Stephen, you'll see there's a nice man in this world to understand what you're going through, it's not just a woman that understands, I say. I have this conversation going through my head. Bill's nice, I say, he's got a nice wife and a little girl he brings in here on two mornings. Barbara, you're my best relative, Stephen is saying to me in my thoughts.

IX

There at the bus stop yesterday morning was Paul with his briefcase waiting for the same bus as me. I thought you took the other bus out to your classes, I say. He says he has to go into Boston instead to straighten out his visa. And you're off to work, aren't you? he asks so I start telling him about where I work and he thinks he knows where that is, down Milk Street over near the big project. I say it's counseling for disadvantaged people. Ah, disadvantaged people, says Paul and he wants me to show him how I go on the map.

All these new Plexiglas shelters have this panel showing a historical map of Stinted Common put up for the Bicentennial. There's three kinds of shelters, these newer ones, then the ones they built when I was in junior high out of concrete blocks they had the kids do murals on, and then there are still a couple of the very old ones from when I was little made of that grooved kind of boards with wooden benches but they're all rotting out. It wouldn't show the Center on that map, I tell Paul, that's of a hundred years ago, it just shows the hills and a few streets. A hundred and twenty-five years ago to be exact, says Paul. I study this map every morning, he says, or should I say I study the identical map at the other shelter across Milk Street? He always says should I say or I fear. See how empty it was back then among these seven hills, Paul says. You know it's called Milk Street because that's the way they brought the milk into Boston from the western farms and that was Paul Revere's ride, he shows me. And these cross streets, he says, were called rangeways dividing up the common. I'm thinking how they taught us all this in school probably but I wasn't paying attention then. This was all grazing land, Paul says, and they kept it in common and parceled it out to the townspeople in stints, they called them, depending on what you needed for your cows. I can't help looking up the history of wherever I am, it's

what I study in graduate school after all, he's telling me
and staring at that map. I'm suddenly afraid he'll recognize
over in the corner that I wrote there some of the things he
said to me in our front hall. I love maps, he says, I can
dream myself into them.

On the other side of him on the bench there's a lady with
a wig under her scarf who's looking at me for talking to
this black man. Then a bus pulls up. The Center is sort of
there, I say finding the spot between those rangeways
where the bottom of Autumn Hill is. Oh then I fear we're
taking different buses, says Paul, I'm headed this way, and
he runs his finger along where Revere forks off Milk and
the bus runs over Asylum Hill to get the trolley to Boston.

X

I love you, Barbara, says Julia when we're sitting around
Ma's yesterday late and it's raining out. Stephen's back at
Catherine's again and now Ma misses him so Pa said let's
have Julia over for supper with Barbara tonight. Julia's
proud to be the one asked by herself for a meal without
Quintus. It used to be either the other two girls would
come or all three girls or Julia and Quintus together. Only
Lucius ever got to come on his own when he was younger
but that's what I mean about Pa liking kids up till they're
through junior high. You got to stop treating them like
kids, he says. It's somehow his way, the way Nonno did
with him too, I bet.

At dinner Ma's latest thing is how you can tell when
there's Portuguese moving in because they got the yellow
robe for the Virgin not the blue in front of the house. Ma,
I say to her, what difference does it make? Well when did

you go to Mass since Tessa's first communion, what do you care? she says to me.

Then there was Julia looking soft cuddled up on me on Ma's sofa. Ursula and Celia at her age already said all the bad words and Julia doesn't. I don't understand how it goes with some kids. It was Catherine that did all the bad stuff when we were little but the boys were better. Peter always got in trouble but not in any dangerous ways and Gregory and me never got in trouble much.

So yesterday I'm stroking Julia's hair and thinking about how to somehow keep her this way. Do you know how much I love you? I ask her. How much? she says yawning like she was almost asleep. Well you know I'm a big person, I say. She's humming something to herself. So when you're big, I say, you have more love in you because love is in every part of your body. Behind your knees? says Julia and I say yes. How about in your nose? she says. I have it in my nose, I say and I pull her up and bounce hers against mine. Then she puts her head on my shoulder. Barbara, I don't want to have boyfriends, she whispers in my ear. I know that girls say that when they're her age. She's falling asleep, I'm thinking, so I let my cheek touch her warm head and let anything come into my mind. That head against this cheek, I'm thinking.

X I

They dragged me to one of their baseball games after all. It's because Quintus's team was playing his cousin Tommy's so I had to be a good aunt and go. Gregory and Gwen started having their kids just after Peter and Camilla finished having the five of theirs and Gwen says she's stopping with just the two so everyone kids me now about being slow to pick up the ball. Of course Catherine had Stephen before any of them and she can't have any more. She wouldn't want to anyway with William.

Gregory picked me up at work. We're taking the kids for burritos first because I don't like to cook on baseball nights, smiley Gwen leans around to say when I get in back with Tommy and Tessa. Tessa always would rather eat out, says Gwen, and Tommy's too nervous to sit still at the table anyway. Tommy is pounding his mitt and tapping his feet. I wish I could stay and work on my insect project, Dad, he says. I want a beef burrito and a chicken burrito too, says Tessa. Wait'll we get there, says Gwen, keep your eyes out for the turtle with the chef's hat. You can see him over the trees coming down the hill, she says, who's going to see him first? Tessa says, I hope Julia comes sits with me for the game. She'll be for Quintus's team, Tommy says, but you have to be for my team. Tommy's a little bit chubby like his father was back then but with milky skin like Gwen's. Tessa's even almost blond from Gwen's side. I want to sit with Julia, Tessa says. Theresa Orsini, shut up, says Gwen.

To be fair I have to change sides each inning. But Lucius comes along with me back over to Tommy's side for the fifth inning. He told me he thinks he's a good sport to be going to Quintus's game when he could be watching a game across the park of his own league. Quintus is more into baseball than Tommy, I say looking at Tommy out in right with his head twisting around looking at things instead of standing with his legs apart and his eyes on the batter like Quintus does in left.

You like coming to games, Barbara? Lucius asks me. And he looks now sort of like I remember Peter looking once too, the one in the family with the curliest hair. I wish I could root for one team for once is all, I say. So come to my next game, he says. Hey Barbara, you know what I'm thinking lately, there's this Wilderness Summer program they have I'm thinking of signing up for, he says, but Dad wants me helping him on that renovation and he's not too big on me going so I was wondering, do you know anything from your job about Wilderness Summer, like brochures? Maybe you could tell Dad about it, that it's a really good thing? I'll ask Bill Potts at the Center, I tell Lucius. I don't know yet what they do for that program since I only just started but Bill leads groups of kids on weekends I know, I think he's involved. Anyways it'd only be a couple weeks in the summer so you could still work with Peter, I say. Yeah but Dad says it's just kids from bad homes. No it's not, I don't think so, I say, it's for anyone in Stinted Common. Dad says wait till his vacation and we'll all go to the country in the van instead, Lucius says.

That inning nothing came out to Tommy. When they were at bat he came and sat on the bench in front of Lucius and me looking relieved. Hey Tommy, says Lucius, you're looking good out there. Since Tommy's just nine it's good Lucius says things like that to him. Tommy tilts his head to one side then the other like he's embarrassed. It's Quintus out there who makes a great catch way back by the fence. And that was the best play of the game. Lucius says, It's a good thing I hung around to see that or he'd be griping for the rest of the season at me missing his big catch. Lucius doesn't get excited, he just watches close, but Peter's yelling from over on his side: Hey Gregory, get a load of that! and everyone on Quintus's team is jumping up and down. Gregory who's standing down by the back-stop shoots Peter the finger and Peter's shooting both fists in the air. Gwen's sitting on the grass with Tessa and they're pointing at me to come over. I guess I'll go back and shut up my dad, says Lucius. Then Tommy's up and that's the last out of that inning but I stayed sitting over with Gwen instead of going back around to Quintus's side.

Your ma says Stephen's getting it bad again, Gwen says to me quietly so Tessa doesn't notice. I guess so, I say. So it doesn't make sense why doesn't he move out and stay with his grandmother? Gwen says. And I say, Why doesn't Catherine move out from William is what I don't get. So why doesn't she? says Gwen. I see it all the time at the center, I tell her, people stuck like that. So why doesn't she go talk to someone at the Center? Make her an appointment, Barbara, and make her go. She's got to get away from that guy, Barbara, Gwen tells me like I didn't know. We'd take Catherine in and Stephen too if we had more room, she says, but I think your ma should take them in really.

Tessa is staring up at us figuring out what we're talking about. See what I don't understand is how Catherine could put her own kid through that, says Gwen. She's putting herself through it too but that's her business but how's she putting a kid through it? And all these years, she says, and it's all he's ever known. You ask me, some women, they don't stop to think of the consequences of what they do. If she says she can't leave him, well where does that leave Stephen then? That's what I'd like to know. And then Gwen shuts up and looks over at me out her big glasses that are shaped like two TV screens I always think.

You know what, I say to her, there's so much going on over in those projects you wouldn't want to know. But when it's your own sister, says Gwen. That's what I mean, I say, and we think we're so much better than those people over there and it could be your own sister. Well she's just got to stop putting up with it, Gwen says. Tessa, you run over and sit with Julia, your brother won't mind.

Gwen could talk for hours to me about what's going on in the family. Most of it's usually what's going on in her own family, all her brothers and sisters up in New Hampshire, I can't keep them straight, they're running around and getting divorced. She doesn't care about watching the game at all and she'd be talking to some other mothers too if it wasn't such a small group there that night so she's yapping at me. I keep my eye half on the game, especially when Quintus is up and he's got that furious look on his face or when Tommy's up looking nervous. Half the fathers from Quintus's team grew up on our street with Peter and us. There's Tessa over there squatting down next to Julia making Julia look large to me. I don't know any of the fathers on Tommy's team since they're from their new neighborhood out the western end. What would Paul make of a baseball game like this?

XII

I feel something coming to me in the middle of the night in the corner where my bed is. Lights from the street pass around the corners of the room and I get the feeling of that smooth clean box again. It's not that I see the walls moving or the lights themselves moving actually but that there seems to be a motion inside everything in the room is the only way I can say it. I mean when I hear a late bus shifting down on the street and its lights pass up past the window seat and over the kitchen area, it's not the lights or the wall that seems to move across anything but inside the wall, inside the light there's a feeling of it moving. I feel that everything around me is moving inside and it's all coming to me in the middle of the night when I wake up from a dream. This isn't a scary feeling at all.

In the morning the sunlight comes in and makes everything look flat and still again. I get out of bed and choose the colors I'll wear that day and have my cereal and toasts and juice sitting on the window seat. I watch the early people on their way. The Center doesn't open till nine unlike the animal clinic or even worse the doughnut shop. I have a lazy life now.

I realize it was getting on to the time when the benefit was going to be and I did tell Camilla I'd buy the tickets off her but I didn't ask anyone yet. I knew if I waited awhile it would make me more ready to ask Paul but it would be hard to ask him right off. Camilla told me about Dom's sister the singer who's just arrived and what a big lady she is, a real Italian mamma. I bet she's got a lot of voice in there, Camilla says. She doesn't even think about me being overweight too when she's telling me about how big that lady is.

I didn't know how I could explain what this concert is to Paul. I also didn't know if coming there with him was the best thing regarding my family. Peter's going to get all exercised about me having a date, maybe Gregory would too, and Gwen wouldn't stop talking about it wondering what everyone thinks of me being with a black man. And then Ma and Pa would worry themselves crazy but they wouldn't say too much, I bet. Instead maybe I should take Stephen, I'm telling myself, or I could see if Alice McKeever would go, she probably likes that kind of music. I can't see asking Stephen though. He'd go along but it'd make him feel funny being out with me at his age. Alice I figure would feel funny coming too, we have more of a business relationship is what it is. Wouldn't it make Paul feel funny too maybe? But I had the feeling about him that it wouldn't somehow. He's not like the blacks you see at the Center who look like they don't dare go out around here except in a bunch. Paul doesn't look that way. He says he studies the history of all the places he goes. He walks around with his briefcase like he's not scared. He's always got something to say about things and he doesn't look dead in the eyes like so many people I see do, black and white both.

So yesterday I go knock on his door when I'm coming in from work. I don't almost realize I'm doing it. He asks me who it is and I say Barbara Orsini from upstairs. The door opens and he's crinkling his eyebrows out at me. My sister-in-law gave me tickets to Italian Opera Night at the Atherton which was in the paper, you may have seen, I say. It's a cousin of hers who's a singer, I don't know if she'd be any good but I hear you playing your radio, I say because I suddenly remembered the music I hear some mornings coming by his door. He's nodding. So I told him when it would be and asked him if he'd want to go, I was inviting him to come with me. He said it sounded very interesting. I fear I have a limited acquaintance with Italian opera are exactly the words I remember he said. But when he was a schoolboy, he said, he did have a part in an actual opera once and he started to smile with his big lips. He said his part was to go around setting off firecrackers which doesn't sound like what I thought of as being an opera. And I sang as well, he said. Then he asked me in but I said I was on my way over to my ma's. I said I'd stop by sometime or he could stop up. But he did say he would like to go with me to the concert and he went to write it down on his calendar. It's a pleasure to know you, Barbara, is the last thing he said before he shut his door.

In the mornings before I get out of bed I think about the day before. It's how I find myself back in things each day. If I didn't stop and think about yesterday I'd just go out and not know where I was is what I'm afraid of. It's that I'm slow to wake up and it helps me get back where I left off. Because when I'm sleeping I'm not exactly me. I don't believe in visions and miracles, I don't even think about God lately, it's really only Ma who does of us all. But I know that when I'm sleeping things do change and each morning I'm waking up with new ideas.

XIII

Now what's happened is that Stephen's got in trouble for being with a bunch of guys from the project smashing car windows. He says he was just hanging around with them and only two of them actually did it. They were walking around late at night up the streets of the neighborhood near there. They had their radios and a couple girls along and there was some drinking. First they were just throwing bottles over people's fences and then someone found a brick and they saw an out-of-state car and he put the brick through the windshield. Then, worse, this other guy who Stephen says no one likes in their group was so drunk he put his bare fist through the side window of a little Japanese car. His hand got cut up and that was when someone in a house had called the cops and they came down the one-way street from the other end and got them.

The one with the bleeding hand was obvious and the cops were throwing him in the back of the cruiser and then he's so drunk he's yelling how this other kid smashed that windshield with a brick so that kid gets all crazy and tries to shut up his buddy in the back of the cruiser. Stephen says he was just standing around watching. The police took all their names and Catherine got called about it but that was all that happened, except to the two kids who actually broke the windows. You know back when we were in junior high school, Stephen says, the kids used to break windows in houses, like back windows and basement windows, well now they go smashing car windows instead. When he was stopping by my place to tell me about it before I heard it from Catherine I asked him why did he hang around with those guys. Us kids in the project stick together, who else should I hang around with? he said. Did I think he likes coming over to Ma's and having the kids on that street looking at him like he didn't live around there? They know it's your grandma's house, I told him, we been on that street ever since before Catherine was born. Not me though, says Stephen. And then you see those out-of-state cars around, he says, and I don't just mean someone's relatives from New Hampshire, I mean Iowa and places like that. What're they doing around here? There's always out-of-state cars out the western end where there's college students, I say. But they're moving in here too, says Stephen. And you know what sort of people now are moving in the project! Nobody likes the blacks moving in there, he says.

Stephen's problem is he goes along with everything. I tried talking to Bill Potts about him after work one day when Bill was staying late at his desk and I stayed late too to organize files. I was asking him what it was like doing those weekend groups and working with kids. I said how I had my nephew Lucius who was wanting to go on the Wilderness Summer and I was describing him and how he's always got plans and he's such a nice kid. And then I try describing my older nephew Stephen and I couldn't explain why I love him too even though he's such a nothing sort of kid. He's your nephew, says Bill, of course you love him. That's why you're good with people, Barbara, he tells me, you don't blame them. We could've hired a lot of people, he says, but we got the feeling in your interview you'd be right for the job. Bill looks still like he was probably once a hippie-type, he's still got tangly hair and you only see him in jeans.

It's a big problem at the Center, Bill says to me then, when the types of people you really can like, they don't need your help so much, it's the ones you can't stand that need it. I mean I count on a kid like that Lucius of yours, he says, to make those weekend groups work, kids like that could almost be counselors themselves. But then there's the nothing sort of kids and if you can just get them to notice one new thing you're doing good. I told Bill I think Stephen's always afraid, he grew up afraid. Because of what you told me how his dad hits him? Bill says looking at me not embarrassed about talking about it which is what makes him good at being a counselor. I'm thinking it's too bad it's Lucius not Stephen that wants to go on this Wilderness Summer. I see it all the time, says Bill, kids grow up afraid of everything around them, everything.

Then his wife Polly comes in with their little Sarah who's always happy to see me. Bill says they'll give me a lift up Milk Street, they're going that way.

XIV

There's that new mall that's just opened and Gwen was taking me there yesterday to get something to wear to the concert at the Atherton. She goes every weekend since it opened but I never been yet. Isn't it amazing, a mall in Stinted Common? says Gwen. I never thought they'd get a mall here, I used to have to drive up to the Heights Mall, she says. What it was is an old brickyard, which is where my grandfather used to work, but it was closed for years and they took some of the old factory buildings and built onto them. Some of the Boston stores you see in the papers opened up branches here. I couldn't believe it at first when Gwen took me in. Since it's on the other side of the interstate you don't just walk there without a car. There's people come down here from the suburbs even to shop, says Gwen and she's wheeling Gregory's big old Buick into some tight space. I was afraid I'd have a hard time squeezing out my side so Gwen says slide over and get out hers.

I got my favorite place for us to go, she says, and then afterwards I'm treating you, Barbara, we'll have a nice lunch at this Bavarian Shop they have. Gwen was strolling along, she loves shopping and getting things done. We'd been talking about maybe going there together for a while and now she was really going to make me get something nice since most of my clothes I got at the More-for-Less. First we're going to check out all the displays, she says, but then I think unless you see something we'll go to my favorite place because they'll have what you want, I just know.

The one thing I couldn't believe was the card shop we stopped in. There was one of a nun showing her breasts and gay cards of naked men on horses there for kids to walk in and see. Gwen's just laughing and saying I'm old-fashioned and what's the big deal. Her favorite store was nice and the lady showed me a nice dress that was colorful but not loud at all. Gwen's telling me all about the fabric and what a great new fabric it is but I don't keep up with these things the way she does. The dress was long stripes in green and gold with thinner white ones. Gwen said it'd make me look slimmer and elegant. Well, she says, so I hear you're going to the concert with a graduate student.

I didn't know if Gregory had told her anything about Paul or if she'd heard somehow from Peter and what he'd told her. I thought probably not much because then she'd be asking in a serious way how I felt about this guy. It's nice you're meeting your new neighbors, Barbara, she says, moving out of your ma's is the best thing you ever did, Gregory says so too. That's what's such a mess in my family you know, Gwen says and that starts her going. No wonder they don't stay married, they're always moving in with our parents, she says. Now Ellis is moving back because her and Henri are having it out and half their kids are at my parents' and half, the older ones, over at Henri's, then you know how Roger and Pam lived at home their first two years married and so how are they ever going to work it out on their own?

We were at the Bavarian Shop but I was resisting the desserts and having a hot pastrami and Sweet 'n Low in my coffee. So you're meeting college types, Barbara, says Gwen again. He's a foreigner, I tell her as the easiest way to bring it up. Gwen's looking through those TV-shaped glasses like she doesn't believe me. I hope he's not Italian, she says, I should know being married to one. She leans her head back and gives a laugh but she's kidding me because Gregory's not Italian-acting when it comes to women at all, it's really more Peter that is. You know what, Barbara, Gwen says, let's keep having lunches together sometimes, I got my friends I have lunches with of course, Patti Donnell and Sue Bartlette and them, but there's nothing like talking to family. So does he speak English or what? she wants to know. I told her what a refined-sounding English accent he has. Hey, says Gwen, this is better than I expected. Then she looks worried and grabs at my hand. Now Barbara, she says, this is serious, don't tell him you got a sister-in-law whose father sends gun money to the IRA, all right? I start to say, Gwen, is your father still sending money to the, but she shushes me. No, this is serious, Barbara, she says, I told you about that group him and my brothers belong to, really don't mention it to this guy, really. She's putting her finger to her lips and shaking her head. I wouldn't anyway, I say.

Gwen does love her conspiracies and her secrets. With her and Camilla it's so different. I get this one sister-in-law that always likes saying just nice things about people and how great all her kids are and then here's the other one that loves ranking on people. She even talks about how her own Tommy's such a pussy and she'll go on about how his father doesn't even try to shape him up. Tommy's only nine, I tell her, Gregory was fatter than that when he was nine and he was more of a pussy I promise you but look how he turned out. And Gregory was the first kid in his fourth grade that hit a hundred pounds, I tell her. One time he meets me on the playground after school when I'm like in second grade and he's starting to cry and says, Come on, Barbara, let's get home. The nurse who weighed them announced it aloud to all the kids waiting in the hall and they were all cheering and ranking on Gregory. So we're walking home and he won't tell me what it is till we're on our street and there's no other kids walking behind us. We were the little fatties of the street, I tell Gwen. Then she goes off on what a pain her Tessa's getting to be now, always running around with the Bartlette girls like wild Indians, and she never goes back to asking me about Paul.

X V

Yesterday I did go to see Catherine after Ma asked me to. Catherine doesn't come over to Ma's like she used to, she just phones a lot, and Ma doesn't think she should go over there herself but figures I could drop in more like it's spur of the moment being sisterly. When I go in the entry that's never locked and up those metal stairs and knock on her door it's unfortunately William who opens. He's looking nice, hair combed, has his green work shirt on with the red William above the pocket. Good for you, he says right off. Good for me what? I ask. Good for you coming by, who ever comes by here except you? he says. You don't see Peter coming by or Gregory coming by to see their own sister, he says. Is she in? I ask. Come on in, Barbara, have a seat, make yourself at home, she's just out, she's coming right back, she's over to the neighbor's. So I sit on the chair by the window in their kitchenette. What you see looking out from there is the dirt in the yard between the buildings that's packed so hard from kids playing there and some orange and yellow plastic bats and footballs and candy wrappers and some paper cups around.

William sits down at the table and rolls up his sleeves and sets his elbows on the table like he wants to be serious now. You heard about Stephen, he says. You mean the car windows? I say. Of course he didn't do anything, William says, he was just hanging out with those kids, I'm always telling him to keep clear of that bunch. William's shaking his head and making his lips tight. So William, what's he going to do when he graduates? I ask to get him off that subject. You know he'd love to get into a place of his own, I say which is risking it a little with William. So who wouldn't! says William and he leans back, stretches out those arms in the air and says, Well I don't mean that for me, we're okay, me and Catherine, but you know how you feel sometimes wanting just to be on your own. Hey I hear you got your own place now, he says, good for you, but Barbara, there's no way Stephen's going to get a place of his own, there's no job he could get that'd pay enough even for a room and he hasn't been willing as you know to train at the Trade, he just takes those nothing courses up at the high school. Let me ask you, what does that prepare you for? William's leaning on his elbows again and I know this is going to go on, one of his explanations how the world is these days. He could talk on and on about it, about how the Trade was good for him, how kids around here shouldn't think no matter how much they do homework they're going to get jobs in computers just because they hear that on TV.

You know, Barbara, he says, they tell you things are picking up but you're not going to see it in this town, things just keep falling down, and he's staring out the window at the building across where there's cardboard over a window. You know what happens in the suburbs, Barbara, when there's a window broken, I mean even like in elderly housing where my aunt lives? They call someone that comes and fixes it, that's what. Isn't that remarkable? he says smiling and nodding at me like somehow I'm in on a conspiracy against him, that's the way William always makes me feel, like I should do something for him.

I know, he says, my aunt lives in this community housing up there, she's got phone numbers to call. There's only one number we got to call here and you know how often there's ever somebody there answering it? I shake my head and I'm thinking I can't listen to William going on like this. He throws his arms up and leans back on the back legs of his chair against the fridge. What's Stephen know about it, what's he care? he says. He doesn't think past tomorrow. You ask him about politics, you know what he says? Joan Ippolito's a Lesbian! William laughs real hard at that. That's all he says! Now where's that going to get him? He doesn't take an interest in politics, he doesn't take an interest in training for anything, he doesn't take an interest in sports even, you notice that, Barbara? He doesn't even watch sports on TV. I don't even think he takes drugs, I don't even think he has sex! What does this kid do! William goes on louder, leaning still on the fridge and stretching his arms around. What does the kid do, Barbara? he says. He's waiting, that's all, he says to answer himself because I don't say anything, he's waiting till someone comes and says here's your job, here's your money, here's your apartment, here's your girlfriend, here's your cable TV, here's your Pontiac, here's your— William just makes a face tightening his lips. You think I'm hard on the kid, Barbara, you and your mother and all them do, he says. I know what you think of me as a father. You think I don't hear Catherine on the phone to her ma whispering away? Barbara? His chair tips forward and he slams down his elbows on the table and stares at me.

It always goes this way with him. You can tell from how long you have to be with him alone how far he'll go in getting furious and then if you see him through that he gets to his next thing which is getting sad, like the time he told me how all he's got is that aunt who doesn't even like him and our family never liked him and he works hard and what's Catherine do for him and one thing or another I heard a dozen times. Yesterday he doesn't get that far because Catherine comes in.

We hear the door and I look around and there's Catherine

looking worn out, her hair hanging straight down almost over her face. She's looking at something on the floor just inside the door and she doesn't see me yet. Those tiles, she says shaking her head. Your sister's here, says William. Catherine raises her head and her hair falls back from her face but she doesn't move over to me. She almost looks like she doesn't care I'm there. She sort of heaves out Hi Barbara with a sigh. What about those tiles? I say. It looks like they somehow got pried loose, she says. I look sideways at the floor and I can see how the edges of some tiles bend up like when Stephen was prying up the tiles in my kitchen area. Catherine presses her shoes down on the edges, all around each one but they sort of pop out again. Take off your coat and stay awhile, says William to her. She just looks at him. I know he's not going to leave us alone to talk, he's just going to sit there and complain how we probably wish he wasn't around.

There's one minute first though when they both go in the bedroom and just out of the corner of my eye I can see him hug her from behind and she leans back against him and they're standing there close for a while not saying anything. Then the mood's a little different when William follows her back in saying he'll make his oatmeal cookies and we can sit around like we used to when they were first married and I was a little girl Julia's age and I'd come around to their first place, that apartment up Sugar Hill that looked out into the willow tree.

XVI

Yesterday after dinner at Ma's when Gregory was there without the kids or Gwen he made me go down the cellar with him to see if I remembered something, he said. What are you talking about? I'm saying and he's laughing saying this is something from our past, something he found. He's telling me how Pa told him to get him in the spirit he should listen to some of Nonno's old records before we all go to the Atherton concert. So last weekend, Gregory says, I'm down here trying out a few and then I hit this one and I could remember Nonno singing that exact song. Out in the garden? I say. Well what I remember is him singing it to me sitting on his lap when I'm maybe Tommy's age, says Gregory.

In a dark corner behind the furnace is where Pa put the big wooden case that's Nonno's old phonograph. I don't really remember it except when I look close at the knobs and they look somehow familiar from when it used to sit up in our living room. Gregory pulls back the plastic sheet over the old records on the bottom shelf. Ma was going to throw this all out last year straightening up but I told her to let them stay, says Gregory. I figure they could be collector's items, he says, someday I'll find somebody who knows and she'll get good money for them I told Ma. But you're saving them, I say, from our past. Yeah, he says, you won't remember it but I do.

He pulls the cord out from inside the phonograph case and plugs it in the socket in the ceiling. Then he pulls out one of those heavy old records with a red label that says the title in Italian. The Masked Ball, says Gregory as if he knew anything about operas which is the way he did so good in school always, acting like he already knew things. It's the end of this song that I suddenly remembered when I heard it, he says. He puts on the record spinning fast and he lets down the needle almost at the end. I remembered exactly the Italian words Nonno sang when I was a little fatty on his lap, says Gregory, these words right here.

Hopes of love is what it means, Barbara, O lost sweetness and hopes of love, Gregory says. Listen, he says, and it's almost like it's Nonno's own voice singing it in the past. Out of the crackling sound comes a man's nice voice. It feels funny for me to hear it because I do remember our grandfather out behind the house way in my memories but I'm sure he didn't sound as good as this man on the record.

Upstairs I asked Gregory to spell out those lines on a piece of paper because he took a little Italian at Boston State. I'm thinking I should start writing some things in Italian too on the bus stop shelter. It feels like something that might've come to me in English anyways: lost sweetness and hopes of love. It makes me think of Mrs. Guimond and Annie Randall and Mrs. Velis and even that long-haired woman who started yelling at me for not knowing what it was like for her with a man.

It makes me feel shaky, says Gregory as he's writing the words on Ma's grocery list pad and rubbing his mustache the way he always does. I didn't know I remembered exactly something Nonno sang, he's saying, maybe I'll go through all his old records once and find even more things. They're antiques, like from the thirties, they're definitely valuable.

I watch him write over his shoulder: O dolcezze perdute, O speranze d'amor. But we're saving them, I say, aren't we?

Saint Something

I

It was my time to go see our grandmother. I go with Ma and Pa Sundays and other times but I also go alone sometimes even if she isn't sure it's me. She was sitting on a plastic chair by a window with a cushion under her and one behind her. She was still in her bathrobe like on most days. There's not too much you can say to her. Nonna, I'm going out this Friday, I tell her. That's nice is what she says but she's looking off. You know about the concert? I ask her. You know about Dom's sister the singer, Dom, Camilla's cousin Gina's husband? Ma was telling her about it I know. Nonna's smiling out the window and also out of the corner of her eye at me a little but as if she didn't know me for sure.

I'm going with a man, a black man, I say. Her face doesn't change. He's very nice, I tell her. He's from an island in the West Indies. He talks very beautifully. I've got my hand on her shoulder but just a light touch. He likes me and I can tell we could be friends, I say to her. If you were blind you'd like him, Nonna, I know, just from the way he talks. You like the black man who cleans up nights here, don't you? You got to be friends with him. I hear you joking around with him. I saw him wheeling your chair down the hall for you and you were laughing about something with him. What's for supper? Nonna says to me. Where's Frederick, where's Margaret? she says. They're home, they're coming tomorrow, I say, Pa was here earlier today, wasn't he, Nonna? She looks like she doesn't know and she's pretending it doesn't matter. She puckers her lips up and shrugs. Then there's some spot she sees on her bathrobe she tries to rub at. It's a slightly darker spot on the pink. It's nothing, I say and I touch her shoulder again.

His name is Paul, I say to her and then I remember of course my grandfather's name was Paolo and they called him Paul but she doesn't say anything. When's supper? she says. Soon, I'll take you in, Nonna, I say. I have to get her up and shift her to her wheelchair that was over against the wall. How's Marjorie next door? she's asking.

II

So you're going to a concert, says Alice late yesterday. Tomorrow night, I say, how did you know about it? Annie Randall told me you were telling her all about it, Alice says. I forgot I been talking to Annie in the waiting room earlier. I tell Alice how Annie was telling me about her singing in her church choir, she's a Presbyterian, and then I was telling her about my sister-in-law's cousin from Italy who sang opera on the Rome radio.

And I also hear you're going with someone, says Alice. I was putting back the files from the day and I feel a little embarrassed somehow. No one's there in the waiting room, just Mrs. McVeigh in seeing Bill and we're about to close up. And Annie told me about your new dress too, says Alice. So I think you're counseling Annie and you're both in there gossiping, I say and close up the file drawer. Alice laughs and walks over to look out the window at the street where lights are coming on, the sandwich shop sign and the blinking liquor mart signs.

It does Annie good talking to me about you, says Alice, you know Annie, it's hard getting her out of herself. She loves the way you chat along with her, Barbara. You know she sometimes goes a week not talking much to anyone? Her mother doesn't talk to her at all for days and there's no father. It's only at her church she talks and then she's mostly singing. She says she comes home and just sits, Alice says. Her mother's depressed but we can't get Annie to bring her in here. These two ladies and they're not young, Annie's in her forties and her mother's quite old, and they sit there at home in silence, no TV even, Alice says. She never tells me about all that, I tell Alice, but I see in her file what you wrote sometimes.

So who is it you're going with, Alice asks then, that man in your life you were mentioning when we had lunch? That's who, I say. His name's Paul, right? asks Alice. Annie told you his name even! I say. I think Annie dreams about you, Barbara, Alice says, she tells me Barbara has a life, Barbara's the way she wants to be. Skinny Annie wants to be me! I say.

Alice is walking around the waiting room lining up the chairs and putting the curled-up magazines in a neat pile. I decide to ask her: So then what about a man in your life, Alice? You don't mean my ex-husband, says Alice. No, I mean now, I say, isn't there one? They're hard to find,

Barbara, I mean the ones you like. You know, Alice, I say
quietly to her something I been thinking of telling her, I'm
not a virgin actually but I practically am, I mean all I did
with a man was with the doughnut shop manager when we
were alone there some nights closing up a couple times but
he fooled with lots of the girls there. I know what it feels
like but I don't really know, from the way it was with him,
I tell Alice. It isn't just because of being overweight, I say,
there's plenty overweight girls in my high school class that
got pregnant and left school or just were probably trying to
be popular. But I wanted to be home more and not hanging
out at night with kids. It wasn't the church or Ma or
anything but I didn't feel I could just go out like that back
then. The boys I was friends with were shy mostly and
they didn't want anything and they went off to the service
next. This is the first date for me in years, Alice, I say.

She's standing now in front of my desk and leaning
forward. Are you a little scared, Barbara? Alice says. I tell
her no I'm not really but I worry because I have somehow
hopes of love sometime, then I find myself with tears
under my eyelids. Alice puts her hands out on either side
of my head and rubs at my cheeks. In Bill's office I hear
Mrs. McVeigh screaming at him about something and I
hear Bill's low voice very calm talking along to calm her
down.

III

Yesterday must've began with my dreams that turned
into thoughts when I woke up. Then remembering the day
before and catching up with myself I remembered it was
now, the day of the concert, the day to be with Paul. And
then I got up and went and soaked, thinking about his

hands and his face which are the only parts of the actual him I've seen. And then I had my juice and toasts and cereal with half-and-half on the window seat. It was rainy yesterday morning but a misty kind of rain all day that didn't matter to anyone. We would be meeting after my work. He said to come down and he'd make us a supper before we went. Ma wanted me over there for supper with everybody, Gwen and Gregory and all Peter's kids since him and Camilla were going out with Dom and Gina, maybe even Catherine would come. But I told Ma no and she was grumpy at me all week.

Alice and Bill told me to leave work early even though it was a bad day with Jack Velis throwing a tantrum when I left. I waited for the bus and read some of the things I wrote before on the shelter but didn't write anything new. Some of them I wasn't sure I actually wrote but they were my writing. Like I didn't remember New children coming along every day. Why would I write that?

I took a long time changing. The dress looked not quite so good on me as I thought it did at the mall but that was with Gwen there telling me how great I looked. I put on my high heels which I'm not used to and decided to wear low heels instead though Gwen told me definitely not to. I went easy on the makeup. Alice told me at work she thought it was better to look more comfortable and like my regular self which wouldn't be Gwen's advice at all. She likes to really knock them out.

Paul opened his door with a sports jacket on he probably got at the Goodwill with a crest on the pocket and a folded handkerchief in it. Good evening, Barbara, let me take your coat, he said and he took my crushed velvet coat I had over my arm. That's a lovely frock, he says looking at my dress. Frock's not a word I'd say, I'm thinking. His apartment is very small, just a room with a bed in the space under where the staircase goes up. Then there's just a double hot plate and a toaster oven and a sink but no bathroom. Where's your bathroom? I ask. I have the key for the one in the hall, he says. This was meant once to be the caretaker's room, he tells me, when this was a more elegant sort of building. He told me how cheap he got the room for and that it was entirely adequate for his needs was the way he said it.

Won't you sit, Barbara, and let me get you a glass of something? he said and pretty soon I was sitting with a glass of wine on the soft chair in his room. I think I saw it last week on somebody's trash pile down the street, one of those Danish-style chairs with a cushion to sit on and one to lean back on that they used to sell cheap at the More-for-Less.

What we had for supper was sort of a stew he heated up on his burner. It was probably a West Indian dish with little pieces of chicken or maybe fish and I think even peanuts, it was hard to tell with the spices. He sat on the wooden chair crossing his leg so I saw his bare brown shin above his black sock and we ate out of bowls on our laps. He kept apologizing for not having a proper table like he said. Oh I always eat sitting on my window seat, I told him.

I never was in a black person's place before and for some reason I didn't expect it to be like it was, like maybe it'd have strange things I didn't know about in it or strange smells especially since he was from a jungly island. I asked him about his island and he said it wasn't really what you think of as a jungle in the movies. It's very dry there, he says. People have barrels on their roofs for catching the rain and then you let it down into the house through a hose apparently. They're actually houses with roofs not like in Haiti? I asked him. He wondered if I'd been to Haiti but I said oh no, I heard it from a Haitian woman who comes to the Center.

You mustn't be misled, Barbara, Paul says. He says my name always when he's talking to me. But I fear, he says in that typical way of his, that some people in Haiti live very well indeed. But there's some in cardboard boxes Mrs. Guimond says, I told him. Undoubtedly so, says Paul, it's not so different after all from here, he says, except the rich seem richer because the poor are so much poorer there. And then he looks at me with a kind of smile I don't exactly understand. It gives me a little shiver. It feels like he means that this is a very strange thing but we two are both understanding it. It's not like William when William tells me about the world and he makes me think it's somehow partly my fault. It's remarkable, isn't it? says Paul and I'm still looking at his smile feeling shivery.

Does it seem strange for you up here in America? I ask him. He says it would seem strange except that he's studied things and he has an idea, he says. When you have an idea, Barbara, he says, it helps matters along, doesn't it? It helps matters along? I say. When you have an idea, he says, an idea to turn to, an idea to make sense of things. So what's your idea? I ask. And then he says in a soft voice coming out his soft big lips and smiling in his careful way, he says, I hope it won't appall you to learn that I'm a communist.

There I am, spooning that stew gravy, thinking here I'm going out this evening and my family's going to all be there and I'm with a black man and that's not even the worst of it. It does appall you, doesn't it, he says. Appall? is all I can say. I don't know what to say to him, I'm looking at his shin. But you like it in America, I finally say. Yes and I like it everywhere, Paul says, I like the whole world. You wouldn't tell people you're a communist when you meet them right off? I say. But I'm getting to know you, Barbara, he says, so I wanted to tell you now and explain.

All the way over to the Atherton walking over Sugar Hill to Willow Street with his black umbrella he talked about his home. All the islands where he comes from are named after the saints, he said, and they used to belong to England but now they're free. They're all different, he says. Some have Americans coming down on vacation and big hotels but his island is too flat and doesn't have good beaches. There were some Americans who wanted to bring in gambling but the people didn't like that so they had a little revolution, he said, and got rid of the prime minister that wanted the gambling and the English had to come back in with a few helicopters. And now we're free a second time and our new prime minister, he says, is what you Americans call left-leaning, I fear. What's left-leaning? I ask him. Paul leans close to me and smiles in the light from the streetlights then he whispers communist in my ear as if it was a bad word.

So that's how come you're a communist then, you have to be, I say. By this time we can see the lights on the Atherton lit up down the street for the first time since I was a kid and I want to get this conversation over before we meet my family.

May I take your arm, Barbara? Paul suddenly says when we're crossing a street and I feel his arm around my elbow. No, I was always a communist, he says, even when I was a boy. So was my father, he says, and he's a minister in our present government. But why did you come to America then, I ask him, when you know they don't like communists? There's so much to learn here, he says and he squeezes my elbow in his arm. Maybe you won't be a communist still when you leave, I say looking at him crinkling up his eyebrows. I don't rule anything out, Barbara, he says.

There's a lot of people going in the door but no one's standing around because of the misty rain. Under the old marquee I untie my rain hat and I'm hoping my hair still looks all right. There's posters saying Italian Opera Night at the Atherton, Benefit for the Renovation. Dom's sister's name, Marianna Antonelli, is in big letters, Soprano from Rome, it says underneath. This is exciting, isn't it, says Paul tightening his arm again and I'm looking around to see if there's anyone that knows me. I have the tickets ready in my jacket pocket.

It's Peter we see first giving out programs behind some lady taking tickets. Hi Paul, he says, hi Barbara, here's your programs, can't talk now, hope you enjoy it. Paul's nodding and smiling and I notice he's nervous himself, not scared but a little confused like he's wondering what's happening next. Ma and Pa are in there already, Peter yells back at us.

The lobby's not like I remembered from going to movies. The paint's peeling and the linoleum's patched funny. Where the snacks were it's just an empty counter and then you get to the carpet that's not soft like I remember but all scuffed up. I used to think the Atherton was the most luxurious place I'd ever been. Saint Vin's was more beautiful but the Atherton was more luxurious.

I can't believe it's Ursula there being an usherette. So Camilla's got the whole family working, I say. Ursula's just staring at Paul. Mom said you got balcony seats, right? she says. I looked at the tickets and they said balcony. Grandma and Grandpa are downstairs, Ursula says. Then:

He's with you? she says looking at Paul. This is Paul and this is Ursula my oldest niece, I say. Paul's nodding and his arms are wobbling around in a nervous way like he wonders if he should shake her hand. Julia's upstairs showing you where to sit, Ursula says.

We go up the stairs with that same fancy railing I remember. You had to be over twelve to be let up there. Me and my girlfriend would watch Peter making out from the balcony when we were in junior high, I told Paul. Isn't Ursula a pretty child! he says.

There's little Julia at the top of the stairs and she yells, Barbara! She's hugging me before I get up the last step. Hello Julia, says Paul, because downstairs he heard her name and Julia looks at him like she doesn't understand how he knows her. Then she says, Oh hi Paul, and Paul opens his mouth looking surprised too. My dad said for me to say hi to Paul, says Julia to me whispering. Paul puts his hand on her hair. Something tells me you're rather fond of your Aunt Barbara, Paul says. Julia's already leading us into the theater. I know already where your seats are, she says, I was warming them up for you.

There's not many people in the balcony at least yet. We're in the front row where I used to always sit. Are you going to enjoy this concert? Paul asks Julia when we sit down and she's just standing there looking at us. I don't think so, says Julia. She's looking Paul over very carefully. Mom said I could go find Ursula and she'd take me over for ice cream, she says. You know Celia wouldn't come but you know what else, Lucius gets to be backstage. If you get sleepy, Julia, I tell her, you can come back up here and maybe if there's an extra seat here you could take a little nap on me. She runs off because more people are coming in. Paul is reading his program. This is exciting, he says again.

The curtain's still closed and the lights are on with people finding seats but I'm already excited too and I never been to an event like this, I'm thinking. What do you suppose this part will be? Paul asks pointing to the first thing on the program: Opening Remarks by George Ippolito. I don't even want to try to explain who's George Ippolito and all that crowd. He thinks he's a big deal around here is all I say.

When it starts there's applause for George but he doesn't say too much, just to ask for contributions and volunteers and then he introduces the mayor who makes a few jokes and says how proud he is for our city and then the mayor introduces Dom. That's Camilla's cousin Gina's husband, I say to Paul. Paul's been listening to every word they're saying as if he was really interested. From the balcony Dom looks short and nervous in his formal wear. Some of us around here have a dream, he says, and we hope tonight you'll get an idea of what I mean. He's shifting on his feet and he's shuffling some cards in his fingers trying to sound like he's casual on TV. We're proud tonight to have Marianna Antonelli here in Stinted Common to sing for us, he says not even mentioning she's his sister. I'm here to tell you, when she opens her mouth, Dom says, it's like a trip to Italy. For all you Italian-Americans here these are sounds of home, he says, and for those of you who aren't of Italian extraction perhaps she'll make you feel a little Italian too. Some people applauded. Julia's sneaking down the steps to our seats and she climbs over Paul and squeezes in next to me even though there's someone now on my other side. What my dream is, Dom's saying, is someday we'll have a whole Italian opera production on this very stage, not the sort of productions they have downtown over in Boston that costs an arm and a leg but opera for the people right here. Maybe tonight, he says, is just the previews.

I V

I had to tell Camilla right away when I came in yesterday morning and she was doing the breakfast dishes in her pink kitchen that it wasn't what I was expecting at all. So how'd you like it? she's saying while she scrapes off the egg. I thought she was going to be more wobbly, you know, like the lady who sometimes sings at Saint Vin's, I say, and it's not like when you hear it on TV coming out the speaker, you know? She didn't even have a microphone. I told you she's a big lady, says Camilla. It's true she was the biggest thing I ever saw on a stage, that's for sure, I say since I might as well joke, she made me even feel thin! Camilla doesn't laugh though, she just says, So Barbara, how was your date? Didn't you see him after? I ask her. She didn't because she went right backstage and Paul and me just left pretty soon and went for ice cream before too many other people got the idea leaving the theater.

Julia told me he was a nice man though, Camilla says. Your Julia slept right through it all, I tell her and how she was scrunched on my lap and she had her knees up on Paul's knees. He didn't mind? Camilla says. He loved everything last night, I tell her, he thought it was the most exciting thing he'd been to ever. He never heard a real opera singer either but he knows more about it than me because of his part in the opera back at his high school. Where he comes from! says Camilla, you're not telling me they put on an opera in the school where he comes from!

He told me so, I say. Well he's putting you on, Barbara, Camilla says like she knows for sure. I mean even here you see what they're putting on up at the high school and Ursula's going to be in this spring? she asks me. You seen the numbers she practices for? That's sure no opera! But where he comes from, Camilla, I say, it was owned by England and they're more strict there in education. Barbara, she says, you can't tell me you've got a bunch of excuse me colored kids on an island down there singing opera. All I know is he said he had to set off firecrackers in it, I say. That's what I figured, says Camilla, he's calling it opera but what would he know about opera? Well he listens to the classical station in the morning to wake up, I say.

Then Camilla stops wiping the plate she's on and looks over at me suspicious. You didn't sleep over with him, she says wincing her eyes. I could've told her no, I hear his radio out his door in the mornings, but I just stare back. What do you think? is what I decide to say. Julia's in the house, Barbara, don't say anything out loud. You're the one who said it, Camilla, I say, I didn't say anything. Her mouth drops a little and she holds the dish towel up to it. I'd know it if you did, she says, I could tell, but you didn't, I know for sure, I would've known right away. Then don't get all exercised, I tell her. Barbara, your mother would die, Camilla says.

She's right it's Ma I'm more worried about going over and talking to. She's mending upstairs when I come in and Pa's out. Saturdays he goes to meet some of his old buddies from work for their big breakfast up the street at Totney's. Ma looks up at me like she just noticed me in the door though she definitely heard me coming up the stairs. Was it a nice dinner you had here last night? I ask her first.

The kids were terrible, she says, I can't manage them all together anymore. Except Lucius wasn't there, he would've helped, but he was already backstage at the Atherton helping with the lights, Ma says, Lucius being her favorite. That's good for him, I say. What you mending? She just holds up a pair of Pa's trousers she's letting out in the seat.

Wasn't she beautiful? Ma says after a while. I'm sitting on the edge of her side of their bed. I always think of her mending in that low chair when I was a kid. Dom's sister? Her voice was, I say, she was one big mamma herself though. Ma twists her lips at me and says, I almost didn't notice her size when once she started in to sing, a woman with a gift like that.

I'm sure Ma liked most the first couple songs which were religious but I liked it more myself when she really knocked them out with those fast ones at the end where her voice went zooming all over. I certainly never heard someone sing that loud by themself, I say, it looked like the guy at the piano couldn't almost keep up. Ma explains he was the new music teacher they just got at the high school.

But you know what I liked? Ma says. Those two songs she called the Willow Songs. Those were two kids from the marching band, Ursula's class, playing the flute and the clarinet, Barbara, could you believe it? Yeah, they looked so nervous, I said. But weren't they good? says Ma, why doesn't Peter get any of his kids playing instruments? Best we can get is Ursula wiggling her rear in that silly show! Oh Ma, I say, not everybody's so gifted, you know. You'd think some from your grandfather would've come down to you kids though, Ma says. I say I think all that music side of Nonno went to Aunt Anna and she took it off to Arizona with her for good. Don't mention her, says Ma but she's smiling now, not so serious. She's pulling the thread around and around in and out tightening up her new seam.

The one with the kids playing was Rossini, she says. Did you read your program? You should know Rossini, Barbara. I know Rossini, I say but I don't really know him. And the long one was by Verdi, the one the Ave Maria came after, says Ma, you should know Verdi, you should know your cultural heritage. Oh Ma, you never played Nonno's records either, I say, and you were going to throw them out Gregory told me. That Ave was so beautiful, Ma says not answering me. That's what you'd like best, Ma, I knew it, I say. I don't know what it is with these Willow Songs, what that means really, she says, I suppose it's songs that are sad like a weeping willow. I finally say, Are you going to ask me about my date, Ma?

She leans back in the low chair and looks out the window to the back. I bet that's Quintus and Lucius behind Peter's, she says and we can hear a ball bouncing. Then she says, What can I say, Barbara? I didn't say say, I said ask, I say. There's something tight I feel, I almost feel Paul's arm tight on my elbow. Did he enjoy the music? Ma says. He certainly did, I say, that's the kind of music he knows about, he has a good education, Ma, you'd be surprised. Didn't you think he was nice when you shook his hand after? I ask her.

Now Ma gets up and goes to her dresser. She's just going through her morning the way she would anyway if we weren't talking. She's finding a scarf or something and then she's tidying up the things on top. I'm glad you had someone nice to take you, Barbara, she says, I'm glad to see you meeting new people. And your Pa convinced me it's nothing to worry about yet and your job is good for you and your apartment, I think it's all good, she says very seriously, so don't go thinking your Ma doesn't think so. But it's hard for me to act like it's nothing is all, you try and understand, Barbara.

I get off the bed and go give her a hug from behind and there I see us, short Ma and her big daughter behind in the mirror over her dresser. Your hair looks nice, she says, you looked nice last night in your dress, Gwen made you a good choice. You know what was funny, Ma? I say. Me looking down over the balcony and seeing you and Pa and just down in front there was Peter and Camilla with his arm around her like in high school when I spied on them. And there was Gregory too and his family looking so dressed up, little Tommy looking like Gregory did and little Tessa squirming around. Except for Catherine and Stephen we were all there which I don't think we were since when you and Pa sometimes took us to the movies there. And Julia was sleeping on my lap and I had a date there with me for once, that's why I didn't really care for those Willow Songs and those Ave Marias, that's why I liked it so much more in the fast parts where she let fly, Ma, I couldn't believe this one woman was doing that, she made me think she could do anything next, and with that red dress she had on like a tent and her fat arms out in the air. I was shaking inside, I say to Ma hugging onto her still with my chin up against her hair.

When I go out back later and the boys are still there playing catch Lucius says, Hey Barbara, wasn't that great last night! and it makes me want to go squeeze him that he liked it too. And how about those lights! he says.

V

Yesterday after Ma and Pa were back from Mass we were sitting in the living room reading the Sunday paper and Stephen was over. You missed a good show, Pa says to him. You wouldn't get me at one of those concerts, says Stephen, unless it's Def Leppard. Ma's fixing him his second breakfast, she says but I know he didn't get much of a first breakfast from Catherine, just cereal is all she ever gives him. Your cousins enjoyed it, Pa says, they were all talking about it still after Mass. I talked to them already, Stephen says, they didn't like it, Celia didn't even go and Ursula went out for ice cream she said. Pa told him Julia stayed the whole time though and that Lucius was backstage. They're kids, said Stephen. Then he looks over at me and shakes his hair which he always does though it doesn't change the way it looks, it just fluffs up and then falls back the same way it already was. They said you had a black boyfriend there, he says in a quiet voice.

I was looking through the Personality Parade but I saw him looking at me. I went with a friend who's black, Stephen, I say. So he's your boyfriend, isn't he? he says. Why should I tell you if he is? I say because Stephen aggravates me with his way of acting like he doesn't care. When did you ever care about my private life? I ask him. So I'm asking you, he says. No you just wanted to say he was black, that's all you wanted to say and you know it, Stephen, I say. I don't have to say that, I know that, Stephen says, I'm just asking you about him, Barbara. You take everything wrong, he says staring across the room at me from the couch. Leave Barbara alone, Stephen, says Pa from behind the movie section in his chair.

Ma brings in a plate of eggs and sausage for Stephen so he

moves to the table and there's doughnuts she got from my old shop on her walk back from Saint Vin's. There's one more for you too, Barbara, Ma says and I can't resist since it's a slow rainy Sunday. Stinted Common did itself proud Friday night, says Pa. It turns out he's reading from the paper, the report of Marianna Antonelli which later I cut out and put up on my fridge with a Smurf magnet. I didn't expect they'd cover it in the Boston papers, Ma said. Pa went on reading for us: A singer of some repute in Rome, the guy says, though known to me only from two small roles on recordings pirated from RAI. What's that mean? asks Pa. The reporter stole the records, says Stephen. He wouldn't say that in the paper, Pa says. RAI's the radio in Italy, says Ma from the kitchen. Well so does he think she was a good singer? I ask. Then Pa reads the part that goes: Though her girth prohibits her from making a truly convincing, how would you pronounce this, he says, Desdemona? Oh no, Desdemona! says Stephen, we had to read that for the Advanced, it's in Shakespeare, that's not Italian. What's her girth? I asked Pa. It means she's large, he's being polite this reporter, Pa explains to me. Though her girth prohibits her from making a truly convincing Desdemona, whether in Verdi or Rossini, she managed the pianissimi, there's a good Italian word, says Pa, she managed the pianissimi quite effectively.

Stephen went back to loudly turning the pages in the want ads. Pa was reading on for Ma's sake who was in the kitchen: Her voice ran away with her in the more florid numbers that closed the program, he goes. I wasn't sure what florid refers to but really that's what I liked about it when she let her voice run away. And then the article goes: However, the recital provided a rare glimpse into the native spirit of Italian opera that we in America usually miss in these days of the international star. And then comes the part I like most to read over: It's a healthy sign, he goes, to see a recitalist drawing such an enthusiastic crowd to an old theater, previously condemned to be turned into bowling alleys, in one of the least likely urban locales in the greater Boston area. Dom must be proud, I'm thinking. Pa said over to me when he finished reading: It must be something to be referred to in the paper as an international star.

VI

Yesterday when Bill dropped me off at my block I had to go look again at the bus shelter to see if that morning I wrote what I thought I did there. It was squeezed in a small corner darker black than my other ones: Her girth prohibits her. And then underneath it says: It helps matters along. I had to laugh for writing those sort of things there. I don't even know why it comes into my mind. It comes straight out of the marker almost and I'm not even thinking. I had to laugh too because yesterday was so bad at work and I just felt like somehow laughing after all that.

First it was Jack Velis again screaming at his mother and hitting her when they were waiting and I was trying to get him off her and keep her off him and all the other people waiting were crowding around. So then Bill handles that but then some new lady Mrs. Montagnoli is talking about her husband who's gay and no one wants to have to hear all that out loud in the waiting room. I'm going to kill him next time, she's saying. What do you mean next time? says Mrs. Velis. There's kids in here, says Mrs. McVeigh. It's too much for me, I just go back to the desk and wait this one out.

But that's only the start. Then the police bring in some girl, she really looks like just a girl though later I find out she's older. She's not even talking and they have to almost drag her each step of the way. Everyone gets suddenly quiet. It's Larry Walsh from my high school class who's on the force now and he's whispering: Barbara, just let's get her in to see Alice, we can't deal with her down the station. Why don't you take her to the hospital? I whisper to him. There's nothing they'll take her in for there, she was fine, she was just sitting, she says she's not going to talk to any man about it and then she just shut up. The other policeman's nodding. There's Betty down the station isn't there? I still whisper. Betty's off today, Larry says, and Diane's over in court. All the ladies in the room are looking at us and her but like they aren't trying to look and the kids are quiet. Then one baby screams. Alice heard something was going on so she slips out of her door when I'm telling Larry she's in there with someone. Just have her sit a minute, Barbara, Alice says, we're almost done.

Then when Mrs. Tavares leaves and he goes in with this silent woman to Alice's office and the other policeman goes down to the cruiser, then Mrs. Montagnoli starts carping. It's my appointment next, she says, I'm not sitting around waiting for them dragging people in off the street. There's sometimes emergencies, I explain. So who hasn't got emergencies! says Mrs. Montagnoli. Well I'm sorry, says Mrs. McVeigh, I'm not listening to all this, I'm going, I'll come sometime else. All I have time for is to say, You call me for a time then, but she's off down the stairs. What's wrong with her? Mrs. Montagnoli says. Just shut up and stop talking about yourself, says the lady with the baby I forget the name of.

Then Larry came out and we were sitting talking about

high school days and he was reminding me of that boy Robert Santangelo who was my friend who'd dance with me at dances. He's gone into police work too, says Larry, he's down in Texas I think it is where his whole family moved to, I heard from another kid who knew him. He was real nice, I tell Larry. I'm just talking to Larry and letting all the waiting people wait, I tell myself. Kids are back yelling at each other and climbing in and out of the cardboard box the fridge came in which we were going to get rid of but now it makes a good way to keep the kids busy. How's your wife? I ask Larry. I feel bad since I can't remember her name but she went to the Catholic school not the high school. Susie's fine, says Larry. So I moved to my own place, I tell him. Hey Barbara, he says, no wonder I drive by your old street and I never see you. Oh I still go over to Ma's but it's great having my own place, it's up Milk Street. Too bad that's not in my ward anymore, Larry says.

Then there's noise coming out of Alice's door and there's also noise coming out of Bill's. It's that old couple in seeing him still, Mr. and Mrs. Donovan. Of course I go out to sit in the car! you can hear him yelling, I can't stand it in there with her! Then there's the window breaking in Alice's. Larry goes right in the door. It was Alice's little cassette recorder she has that the girl picked up and threw right at the window which broke it and out goes the recorder. The girl's back sitting down on top of her hands but Larry stands there next her. Alice doesn't get upset. She explains how it happened like it was a normal thing but the girl is looking at her like she hated her. Did you get her to say anything? Larry asks. She's not from Stinted Common, says Alice, she doesn't have a place to go. There's Mrs. Montagnoli at the door leaning in and she says, You should arrest her for vagrancy, Officer. Larry smiles in a calm way and shuts the door softly on her. I'd go back to my desk but Alice says wait.

We were all standing there thinking is the girl crazy or is she sick or is she just real poor. They didn't find her at night somewhere or find her trespassing, she was just sitting at a bus stop and the weather's been okay so she wasn't cold but Larry noticed her there all day. Larry said to Alice he could've let her sit and maybe she'd be gone by night but he was asking if something was wrong and all she could say was she wouldn't talk to any man. He asked her if she'd go to the Center and see a woman and she didn't say anything of course but she went with him. That's all he knew. Then all Alice knew was that she did start talking and she said she hadn't been raped and no one had tried to hurt her and she wasn't on drugs or drinking. She just wanted to sit forever is what she told Alice. People could move her but all she herself was going to do was sit. How long she's been doing this, does she say? I asked. She was saying she just started today and then she saw the recorder, Alice said. This girl threw the recorder because she thought Alice was running it when she got her talking but Alice wasn't.

I'm going to call Betty at her home, Larry says and he goes out to the waiting room where everyone's talking loud now and Mr. and Mrs. Donovan are leaving with Mrs. Donovan wiping at her eyes. The door closes after Larry. I better stay with Alice. We don't say anything. I look at this girl, this woman really, you can see up close she's not so young, she's just small and thin and has her hair back in a ponytail but all around her eyes it's wrinkled. The other policeman knocks and comes in with the recorder he picked up from the sidewalk. Then him and Alice tape up some cardboard over the window for now. Usually people throw things into windows from the outside, he says, but this is a new one. Stephen and his friends I keep thinking of.

I'm back at my desk when Betty comes up. She was a friend of Catherine's when they were in school. They go in and that's all I know and I'm back acting to everyone there like it's a normal day at the Center. The people coming in now only get the story from the ones who've been sitting for a while. It's piling up because Bill can't handle everyone, especially since Mrs. Montagnoli wants her full appointment. Larry and Betty finally take that silent woman out and Alice sees Mrs. Montagnoli. At five she tells me to go home when Bill leaves but she'll stay late and see people so I left not even knowing what ever happened.

Bill dropped me off on my corner on his way to pick up Polly and Sarah so I catch him up in the car and he can't believe the day. The police never know what to do with people, he says, but I say that Larry's new on the force and he's the nicest guy, he was trying to do the best thing. Paul's light isn't on when I come in. I know he's off studying because he said he had big tests coming and that concert was his last treat for a while. I look up the dark brown shingles to where my bay window's sticking out. This time of day there's no sunlight on this side.

VII

It's just like Pa, giving me a birthday present early and he doesn't even warn me. Yesterday I would've been gone to work in half an hour but he knows the installer from hanging around Totney's so he was sure to have him get there early enough. I open the door and there's a guy saying, Miss Orsini here's your phone. I didn't know anything about it then he gives me Pa's birthday card. So now I got a slim-line phone installed and Pa says the bills are going to him.

Who do I call first of course but home. Ma answers and I say just put on Pa. Pa, I say, are you crazy! Crazy for you, he says. Pa, but who am I going to call? This way we can call you, he says. So when I get home from work then I call Peter's house and get Quintus who just wants to tell about his baseball and then I get Camilla on but she's busy cooking. Then I call Catherine's but no one's there so I call Gregory's and he's the one that answers. He knew all about the phone already and he was trying calling me to be my first call but it was always busy. I say I had to call Bill Potts about work because I didn't want Gregory thinking I tried him last.

We got an idea, says Gregory, we're having some people in for brunch Sunday and Gwen said why don't we get Barbara and her new friend. Not really, I say and he says, Yes really. You mean the Bartlettes will be there? I say figuring he wants to show off his sister with the black boyfriend. The Bartlettes and the Donnells probably and some others, Gregory says. He's busy studying for tests, I say, I didn't see him since after the concert. But brunch is no big deal, just Sunday noon, Gregory convinces me. Well I could ask him, I say. Gregory asks where did we two go after so I tell him how we went for ice cream. You know I like that Paul, he says, we were having a nice talk there when you and Gwen were yapping in the lobby. You know what he told me, Gregory says, he told me the concert transported him. So then I asked where it transported him to and he said it wasn't to a place, it wasn't to a time even, it was to a state of harmony, he said, it transported him to a state of harmony, Gregory says over the phone, that's nice, isn't it.

My phone cord reaches so I can sit on the window seat but also the other way so I can take it in by my bathtub. I feel like my apartment is more part of the world now. Pa knows how I feel about things and maybe he did it because he wants to be able to call and probably Ma told him she wished I had a phone so she wouldn't worry about me as much. But Pa really got it for me I'm sure because he can tell how good it'd make me feel and he knows I'd never do it for myself.

VIII

Yesterday after I been home for dinner and got back to my place and was just fixing a snack there was a knock. It's Paul Felice, Barbara, I hear him say. There he is when I open up with slipper socks on and a brown cardigan. You know your last name would be Italian if you said it Faleechee, I tell him while I'm thinking of it. It's a French name, he tells me. So how does he get a French name I want to know. I'm leaning on my door and we're just talking in the hall in this neighborly way. Paul explains how his island was first French way back before it was English and there was even Swedish people on this other island there and there was Danish people and Dutch on some other islands. I say how it must get confusing down there. Well we're a very mixed lot is what he says. His great-grandmother, he said, was a daughter of a Swedish sailor from Gustavia which is what he can see at night across the water from the tip of his island. He described it with his hands pointing down the dark hall to where there's light under some old lady's door. Like that, he says, a line of lights in the distance, it's quite beautiful, he says as though that crack under the door was actually this Gustavia. I ask if that's another island but that's the town on it, he says, it's named for the king of Sweden back then. Somehow you know about so much, I say and that reminded me to ask him about his tests. I took them just this morning as it happens, he says. Then I realize I shouldn't keep him just standing in the hall. Then you should come in and relax and have a snack, I say.

He looks in my apartment and says, If I may? Ah that's your window seat then, he says. He tells me how he always looks up at the building when he comes home and he wonders which window belongs to me. It's got a nice view in the day, you can even see down Milk Street to the Bunker Hill monument, I say, and it's the only bay window in the building, sort of decoration, I guess. From his window, Paul says, he only sees the All-Night sign blinking. Even when he sleeps and the shade is shut there's blinking all over his walls, he says. I can see him tucked in his bed there under the stairs with his covers up to his chin. I always think of Paul as being bundled up somehow because it's too cold for him up north here.

If I may? he asks again before he sits on the window seat. I was making popcorn or you could have a slice of pie I have in the fridge, I say. I didn't expect to be fed, Barbara, he says. I offered him Tab or a Seven-Up but he said just a little popcorn would be plenty. So the test was okay? I asked. He'd know next week but it was only the midterms not finals. I'm sorry I had to disappear all weekend after you were so nice in taking me to the concert, Barbara, he said then. I brought the bowl over and sat on the other corner of the window seat and remembered what Peter said about the beams going back into the building.

Were you really ever in an opera yourself? I asked him when we're eating. Indeed I was, he says. But not in Italian, I say and he says, Oh no in English. We keep trading off putting our hands in the bowl between us. Mmm this is buttery, he says. I tell him it's the only way to have popcorn. He goes on telling me about his school down there. He didn't think they had that kind of schools in Stinted Common, just for boys where you lived at the school. One of the finest boys' schools in the Caribbean, he said. So I told him about how they were thinking of sending Lucius to Boys' Catholic because it's a good education and there's more sports facilities but it means him commuting because there you don't live in.

It's mostly only blacks now in his old school, Paul said, but there was a few whites still when he was there. The son of some Russian ambassador was there, he said. And there's a girls' school too which they put on shows with. Then it turns out that their music teacher, or music master he says, was a communist too even though he was a white. And the opera he got them putting on, Paul said, was anti-imperialist and anti-capitalist. It gave me a shiver to hear him saying those words which usually you hear only on TV coming from some Cubans or whatever. But he was just scooping up popcorn and smiling like he does and saying those words.

We were getting down in the bowl to the half-popped kernels which actually I sort of like and our fingertips were greasy. They even touched when we were both rubbing the sides of the bowl. Excellent popcorn, says Paul. You may be sick of my family, I say deciding I might as well ask him, but my brother Gregory you met is having a brunch on Sunday and they wondered if I could bring you. Paul looked over at me looking so relaxed in his cardigan leaning on a pillow against the window and picking a minute at his teeth with his fingernail. What exactly is a brunch, if I may ask? he says. After I explain it's a late breakfast but with more lunch-type food, he says, You know, Barbara, I find it so pleasant being with you. I lead a rather lonely existence here, he says but not in a sad voice, and I would love to come to your brother Gregory's, I would love to do anything with you and I promise you the very next invitation will come from me. I told him it doesn't have to be like an invitation, it can be just like neighbors dropping in, like friends. It's difficult to say, Paul says, but this visit has been, he's looking at me and thinking of a word and then he says: memorable. I'm thinking how it really is memorable for me too. Then he says it's been like looking out at a new view where things in the distance look more beautiful now but he says it not looking out the window but looking over at me.

IX

Catherine called and then she came over. I haven't seen her for a long time just us and she didn't sound good over the phone. You there, Barbara? she says and then: I'm coming over. When I let her in I pointed to Paul's door and whispered that's where Paul lives but she nods and doesn't look too interested. We get upstairs and I show her my place which she didn't come over to see before. I slept late it being Saturday and took a long soak so I hadn't even got dressed yet and my hair was up in a towel. You still have that red bathrobe? says Catherine feeling it between her fingers where it's wearing out. You had that back in high

school, she says. Hey you know who I saw? Betty! I tell
her, she came in the Center to take some crazy woman
away. I thought they just had Betty behind the desk at the
station, Catherine said.

She sits on my chair not the window seat. I'm making
her some tea. There she is my own sister and we're so
different. She's looking more and more like Ma but taller.
But she has the long face with the long nose not like mine
and the hollows in the cheeks. My round cheek would fit
right against her hollow cheek, I'm thinking but Catherine
and I don't hug each other that way ever now. I hug Gwen
and Camilla more though they still don't feel like sisters
like Catherine does.

The best things are remembering Catherine and William
back when they got married and when they lived in that
apartment especially before Stephen. Then when Stephen
was a baby I'd go over there and learn to diaper him and get
him to fall asleep on me. It was my main thing to do back
then in junior high. They could always get me to baby-sit
Stephen and they'd go out to a movie. Catherine didn't
have me sitting as much for Ursula when she came along
or Celia but for Lucius I did so she could take the girls with
her for shopping. I guess it was the boys I knew better at
least till Julia and by then I graduated high school and I was
usually around Peter's more because they moved into their
house right next door to Ma. But Quintus I couldn't handle
he was so colicky. And it was always too much of a thing
to go sit for Gregory's kids though I did sometimes but
they had kids on their street they paid or they traded off
with other families. And Gregory was into taking care of
his kids himself more than Peter was ever, that's one thing.
Gwen was always going out with her girlfriends at night
and leaving Gregory to sit but Camilla was always home.

Anyways things didn't go good for William and it already got different going over there and then they moved one other place and finally into the project. I think William was changing then but I was too of course, going from a kid to graduating, so everything seemed different. It wasn't like Gregory or Gwen who got married when I was already older or even Peter and Camilla who knew each other all their lives and they still act the same now together as they ever did. But Catherine's all different now, William's all different, and I can't look at Stephen and think of him being that baby I held. Even Ursula I can see being a baby still but not Stephen. Now he's so skinny and wiry like he's always tense and like William he's got really hairy wrists and the backs of his hands and ankles and it's sticking out his shirt at the neck but he's got Catherine's build, the hollows and that look off in the distance.

When Catherine was in my apartment yesterday morning I was thinking I wish she was more alive somehow but she's just sitting there. I gave her the tea and I got up on my window seat in my old bathrobe. It was all sunny there. You look happy these days, Catherine says. I'm pretty happy, I say back. You weren't so happy before, she says, but it's this place and your job and your new friends, right? How's your job? I ask her. Well one of us is working anyway, she says. I thought William was back on, I say but she tells me he got laid off again, it was all some foul-up. That's some way to foul up, can they do that? I asked her. They can do whatever, she says.

So that means he's around home again, I'm thinking. How's it between you two? I ask her. I was going to that concert too, you know, Catherine says looking at the clipping on my fridge, I was coming over to Ma's before for dinner too and then William tells me I'm not going and that ended up in some fight so Ma's on the phone all week as usual and he's telling me to stop always talking to Ma, it's bad for me, so I say I suppose he's good for me. So that's another fight, that was worse. Catherine's telling this all looking at her tea not drinking it and making a sigh each time she stops talking.

You know who you should talk to is Alice McKeever at work, I say because Catherine's reminding me of all those people in the waiting room. You said that before is all she says.

Then I'm looking out the window at the bus going along Milk Street and when it stops the old ladies get on to go do their Saturday shopping. And there's a pack of teenagers hanging out in the spring sun at last. So Barbara? Catherine says. So what if I said it before, I say aggravated at her, you want me to say it again even? You tell me one thing this Alice McKeever could do for me and Stephen, she says, she's not going to change William, she's not turning him back the way he was before, she's not getting Stephen out from home. Don't listen to me then, I say, I don't have any other idea. Why don't you just do something yourself to help me, Barbara? she says and I can tell now how she came over here mad at me somehow already. People don't help each other in families enough, she says. So who helps me! I say. You're not married! she screams back at me suddenly.

We look at each other and she's sitting there dark and crying. You're coming in to see Alice, I say. I'm taking you on Monday. I'm working, she says. You're coming on lunch hour and you know you can and I'll switch somebody's appointment around. I'm on the register at lunch, she says. You're calling in sick, I say. I am not, Catherine says. I'm calling in then and telling them you're sick, I say.

No you're not, Catherine says still with tears on her face.

I go over and stand behind the chair and hold her shoulders while she sniffles. Something's happening to me, I start telling her. I'm learning things, I say just talking into the air while I rub her shoulders and words start coming from my mouth out loud. It's all right for some people being a communist is what I say first. I don't even know if Catherine's listening. I feel her shoulders give a shake when she tries to breathe after crying. Then I say out loud: There's people living so poor it would make you feel richer than I ever thought. Not here maybe but down in Haiti, I tell her, and on all those islands named for saints where Paul is from. Then I keep rubbing and she's quiet and it feels almost in a dream so I just say words: his big black lips, I say, his black shins, there's barrels on the roof there for catching rain. I'm rubbing where her shoulder blades are and she's just making a few sniffs. The lights across the ocean in the dark, I say half out loud. Then we're quiet for a bit. Music makes me feel in the state of harmony, I say. I hear Catherine say, What do you mean music? You would've liked the Willow Songs, Catherine, I say, and those nervous kids from the marching band playing along. And Lucius back there learning to run the lights and Julia sleeping on my knees. I didn't sleep at all last night, Catherine says.

So I told her to take a nap in my bed and then take a bath in my tub and I was going out to the store and when I got back I'd make her a second breakfast. I'm already leading her to the bed and pulling down the spread. Hey this was Nonna's spread, she says. Ma let me take it, I say. I remember always going and sitting on Nonna's bed Saturday mornings early back when she lived with us, Catherine says. I even think I remember doing that too, I say to her, just before they moved to their apartment. You were real little then, Catherine says.

X

How to get over to Gregory's on Sunday was the problem since buses don't run as regular and it's crosstown anyway from where the buses run. I didn't want Gregory having to come get us when he was getting brunch ready so I didn't say anything to him. But then Paul had some graduate school friend with a car who was going out anyway to play soccer so he said he'd come by for us. I was ready, just a sweater and skirt for brunch I figured since it was a real spring day again luckily.

When I came down Paul was out front with a book he was reading in the sun but when this rattly Volkswagen drives up he runs and puts his book back inside and then we walked side by side over to his friend's car. It wasn't a black man but some blond guy with a trim beard and a smelly gray sweat suit looking sleepy. Paul said he'd get in the back but I said I would. I said hello when I squeezed in back next to a muddy soccer ball. Paul said, This is Horst my Namibian friend. After saying hi again I asked if he was a graduate student too for something to ask. To my dismay, said Horst laughing.

The car started rattling along Milk Street and I was just hoping we'd get to Gregory's safe. I had to explain to Horst where to turn but since I don't drive I got mixed up with one-way streets. We don't want to make you late for your game, Paul said being polite but this Horst was just laughing and backing into people's driveways to turn the car around. I love it when I'm getting lost, he says with some kind of accent, I'm spending my entire life doing it.

Then he screeches up to a stop sign and I realized we were back on Milk Street where we started.

But he finally got us to Gregory's and he told us we had to come play soccer with him some Sunday. Best way to be waking yourself up after a heavy night at Clooney's, he says which is the bar in Endicott Square Gregory sometimes goes to. I'm thinking how Paul and me probably wouldn't be too good playing soccer even with this hung over Horst but it was nice for him to ask. His Volkswagen drives off clanking its tail pipe on something and when we're walking up Gregory's steps I say to Paul: Horst sounds sort of like Nazis on TV. That's just his accent, says Paul but I'm thinking how there's so many foreigners around from countries like this Namibia I never heard of.

Tommy opens the door in his church clothes with his collar too tight squeezing his neck pink. So you're the butler, says Paul giving him a handshake. There's people already in their living room talking. We don't have coats it's so warm out so Tommy leads us straight in. He's been sitting on the front steps earlier, I can tell, because the seat of his pants is dusty.

It's little sister! Gregory yells coming in from the kitchen with his electric skillet. Just in time for my famous pepper omelettes, he says and he starts spooning it out on some plates. I met the Donnells once and I seen the Bartlettes though I didn't meet them before so we all got introduced and I introduced Paul and explained we lived in the same building. You should see Barbara's gorgeous new place, she's got a view almost to Boston, says Gwen. She's nudging over on the couch to make room for me and points to the kitchen chair she pulled in for Paul. Mr. Bartlette's into real estate so he wants to know where my place is and then he says, Oh I know that old building, that brown shingle on the corner with the precarious-looking bay window? That's a DiNapoli property, he says.

I can see Paul being nervous when he crosses his legs and looks around the room. It's a lovely place, he says to Gwen. She's smiling away, happy for all these people being over. It's Gregory who does the cooking for brunches and next he comes in with a bread basket with his latest thing, crumpets. This is something you're going to like, Barbara, he says, I'm getting you hooked on a new breakfast treat. Alice sometimes has one with her coffee, I say but it's true I never did have one myself before. Alice McKeever I work with, I explain to Patti Donnell. They're very good with lots of butter, Paul says when Gregory passes to me next.

It's different being at Gregory's for a change. At Ma's on Sundays there's Pa in his recliner with the paper and as usual all the drapes closed in the front, Ma always likes to keep private from the street. But Gregory's got his blinds up and even one window open a crack and there's his plants hanging in the windows. He takes care of them too and I never can figure what Gwen actually does there around their apartment. So where's Tessa? I ask her. Out back with the Bartlette girls, says Gwen and then suddenly they all come in, two little black girls and Tessa wrestling in the kitchen.

Gregory's out there getting them omelettes without peppers but Tommy eats with us sitting quiet on the rug and the Donnells and Gwen start talking politics. Did you want to see my newt? Tommy says after I'm finished with my helping so I go off down the hall leaving Paul there for a minute to see this little red lizard Tommy has in a bowl by his bunk. It's still in the eft stage. He explains to me all about it. Tommy, you're smart in school, I can tell, I say. Tommy's not like Peter's kids with me. He's shy and likes to explain things but he doesn't come zooming in and jumping on me.

Pa always says how his grandchildren's hair keeps getting lighter. I mean there's Stephen who even though he's so pale has got the blackest hair I ever saw and then there's Peter's kids with their dark skin, like Camilla's, but slowly getting lighter hair till Quintus actually has even these light brown highlights. And then comes Tommy who's really got all light brown hair and Tessa you could almost call blond at least when she was littler. What if I had a baby with Paul, I'm thinking, well Pa would really have to change his idea fast. What're you smiling at, Barbara? says Tommy catching me thinking about it. You and your bugs and newts, I say. If it was Quintus I'd probably give him a pinch somewhere but not Tommy.

Then I come back to the living room and it's Paul who's talking now. Well I have an African friend, he's saying mostly to Joe Donnell but everybody's listening, with whom I discuss this very subject, says Paul. What? I say squeezing in next to Gwen again and Gregory passes me another of those good crumpets. Try this one with apricot jam, he says. Joe Donnell explains what Paul's been saying about how in the world there's places where the only way out is, you know, like the IRA, says Joe. What way out? I say looking over to Paul. Well I was speaking of this African friend of mine, he says, and that he can't go back home now because of his association with, I don't mean to appall anyone, but with, then Paul looks at me with his black gentle face and a hand gently over on my plaid skirt and he says: with what you might call terrorist elements. Terrorist elements? I say. And, all the worse for this friend of mine, he's of an old colonial family! says Paul to the others. So his allegiances are complicated, he says.

Paul! Gwen says leaning forward over me like she just found a new friend, I have to tell you something! It's something everyone here—oh Tommy go out and shut up those girls, she yells. Then she looks around like she loves it we're all in on her conspiracy and I'm thinking please Gwen don't start talking about her father and her brothers and them sending guns or whatever they do. But of course that's what she starts talking about and the Donnells are joining in saying how they're all for it themselves and get out those damn English. Here I was promising Gwen at the mall I wasn't going to mention it to Paul and now she goes herself spilling it out.

The Bartlettes, who are dressed up like they'd went to church first to whatever church they go, they're just sitting there sipping coffee and listening like they were bored maybe. And Paul, says Patti Donnell, you must've had a time getting the English out of your island too, right? In our case they were rather more eager to go, says Paul in his typical way of saying things, indeed we found it necessary to ask them back for a short spell, he says. But what about this African friend? says Gwen still leaning over me to Paul with her elbow jabbing in my side.

Mr. Bartlette then says like to himself: You Irish! no way I'll ever understand your politics! Gregory's in the kitchen yelling back: I'm not Irish! I'm not Irish! Then Paul does tell more about his African friend who was out in the desert of his country helping poor people. And these are people starving in the desert as if they lived in the Stone Age, Paul says. But terrorists are cowards generally and I speak from some firsthand experience, says Mr. Bartlette. I guess he was in the service during something. Mrs. Bartlette puts her cup down so carefully on the coffee table I can tell she'd like him to stay out of it. We're all watching her and she does it so slow the cup doesn't make a sound. Paul doesn't look worried now though. No, he says in a soft voice too. I'm watching his lips move, they're so big it's not like they're even making the words. It's more cowardly, isn't it, he says, to fly your colors in the open air—and then he smiles and says: but from the wings of a jet plane?

This is something we'd better not discuss on a lovely Sunday morning, says Mr. Bartlette like he knew his wife didn't want him to. We all look up at Gregory coming back in then with strawberries and whipped cream. Gregory did go all out for this brunch. Him and Gwen are both that way when they do things, their life's so different than us growing up. His job doesn't even pay him that much more but it's the things they spend their money on like that batik hanging from Indonesia Gwen's so proud of, ugly as it is.

I'm hoping it's the end of all this talk now even though it made me feel somehow excited when Paul would say something. But I didn't want the Bartlettes and Donnells getting into some fight or Gwen going on more about the damn English. It was nice of Paul not minding her too much. The thing about him is how he lets people have their say irregardless but he'll still say what he means too. So then we're talking about everybody's kids for a while instead.

I'm feeling so stuffed by the time it's come to leave. We never did talk about what you do, says Mrs. Bartlette politely to me when we're all standing up. I'm thinking who ever stands up when you come or go at Ma's! I tell her I work at the Autumn Hill Center. You know it's meant to be a sort of drop-in center for family problems, I say, but now it's caught on and you have to make an appointment.

Little sister keeps that place afloat, says Gregory when he kisses me good-bye from under his whipped creamy mustache. That was some brunch of yours, Gregory, I tell him. They're all glad we came. Then Gregory offers to drive us but Paul says the day's turned out so warm he'd like to walk so I say so too.

When we're walking along I point out the Bartlettes' duplex which they own the whole thing and Gregory told me they own also a couple more buildings on the street, not his though. The two floors above Gregory there's students moved in now and earlier he was laughing about how students sure aren't like they were in his day with drugs and parties, now they just want to study. It's so different here out the western end, I say to Paul, I don't really like it, it doesn't feel like neighborhoods, it's more spread apart. He said he thought Gregory's friends were very neighborly though but I explained it wasn't the same as growing up some one place and everybody always knowing everybody.

I didn't know you had an African friend, I say when we're going through Endicott Square. Then I find out I already met him, it was that Horst. I said, But he wasn't African! But Paul said yes he was, Namibia's the only country he ever had. It was his German great-grandparents that settled a colony there, oh before the First World War, says Paul. But Paul, I said, how can you keep track of the world the way it is? I'm giving up! That's when he put his elbow around mine like on the Italian Opera Night. Barbara, he says, I hope I didn't embarrass you arguing with that Bartlette fellow. But I just didn't understand it much, I say, what you all were actually saying. I don't understand it either, Paul says. Sure you do, I said, you know all about world news, you're always studying it.

We walked along the cracked sidewalk looking at the more usual triple-deckers now that were more like my old neighborhood and people didn't have so much front yards along there like they do out by Gregory's. But for all my studying, Barbara, I still don't understand very much of it, Paul says again. I wish I did, he says, I wish there could be one place I did understand. Our elbows are squeezing soft against each other. I don't care who sees us out on this sunny quiet day.

XI

Yesterday at the Center I told Alice how I switched Mrs. Figueroa around till later because my sister was coming in. I didn't know why but Alice looked miffed. I closed the door in her office before anyone was out there waiting and asked her if I shouldn't have done it. I'm just afraid, Barbara, she says, I hope you didn't tell her how I was going to solve all her problems. Alice looks at me actually worried, it's not like Alice. Oh, I say. Didn't you want me to have her come? I ask then. But I'm still afraid of disappointing you, Barbara, she says. But I know how it is here, I tell her, I see how people have to keep coming and things don't get better but they feel better because they're doing at least something, you know? And Mrs. Figueroa on the phone didn't mind at all, I tell her.

We never really talked about your date, Alice then says to change the subject. Like I told you it went fine, I say but she says I didn't say how I felt about him though. I tell how Paul told me he always likes doing things with me but he does have to study too much is one thing. But how do you feel about him? Alice says again. It gets me excited when he talks, I listen to every word he says, I tell her.

Alice squints and looks at the new windowpane with its white putty smeared on it. Beware of the ones who like to hear themselves talk, she says and I get the feeling she's talking about somebody she knows. But he doesn't really, Alice, he's very quiet, I say, he just says a few things in a gentle way. But the big question, says Alice, is does he want only to talk about what he does and what he thinks and what he knows? Alice is looking still worried and squinty. He does talk lots about world news, I say. And I'm sure you're just dying to hear it, says Alice tapping her pen hard on her desk. Oh well, it's not been a good weekend, she says. Then we hear someone coming to the waiting room and when I'm heading out Alice says, Send in the first lion!

When Catherine came at lunch she didn't want to act like I was her sister to anyone there. Have a seat, I said after I filled out her form like I would say to anyone and I hear Mrs. Montagnoli turning to her and she says, I bet you're here because of your husband, am I right, but you ain't seen the half of it, she says. I see Catherine look like she'd kill her and that shuts up Mrs. Montagnoli.

When Catherine goes in I'm nervous so I take out my turkey club Bill got me at takeout and eat it at my desk. I didn't want to go out this lunch hour at all and I already had my Tab in the fridge. Then she comes out later when Mrs. Montagnoli is in seeing Bill this time instead of Alice after she insisted and a whole new group of people is there who look like some kind of Orientals but with Portuguese-type names and I'm going crazy over their forms. Catherine stands by my desk a minute and whispers Alice told her to come back next week same time. Then she hands me a Hallmark envelope and even has a smile between her hollow cheeks. It's a card from the rack where she works,

I recognize it from browsing. To a Very Special Little Sister, it says and there's some chubby little cat being patted by a big one with eyeliner and high heels. I love you, Barbara, she wrote in.

What are we going to do about your sister's file? Alice wants to know when we're closing up. Since she's your sister and I told her everything's confidential, Alice says. You keep it in your desk then, I say. I'm thinking how everything's so confidential lately, like Paul told me it was confidential about Horst and the terrorist elements. But I'll say one thing, Barbara, Alice says just when Bill's coming out his office and locking the door, I think her son should be seen by someone. You mean Stephen? I say. I think it's very serious, Barbara, Alice says. You were telling me about him, weren't you, Barbara, says Bill, your nephew, not the wilderness one, the other one?

The three of us are standing in our empty waiting room, the chairs are all pushed around and the magazines are out of their piles. It's light now in the afternoons so it doesn't feel so closed in with the liquor mart signs blinking the way they do in winter when we close. I love this center, I suddenly feel.

If Bill could maybe see him, says Alice and she sits down on the edge of the rickety green chair looking tired. It's what I feel we really could do here, she says, talking to the kids. It's harder talking to mothers, it's harder talking to fathers, even when they're the ones we really have to talk to, she says. But I wish I could only talk to the kids or just somehow get them out of there, just get them out of there, she says almost mad like she's been all day.

Bill sits on the edge of my desk and says, It's been getting to us, hasn't it? Lately, I say and I sit down on the comfortable chair. It's the three of us who work there and we never get to just sit around quiet together. It's not like when I had to deal with that doughnut shop manager or when I was receptionist for the vet. It's like here all three of us together run this place and there's so much we all want to do.

XII

The man across the street on the second floor is in his window when I walk up my old street yesterday after work. It's a strange old street. One end you get Totney's where Pa likes to go and see his friends, the other you get that body shop with smashed-looking cars parked all over the sidewalk. Then you get these strange old people like that man in the window or old Marjorie in such an empty half of a house and you get Peter's little single-family tucked in between the usual duplexes and three-deckers. George Ippolito must rent out half of them including Peter's too. Then just about everyone here you recognize but it's not like over near Gregory where you'd invite them in. Here you always know them from being on the street together and talking over the fences and it's like everyone belongs here but everyone's private still which I like.

Lucius's baseball season's going great and I finally have to definitely go see him now at shortstop. But it's going to be another one of those dinners with Camilla telling everyone to eat their food and shut up and Peter acting like one of his own kids. There's Ursula on their front step with some boy who has a dangling kind of earring in one ear. He's a new one to me. When I say hi she says hi but doesn't look like she's going to introduce me to this boy. He's got a cute smirk on his face and he's leaning back casual the way those kids always do.

I walk in the kitchen and there's Peter not Camilla. What's he doing home I want to know. New schedule, get off early on Wednesdays since I work more Sundays now, he says washing something in the sink. I look in. It's carrots. Peter, you're not taking up cooking, I say. No, Stuffs, he says using his old name for me, I'm getting things ready is all, Camilla's off with Celia and Julia going shoe shopping at the mall. And you know how dangerous that could be? he says. I sit at the table and he says it's time for a beer, it's so nice and warm out, great baseball weather, just what we need is a cool beer, right? Don't you ever sit down, Peter? I say. Okay, I'll sit down, he says squeezing in beside me so he can poke at me and squeeze me the way he likes to.

I was thinking, Barbara, he says, you know, looking out at Pelucci's back porch and peeling them carrots, I'm thinking back when I was in the service and counting on not being sent over but thinking how I might still be and I didn't think back then I'd end up here with all these kids of mine. I mean yeah, Ursula was already coming along and, you know, Camilla and me planned on lots and giving them all those Roman names like we made up lists of but that was back when I was just a kid really and what did I know? Peter's got his hand squeezing my arm, not tickling, just a tight squeeze like he always does when we talk. And did I think I'd ever be living in this house next to Ma and Pa? Did I think I'd ever have these five great kids and play baseball with them? And have Camilla taking my van out with the girls for shoes and me peeling carrots at home? I mean, come on! And then my little sister dropping in and I got my first little girl out there now on the front step, did you see her, and she's got some dink new boyfriend. It's already like me and Camilla back then and I hardly can imagine it's been so long. It's spectacular, isn't it? he says.

I tell him it is and we're sipping our beers so I decide now's a good time to ask him what about Lucius this summer. You know how he wants to go on the Wilderness Summer and I took him the brochure Bill Potts gave me at work, I say, did he show it to you yet? Are you kidding, says Peter, he taped it to the bathroom mirror, I have to see it every time I shave! So are you letting him go? I ask. It'd be good for him, wouldn't it, Barbara? Peter says. It's something we never got to do, he says, no wonder I like just taking off in the van with all of them. What's the farthest we been away from home when we were little, only just one time Pa drove us all up to that lake place, right, and we rented that cruddy cabin! This family's never going on another vacation, remember Pa saying? We were all terrible up there. Catherine was taking a fit because she's away from William, boy those were the days, and I'm missing my new little sweetheart, you know who I'm referring to, and Gregory's getting picked on at the beach and you're just a fat little sunburn case. This is supposed to be relaxing? says Pa. This is what you call vacation? We get more vacation staying home. Yeah, says Peter, Pa and Ma, they weren't exactly adventurers. You know what this is costing me! I can hear Pa saying.

So is Lucius going? I ask Peter again and he says he told him he could at least apply. Then he's in, I say, but that's confidential between you and me. What makes you so sure? Peter says. I say because I know the right people. Little sister knows the right people? Sure I do, I say. Hey, Stuffs, you know you're moving up in the world. I wish I could get Stephen to apply too, I say. Stephen apply! says Peter, when did Stephen do anything for himself! I don't have any patience for him anymore, Peter says, I'm sorry.

He pokes my side to see how far in his fingers can go. Okay, okay, Peter, I'm saying.

But then look at Lucius, now there's a kid, says Peter, so what if I'm his father! I mean he's a dynamic shortstop and now he's so turned on by that backstage stuff and he's wanting to learn all about it and work for Dom's new opera production next fall and he says he wants to study lighting someday so he can make a career and he wants to go on this Wilderness Summer on top of that. I mean give me a break, says Peter, that's one hell of a kid! So who's the one out there with the earring? I ask. Oh yeah, says Peter clunking his head back on the wall and rolling his eyes. You know it's funny, that earring, I mean what kind of fag kid would wear an earring back when I was in high school and I don't just mean your old-fashioned hippie ring-type earring, I mean your inch-long weirdo earring. But that's what girls go for these days. You know what Ursula tells me? She says, Hey Dad, you seen Ryan's earring, I mean can't you just see why I love him? Peter raises his hands up and shakes them, then shakes his head and rolls his eyes over at me. And that's my oldest daughter for you! he says.

XIII

I keep wishing Paul could be with me more. On Wednesday he did meet me at lunch at the sandwich shop and that was nice and I showed him the Center after. Then we talked on the phone one night when he called from when he was out to the college library studying and just felt like calling he said. So then he did invite me for Saturday going out to dinner. He said remember how he promised the next invitation was definitely coming from him? So yesterday I'm at Ma's for dinner and I really want to talk more about

Paul to her so as to get her more used to hearing about him but I don't see how.

Anyways she's all worried about Marjorie who's in the hospital now. No one knew she had to go and she couldn't even get to her phone to call anyone. Ma just luckily saw the mail wasn't taken in and Marjorie always takes in her mail right away. So I rang, Ma's telling me, and then I phoned up and then I knocked on her back door. All the time I'm thinking thank God for your father, Barbara, him being with me still, I couldn't ever be an old lady alone. So Stephen was coming by after school I knew and I had him climb up over the back porch and look in a window and he says he sees Marjorie down the hall, she's sitting leaning against the wall there. Imagine! Your father just gets back from Totney's and he's got the emergency key Marjorie gave us, Ma says, and I've got Stephen yelling in from the back window and he says she's moving a little. So we're right in up the stairs and I'm calling to the hospital. Oh Barbara, it's awful what old people go through. You know what her place is like inside lately? There's all that old furniture from her husband's mother that used to live there and it's all covered with this much dust, I'm telling you, and the rugs smell like I can't even say, the whole place smells like an old lady who can't control herself anymore, you know?

I see tears in Ma's eyes when she's telling me all this. For once Ma's sitting in the living room with me and not yelling in from the kitchen and Pa's gone out for pizza because she just doesn't feel she can cook tonight after such an afternoon. It makes me think back on my own mother, you know, Barbara, Ma says, going back to Bologna again all by herself. Why she's ever went back there, Barbara? That was a long time ago, I tell Ma. I don't ever forget it, Ma says, I live with it every day, how she comes over here alone with little me and she works and works and then she goes back there all alone and dies. Now Ma is really crying.

They carried out Marjorie? I say. They had to carry her, Ma says, but she was talking. I just been sitting on the floor, she's saying, I was going to get up soon. You know that woman doesn't weigh ninety pounds, Ma says. She always got on me for slumping, I say. Pick your head up, Barbara, that's what I can hear Marjorie saying all the time. And you know what your grandmother's going to say, Ma says, she's going to say well there's another one gone and look at me, in her pink old bathrobe telling everyone what to do. Ma getting on Nonna's case makes her feel better about Marjorie and about her own mother, I can tell.

Then Pa comes in with a big pizza box and it smells so good I take a few deep breaths. What are you two ladies going on about? says Pa. Marjorie's going to be all right, he says, I called while I was waiting on the pizza. But Ma's feeling mad now. And then there's going to be God knows who moving in her half next, she says. And did you see that boy sitting around with Ursula again out there, Frederick? He's out there again all right, says Pa, the two of them right there on the step, hardly said a word. That's Ryan, I say.

Then there's Stephen coming down the stairs smelling the pizza. I didn't know he was up there.

XIV

Yesterday I didn't wake up in my bed, I woke up in Paul's bed, but then I was back up soaking and thinking and it was still Sunday morning and then we were going together for a walk later to follow the old map of Stinted Common and find the places he read about in his history. It was still beautiful weather.

Oh Paul, is all I can think, oh Paul. We did go out for that dinner. It was a nice place over Willow Street and they served Italian food which Paul was sure I'd like and he said this was his treat. But you cooked dinner for me once already, I said and he said from now on we could go halves but not this time. So I said he had to let me cook for him then next week and he held my hand on the tablecloth nodding at me with his crinkled eyebrows. I didn't recognize anyone at that restaurant, Veracini's, where I never been before.

It seemed like I was doing all the talking, it was all about my family I had to explain to him. He already got all their names right from when we went to Italian Opera Night. He asked about each one, even Quintus. I told him about Ursula's new boyfriend and how Stephen was back at Ma's and saying he was never going back to the project but then he goes back over there nights anyways and hangs out, just stays out of his dad's way is all. He asked me about Tommy's newt I was telling him about and what was Gregory's job again? he asks. I tried to explain even though it never did make sense to me exactly that Gregory worked warehousing for some electric parts distributor but he didn't work in the actual warehouse but inventorying. Paul said Gregory was telling him some about computers at the brunch. I think he knows all about them, I said, he checks out inventory with them.

I didn't think Paul cared to hear all that so on our way back walking I asked him about his family too. It's only his father, he said, his mother died. When I was quite small, he said then but he remembers her well. And of course there are lots of cousins, he said. He didn't want to keep talking, I thought, but then he said, She always wanted me to travel. Your mother? I asked. She always wanted me to go to England to be educated, he said. It's what West Indian mothers of a certain class most wished for their sons, he said. I'm glad you came to here not England, I told him.

We could see our building down one block. Before we get there, Barbara, I must ask something, Paul said. Because I can't ask you standing in front of your door or mine, he said. I stopped and he stopped and all the Saturday night traffic was zooming by us, car radios going, the kids out for rides. Perhaps you'd come in tonight, he says, perhaps you'd stay with me, that's what I'd like, he said, if you'd like it.

I couldn't talk but I was shaking I know. So we stood on that corner and then he went on talking. It would be to keep company together, he said, it would be to be relaxed with each other. I'm very inexperienced, I said. But only to be close, he said, right now. Forgive me for asking you on this street corner but I was afraid somehow to enter the building tonight until I had asked you, he said. With all the lights of traffic and stores on his face and his sweater and on my velvet jacket when I looked down at it, it seemed like we were standing there and standing there when everything else was going by. Could I go up to my room first? I said.

Oh yes, Barbara, you could do anything, you could wait, it could be another time, I only had to ask you now, he said. But I'd like to come, I tell him because I couldn't not say yes. I don't have any, you know, birth control, I said then. There'll be time, he said, when we feel right, when we're relaxed. What I want first is to hold you and kiss you, Barbara, he said.

How can I forget any word now he said? I had to begin walking, thinking about him. And he was beside me.

I did go upstairs first and I put my nightie and my robe and my slippers into the plastic bag from the mall. I brushed my teeth and put my hairbrush and toothbrush in the bag too and then I remembered his toilet was out in the hall so I made use of my facilities and sitting there on that soft seat I felt I was all in a long dream that didn't stop. I was so thankful it wasn't my period.

I have something special, he said when I came in. He was holding a cassette recorder like Alice's. I purchased it at the Goodwill, he said, but it works perfectly well. And it was all because he found this cassette for sale at the college store in their markdown department, he said. It's of the very opera I had the part in when I was in school, he says, and I haven't even heard it since. But it's not the little part I sang I wanted to play you, it's the love song I wanted to play. To hear it with real singers and with an orchestra, he says, it's so much more beautiful than it was coming out of our young mouths.

So he closed his shade and like he said the light still blinked around the room from the All-Night. He got into his pajamas on one side of the room when I got into my nightie on the other in the blinking dark. Then I found my way in beside him in that bed under the staircase. We were very close to each other because it was so narrow and we're both wide. But we're soft and we felt good close together leaning up on his big pillow.

Then he reached to his side and pushed a button and out came a quiet song which really was pretty especially when the two voices went at the same time, the man and the woman. Sweet and low, sweet and low, they sang. I could tell what they were singing and they sounded English too like Paul. When it was over he touched the button and stopped it then he said the song to me like reciting a poem he memorized: Sweet and low when all enduring are the songs that lovers sing is how it ended. What does it exactly mean? I said. It means, Paul says, that when it endures all, I mean when it lasts through everything, you know, love need only be sung of softly. I love to hear you talk that way you do, Paul, I say. I got him to say it again, first the whole song and then the way he explained it. It sounded different than saying you only need to sing softly about love, I thought. Love need only be sung of softly, I said again to remember it. When it endures all, he said, when it lasts through everything.

How can this opera be about communists though? I asked him. In the dark I could tell Paul was joking when he said, Even communists must love each other, Barbara, and then he said, my sweet one. We were hugging close then. But was the person who wrote it a communist, are those people communists on the cassette? I asked. I don't suppose so, said Paul. But we'll study it sometime, he said, and you'll see what I mean. Listening very closely to something, he said, you can't help but hear more and more what it truly means. That's how I found my idea, he said, I hear it everywhere.

I'm learning from you, Paul, I said. And how much I'm learning from you! said Paul. But I don't know what though, I say. Oh yes, said Paul, oh yes, I learn, I'm learning right now. He held onto me. Our softness and the smell of him and my toothpaste smell were what I was thinking of. I don't know when I fell asleep but I finally did. Once I heard one of those old ladies shuffling up the stairs right over our heads.

X V

Your boy's all set for this summer, said Bill when he went by my desk yesterday, we got the money from City Hall definitely. Bill's looking very up today. He's humming letting himself in his office. Alice comes out to the fridge to get milk for her coffee. She doesn't look any better though. I'm still thinking of this woman that came in the day before with her little girl all bruised up. They sat there and no one was talking to them. Everybody could tell it was something worse than usual. I'm glad it wasn't during Catherine's time, she doesn't need to think this is a place for crazies.

The woman sat there with her child. They were both ugly anyway, dirty looking, but you could tell what was dirt and what was bruises on the little girl. She was Tessa's age maybe, she didn't even look up at me or take the Tootsie Pop. Because of Paul somehow I don't feel so sad anymore seeing those people. I do feel sad but it isn't at all for me too now. In a way I feel maybe more sad because of that, because I don't feel sad for me, because I can just see how sad those two were sitting there in their thin dresses.

At the end of that day Alice told me the lady herself was the abuser and I'd been figuring it was probably the father. It's the worst to see when they're both sitting staring out at you or at nothing really and you know the one actually did hurt the other and they're sitting there beside each other. I told it all to Paul and I was getting upset telling him.

So Alice was still in a bad mood yesterday too and then the mail came with the really bad news. Annie Randall was there talking with me. She was going on about how she liked my yellow blouse and where did I get my hair done. I told her all that before but it's something we always talk about over and over. Alice took the mail from my desk and went in her office, then she comes out, knocks and goes in Bill's, then he comes out with her and they tell me to put things on hold and they go in her office with the private phone. Annie's just watching them like she thinks they were some kind of geniuses.

More of those Portuguese Orientals are back again but Bill speaks Portuguese of course and Spanish. And Alice speaks Italian and French so they've got it covered except for Greeks but there's no new Greeks coming in and Italians usually speak English too more than those Spanish types. At least the Orientals or whatever you call them were patient, I'll say that for them. I didn't find out till last night what was going on because Alice and Bill left early to go over to Boston. I should've known it was a bad sign.

Alice called me at home from there. Bill and I are drunk, she says. What're you doing, Alice! I say laughing but I already know it's something not so funny. We're out drinking, we wanted to talk to you! she says. But what about Bill supposed to pick up Polly and Sarah? I say thinking what if Alice and Bill were having some kind of affair on the side but I couldn't ever believe that.

We're having a great time, Alice says and I can hear Bill too saying in the background: Tell Barbara to hop a bus down here right now, we need her. They're consolidating us, Alice says, they're consolidating us with the East Center. Can you believe, Barbara, they're consolidating us with East! How many of our people are going to come see us over there! she says. The end of summer and that's it! she says. That's it, says Bill in the background. We're going to the governor, straight to the governor, he's saying. My job! I'm thinking.

XVI

Ma wanted to be sure someone was with Nonna all day when it was the anniversary of Nonno's death. Somehow Nonna doesn't know any other day but she knows when it's that day. If I could've only gone with Paul to see her and let him meet her, instead it's with Lucius I'm going over to do our part of the day, just sit with her and even if she's sleeping for some of it, just keep a watch on her.

All the way over the Sweet and Low song is going in my head the way it usually does when I'm walking somewhere ever since our long Sunday walk Paul and me took up over all the seven hills of Stinted Common. This will keep us in shape, Paul said then, no need for Horst and his bloody football! It's our historical tour, Barbara, he said, the hills and the rangeways, and where Paul Revere rode and where the troops fell back from Bunker Hill and where they raised the flag. The flag of the United Colonies, Paul said when we were standing up there at the fort, first raised here on Shepherd Hill for all to see in seventeen seventy-six.

I don't know what Lucius was thinking about when him and me were walking over to the Home. I didn't think he thought about girls yet but then I realized he probably does since he's thirteen now. And then when I was still hearing the song I remembered about consolidating the Center. Every time I forget about it for a while then it comes back and hits me. Alice says there's probably a job at East too but what about our people?

Nonna's in her room, the attendant says, the white one not the black one who's on nights. We get in there and she's in bed but not really asleep and the other lady's out. Now what are you two doing here? she says and I figure she doesn't know which two we exactly are. She pats her bedspread and Lucius is light enough to sit on the edge without disturbing her so he sits there and I sit on Mrs. Giovinco's bed. My children, Nonna says and we know she means she thinks of all of us as her children even if I'm actually her grandchild and Lucius is her great-grandchild.

Nonna, says Lucius, you know what I'm doing that Nonno would like? Of course he never met his great-grandfather. My child, Nonna says. She doesn't know what he's talking about but she's happy enough to hear his voice and I watch Lucius and how he almost can't stand sitting there, his feet are tapping and he keeps fiddling with his fingers. He has a dark beautiful face I love, just like Julia's but a little longer like a boy's is with more of a nose and his curly hair. You see, he says, there's going to be an opera next year and Mom's cousins are coming over from Italy. And I'm going to work backstage and help Dad fixing up the Atherton and I'll get to work some of the lights during the opera. You get to climb up above the stage and look down on the people, Lucius says, I did it when they had this concert, Nonna, I could look right down on this lady who's singing. And then he checks over at me and says, Right down her bosoms! He knows Nonna doesn't really know what he's talking about and he likes getting away with saying that. Oh Lucius! I say. And they're heaving away when she's singing, he says making his chest go up and down. And then, guess what, I got accepted for the Wilderness Summer, Nonna. Suddenly he stops talking though like he realizes it isn't really fun to keep saying all this to that old lady in bed. It's hard even asking her how she is or something about the Home because she'll just say suddenly: Where's Frederick? or When's supper? Lucius sort of sighs looking sad now and just looks at her.

She says one more time: My child. But her eyes are closing. Lucius looks at me like he'd like us to go. And you know, Nonna, I say, it's all working out good with my friend Paul. Paul? says Lucius. It's all working out between us somehow, you wouldn't believe what it's like. He'd love you, Nonna, if he met you, I say.

Then Nonna says with her eyes closed tight, maybe talking to us or maybe talking just to herself: Being good Catholics we should love everyone, she says. Lucius is looking at me like he's just understanding what I mean about Paul and he looks sort of worried. Pa's coming soon to take over for us, Ma told me before we came. I'm hoping he'll come soon even if Nonna goes to sleep. I'm thinking he must want to be there alone with his mother on the day his father died even if sometimes she isn't even sure if it's him.

The Wilderness Summer

A dream of a soak. Breathing in the steam. The mirror fogs all up. All of me's floating. No one believes it ends up making you cool in this hot weather but after when I lay out on my sheet and a little breeze comes in it does. And then Paul coming over from studying and we'll have our supper later. All this summer's too quick how each day comes and then goes. Got Lucius's card and now already he's getting back Sunday. They only went once to a town where he could mail a card from so that's how much it's really the wilderness. He says don't tell Mom but they get to swim naked in the lake but boys and girls separate then they swim later all together with their suits on. He says he's not such a good swimmer and it's freezing off his you-know-what. At the bottom he writes in: Hey Barbara, you should be girls' counselor sometime up here, love, Lucius. Only I can imagine all the bugs. And Bill was saying sometimes they see a bear getting in their garbage and you hear birds in the lake whooping all night long. I wouldn't be used to those kind of things. Now I bend up my soft round knees and leaning back my head to get my ears under and hear no sounds at all. That's better and it's so steamy over the light bulb and I'm dreaming off. Who knows, right now Lucius probably's floating in that cold lake up there where none of us have ever went, cold and all naked. Paul takes cold showers before he goes in the mornings. For me, forget it. We're different in our ways. Sometimes it bothers us but not too much. Paul sitting around after dinner when we went to Ma's and him and Pa talking about articles Pa reads in his magazines about irrigation. Ma just doesn't act like she minds it I'm with Paul. Then in the kitchen seeing it in her eyes and she's not letting on. I'm thinking, Ma, please just leave off worrying, who knows anyways what's going to happen? And on a Saturday afternoon Paul and me taking Lucius over to where he got on the charter bus and even Lucius was looking worried. Then he's pretending maybe he wants to stay home instead and keep working on the Atherton because he really likes that. And he didn't recognize any of the other kids from junior high in the group, they're mostly from East or over Ploughed Hill, there's even some black kids in there. So off they go, him looking out the bus at us. Then Paul and me walking on over to Herbie's Slush where Celia's working afternoons. Then on along strolling. Paul in summer's more just Paul, his white shirt and his black elbows and with the rubber flip-flops he wears it shows the pink bottoms of his toes. Luckily for Alice helping me with birth control. All those years thinking about Clint Eastwood or whatever and now it's entirely something else, I didn't even know how it'd be, I was way off. Now we got used to us, how we are, we just be together and it'll come on us like we really want to.

Paul's laughing and squeezing and I never pretended Clint would be like that. Seeing Paul just laying there tired out after and him and me calming down our breaths. Don't mind the mess and sweat soaking in the sheet. I'm getting used to how it is, not like it's over before I knew what hit me with that doughnut manager Sam. Something like I never knew could really happen, how everything around me feels good, looking at the walls, feeling a breeze, hearing traffic out there. Our arms leaning across on each other. I can make myself feel this way anytime just thinking of it. Oh Paul, I'm thinking of him being big inside me and all around me and me feeling so hot holding him in. I can't see except for our colors where we each stop. There's this bulge of white out here and this bulge of black out there, it's all of us. Oh Paul, he's happy with me even if sometimes we argued about something stupid like which street took us back home on one of our walks. But we didn't expect ever to know each other, that's why I think we don't fight, instead we feel lucky. There's no hurry with Paul. And going into work to see all those poor women now, why are they all such a mess? Catherine getting married so young way back and then it's not her fault what troubles William had with his jobs. That's what Paul says. Jobs is the biggest problem for people but what are they supposed to do about it? Can't go out and just say I feel like doing this for a living, period, that's it. Like Stephen drinking by himself like I saw him. Wish he'd go drink with other kids if he wants to drink. Easy getting six-packs and they're all going off together standing in alleys yelling and slamming at each other when they get roaring. So he hangs out sometimes too but sometimes takes a few bottles down the river past the project recreation facility and sits alone on a bench. Or him over at

Ma's on hot days around the house looking at TV. He goes in their room because of the air conditioner when Pa's out at Totney's and Ma's out shopping, him just up there laying on their bed. I found him already a couple times. He stays home days more now though what with William on part-time park maintenance for the summer. And poor Julia doing her Arts and Crafts in the Parks program and she's looking over at these loud guys digging for the drainage goofing off on the job like I seen them do and she's hoping her uncle wouldn't recognize it's her at the crafts table working on her Pepsi-bottle bird. William finding Stephen drinking at home, that'll be the next thing. Summer's bad for Stephen with no school, got to get some job. Him being out one whole night in the reeds down the river when it's so late he couldn't go to Ma's or home even. He got under some plastic garbage bag when it started to rain, he told me like it was just fun and I'm not supposed to tell Catherine. But something's going on. I'd make some big dry room somewhere for people to go and they wouldn't ask you questions, just let you sleep. Oh the nights with Paul, us sleeping so good, I go off to sleep happy and he always says last thing: Sweet dreams, and I love you we say to each other. So why's Ma look that way at me? She can just stop bothering over it. Me telling off Annie Randall about her mother too. If you want to go out, you go out, I tell Annie. But she's coming in more regular now and she's driving me crazy she gets talking so much. She used to be mostly quiet with these little shy questions she asks. Now she's yapping away and coming in a whole hour ahead of her appointments so what can I do, she pulls a chair over to my desk and starts right in. Alice is recommending the hospital for some medication, all this talking's a bad sign, she says. So Barbara, how's your boyfriend? Annie starts in looking all pale and skinny and jumpy. So I saw you walking down Milk Street, you were stopping for slush and then you went and sat in the little park on the corner, I saw you, aren't I right? Like she's following us but I never once saw her. Then she's telling me how she wants to get her hair done like mine but when does she ever do anything to her hair? It's all just plans and talk. And I'm thinking how these people don't know the Center's moving in the fall yet. They're definitely not going to go down to East, most of them. Alice is not sure even if I really would get transferred too yet. Part of saving money is they can use one receptionist to do it all, that's what they told her lately after she made a stink. They got a surprise coming how much work it is but what do they care? Now Bill's thinking he'll quit because he got too mad for his own good talking to somebody at the State House, Alice said. Well Catherine's not coming anymore anyway. Everything's going fine now, she tells me last week over her place. Oh yeah, everything's going fine, Catherine! I can just tell when she's not telling me something. Everything is! she says. Yeah, everything is, I say. Oh shut up, Barbara, get off me anyways! she says. Well shut up yourself and don't come crying to me, I tell her. William's working, isn't he, we're all right. Yeah sure, you and Stephen are all right, I say because I know something's definitely going on. What do you know about Stephen, Catherine says, look, William hasn't hit him once this whole summer. That's nice, I say. Barbara, she says, your lip's driving me crazy. You need to get some lip, I say. Just shut up, Barbara, and just get out of here, I didn't ask you over here to hear this, and then she's pushing on me to get me up from the kitchen table. I got other things to do, I'm going anyways, I tell her. You're some sister, she says. So go cry to Peter, he's going to be real sympathetic, sure Peter

is, I tell her. Do you see me crying to anybody? she says. I
forgot, everything's fine, oh yeah, I say. She slams the door
after I'm out and I'm walking down those cool stairs
looking at people's doors, dark and locked and noisy inside.
I'm not dealing with all this, I'm thinking, that's it, and
that was last week. Neither of us is going to call back till
Ma does something to make us. So what. Now slipping
myself down all the way in the tub while it's still so hot
and I see sweat bubbling up out on my knees there. My
forehead all wet from steam even where I didn't put it
under. I want Lucius to come back from those woods soon.
It's like all dark woods to me, cool, and somehow he's
running through there naked, I can see him there closing
my eyes underwater. I never saw him naked since he was
a baby and I diapered him all the time but I see him skinny
and all tan running fast between those trees. Not like in a
park but it's all mushy ground but somehow he runs
through it leaping. Then he stops real sudden like he's
perching and listening. Then comes this darker girl I can
almost see like one of those Puerto Rican girls maybe from
the charter bus and she's standing by a tree with her skin
showing like it's bark through the leaves. I'm hearing her
through the water in my ears making sounds like a bird to
call to him. Now it's more like it was all on Paul's island
or Haiti the way it looks, it starts raining through the
leaves, these light drops falling straight down like you
could start counting them. Lucius is balancing ready on
his bare toes. I shouldn't be seeing him so naked, he's just
little and she's over there with leaves just hiding her. Why
am I feeling so scared for a moment? It's like he wants to
dive onto that girl. If I come up from underwater where I
can breathe better now slowly. How funny I'm thinking
something very strange. Then everything's coming to me.

Suddenly it's all those women I'm thinking of again. I can't get all of them out of my mind. Mrs. McVeigh, Mrs. Figueroa, Mrs. Ortiz. I'm going through whose appointments there is in the morning and all the more I feel my heart going like I'm dizzy. Mrs. Farwell, Mrs. Guimond. The bathroom light bulb is all fuzzy. What's happening to these people, I'm thinking, let's see, there's Mrs. Velis, she's stopped coming, but Mrs. Claude, Mrs. Tavares, Laurie what's-her-name, Annie Randall, Mrs. Montagnoli I can do without, Mrs. Donovan that cries by herself, then that awful woman with the girl all bruised too, and whose appointment comes first tomorrow? And the silent woman who wouldn't talk to a man but she never came back and the woman who couldn't help herself, how it just comes over her and she's got to see him. I'm breathing better now sitting up. Wasn't I just thinking too about Lucius somehow in the wilderness? This is enough of a soak for now.

Utopia Limited

I

I'm never doing that again. Horst kept asking us but we never went all summer so why did we finally go on Sunday? Now I'm going to be aching all week. Paul thought because it's cloudy we wouldn't get so hot running around. Fat chance is all I can say. I'd look too chubby in shorts so we stopped and borrowed Gwen's magenta running suit she never wears and I squeezed into that instead but it was almost worse, I looked like a balloon. My old sneakers from high school that I didn't wear since working at the doughnut shop were pinching my feet too. Paul did have on old football shorts from his school days, he said, and they were so baggy it figures he was more overweight once before he came up here. And he had basketball sneakers from the Goodwill. Did we ever look the pair!

Horst drove us in his Volkswagen and he was saying, Look, everyone is still being being wasted from Clooney's, don't worry about it. We get to this field but it's only us yet so he does some tricky things with the ball on his knees and his head in that same gray sweat suit I don't think he washed since last spring. Then I saw Paul's brown sweat-shirt says Sugar Hill Brownies on the back and I'm think-ing he should have never picked out that one at the Goodwill. Sometimes he doesn't really think about his style. Now he just looks totally brown to me except for those blue shorts.

When the others came me and Paul didn't know what we were doing at all but some of them didn't either. I was the only actual American I think. And then this little Oriental guy comes bouncing over and hugs me and he's yelling: Mees Barbara! Mees Barbara! You help my mamma, you help my mamma, he says. Sure enough he brought his mother to the Center back in July, she was one of those East Timor people. I'm Mikey, I'm Mikey, he says, American name Mikey! So I hug him back but still I don't remember him. It feels nice he knows me though and all during the game he tried not to get the ball when it was coming to me. He pretended he missed it or tripped over his feet just when I thought he'd kick it. I play against you, Mees Barbara! I play against you! he said every time our team got the ball.

It was the Eastern Hemisphere against the Western Hemisphere was how Horst set it up. He was laughing the whole time. I think he really did know soccer but most of that bunch you could tell rather would be in some library studying. This one boy from Peru I think says, In my country I am worst player but here I am football wizard! Luckily there's girls there too but I would say I was older and definitely heavier than the other ones. But they all were so friendly that I would've almost liked gym class if it was like this back in high school. It's just that now I can't keep up so good and I'm wondering how I'm getting up the stairs to start my last week at work with all these aches. Some way to be feeling when there's all the moving to organize.

Paul at least knows the rules too but none of them cared much. Everybody was just screaming and yelling. Suddenly the ball would go one way and everyone was thundering down one end and then it would suddenly go the other way. And Mikey's dancing around me yelling: I get you next time, Mees Barbara! I get you next time! Luckily Paul and me were both on the Western Hemisphere. But Horst's team won because he was the only person who really made any goals.

Now were you not having so much fun? he's asking us in his Volkswagen after. It smells sort of with us three all sweaty in there. Then he decides since the sun's coming back out why don't we take a little ride to the country now. Typical Horst, he gets confused trying to find the right road then we go out through Lexington instead and it all begins looking like another world to me. I don't ever get out in the suburbs hardly.

By God, these houses! Paul's saying. This is the true America, man, says Horst. You never been out this way, Paul? I ask him. Well I've known it to exist, he says, but to drive through miles of it, and it only keeps getting grander, and so green! Wait'll you see it in Concord, I say, it's only the fanciest houses out there. And in another month, Paul, says Horst, this green will all be red and gold like nothing you've ever seen. Paul's just staring out at all the lawns and their big houses going by.

Finally we park at the Concord Bridge where I went in high school for history and when we walk out there with bunches of southern-sounding tourists in hats I feel like we're smelly slobs. But everyone was smelling so bad too back in Revolution times, says Horst.

Paul thinks it's funny how each town around here claims it's where the Revolution really did start, like Stinted Common was where they raised the first flag on Shepherd Hill. We're looking at the Minutemen statue and my knees are starting already to be too sore. Well then we'll go somewhere for soft ice cream instead, says Horst. He does a jump in the air and pretends he just kicked a soccer ball back over the bridge. Goal! he yells and Paul and me look at each other like he's crazy which sometimes I think he is. Paul even told me Horst can really speak English much better, he just likes exaggerating that accent to be somehow exotic, said Paul.

Then we're all licking our cones and rattling along back home. His tail pipe still isn't tied or tight. Paul, says Horst, did you ever hear Americans calling themselves anything but the middle class? I don't believe so, says Paul licking away on his chocolate double-dip. Upper-middle, middle-middle, lower-middle, that's what they are calling themselves, says Horst. Or upper-lower-middle perhaps, says Paul and they're both smirking. Why's that so funny? I say in the backseat. It aggravates me when they get acting like foreigners and there's something funny about America.

But do look around at these houses, Barbara, says Paul. So? I say but they shrug their shoulders and don't look back at me though I see Paul's eyes from the side crinkling in the sun. Two hundred thousand, says Horst, two hundred thousand at the lowest! Hundreds of them, he says, thousands! Middle class indeed, says Paul. Well people at the Center aren't so rich, those people you can't even call them working class because they're not even working some of them, don't tell me about middle class, I say and go back to spooning my sundae out of the paper cup. And I wouldn't want to live out in a place like this anyway, I tell them.

There's a little bad mood for a while in the car. Horst starts telling some tasteless joke he heard at Clooney's about why the Burger King got the Dairy Queen pregnant but they can tell I'm still mad. They just think Americans are all rich but look who's talking. Paul's father sends him money I know and Horst's family owns half that country he comes from, Paul figures, and they just send him here to keep him from getting in more trouble.

Paul, I say when we're home later, you know that African girl, I think she was, that was playing for the Eastern Hemisphere? He says what about her. Then I ask if he finds her attractive, for being black too and thinner. Well she was quite attractive, I grant you, said Paul, but one doesn't compose one's life around an exterior. Oh one doesn't? I said. Him and his one's this and one's that.

Paul just came and squeezed me sitting on my window seat but I didn't act like wanting to be squeezed, like I even didn't like him right then. I promise, sweet one, he said, I'll try to curb my political banter with fellows like Horst. You just do that, I tell him but as usual how long could I really stay mad at Paul even when he was acting so superior because he doesn't mean it that way, he doesn't really think he's superior at all.

It's easy to fall into banter with Horst, he says, but I grant you it avoids the real human problem, doesn't it? So what's the real human problem? I say. How to love all of us, even the middle class, says Paul. So I let him have his hug and then I can feel the madness squeeze out of me like I was melting. It's just that I ached all over from that damn game though.

II

It's working out fine now with Stephen moved into Paul's old room. As long as DiNapoli our landlord doesn't find out he won't have to pay the two months' deposit and all three of us are saving because of splitting the two rents three ways. Was Stephen ever glad to get out finally. We only brought up Paul's Danish-style chair but left all the rest for Stephen. He's happy down there even though he spends most of what he earns now from Veracini's on the rent. But he can eat leftovers at work and Catherine gets him to come home for a bite now that William's finally gone for good. That was some way to end the summer.

I'm sad all week at the Center though. Each time a person comes in for their appointment I'm thinking maybe this is their last one. Bill's definitely quit for good and going to work for the recreation program full-time starting right after he takes Polly and Sarah on his two-week paid vacation he's owed. So it's just Alice going to East and so far they still won't rehire me but they keep saying more funds are coming in September they hope. So I'll be on unemployment just like William always is. Hey, says Stephen, you ought to go out drinking with my dad, and he laughs like he thinks it's a hysterical idea.

I went downstairs to see Stephen yesterday late when he was through work and Paul had to be out late at some international students event I didn't feel like going to. Horst never goes to those things Paul says so I don't see why Paul has to go. Anyways there was Stephen still in his outfit. Hi I'm Stephen, he says, I'll be your waiter tonight. Stephen, I say, you're getting to be a real laugh. Let me tell you about tonight's specials, he says and goes off laughing.

Hey you do that good, I say and he says, Enjoy your meal, folks.

He's sitting on his bed under the stairs with his knees up after he's taken off his jacket. So I sit on the wooden chair and look at him awhile. Is everything all right here, folks? he says. I'm thinking of the Chicken Marsala alla Veracini he told me about yesterday. Don't make my mouth water, I tell him. So when are you and Paul coming there for dinner anyways? he asks. You'll save on the tip, he says. I'll tip you plenty, I say then suddenly I say, I'll tip you right over! So I jump up and grab his knees and tip him over on the bed and tickle him. Hey Barbara, I know what you and that black guy you go out with used to do on this bed, he's saying. So? So? and I'm tickling away. Hey! Hey! Stephen's squealing, get off me! I'm getting squashed, Barbara!

I let him sit up but I stay sitting there with an arm on his back like I used to when he was little and crying about something but now he's only laughing and I'm happy except for how much I ache still from soccer. So what I want to know is, Stephen, do you bring back somebody here yourself to this bed or what? I say. Maybe I do and maybe I don't, says Stephen. Well you just keep it quiet under these stairs when the old ladies are coming in, I say.

Then Stephen looks at me serious. Barbara, he says, how come I didn't use to think you ever talked about, you know, things like that? Because I didn't use to, I say. So how come now you do? he wants to know. It's not that I really talk about it, I say, but you know, what with Paul and me. Remember when you were first hanging around with him, he says, well I didn't mean to bother you about Paul being black. You didn't bother me, Stephen, I say but he says yes he did. I didn't mean it though, he says.

We're leaning back and I look up and there's a Def

Leppard poster taped on the sloping ceiling where the stairs go up. You're more like a big sister not my aunt, says Stephen leaning on me. You're more like my little brother, I say. Who do you go talk to most, Stephen, about things? I ask him. You, he says. Well now, I say, but I mean before moving in here. Nobody, he says. But I mean like your friends at the project? No, he says. Your mom? Definitely not her, says Stephen. Then he's quiet for a while.

You know it's funny though, he says, who I talked to more really was my dad. I don't believe him but he says it's true. Just sometimes, Stephen said, sometimes late when Mom was out and we made cookies and he'd tell me his ideas about things and all about the crummy way the world was, I mean he really thinks about those things, my dad. Then of course next day after school, says Stephen, I'm coming in the door and I get slammed. Or like when he found me once picking at the linoleum with my knife. I don't know why I was even doing it. I always used to do it just a little now and then, just picking away at it. Then he comes in and finds me and so you're the one, he says. Well that was back before things really got bad I guess, says Stephen. Hey I hear Paul I think, I say.

It definitely is Paul's slumpy feet on the stairs. Sssh, I say, then I sneak into the hall and run up and grab Paul from behind and he nearly takes a heart attack. Can I come up too and watch a little TV? Stephen is saying standing down by his door.

III

So Barbara, I just heard, says Annie Randall yesterday as usual early for her appointment. It's a typical crazy day and there's no empty chairs so Annie's just leaning over with her elbows on my desk. Move off those files, Annie, I say. So I just heard, she says again. I been learning to let her say things twice to slow her down. It was in the Commoner this week, she says. Did you see it in the Commoner, the front page? I knew about it a long time, I say knowing she's talking about consolidating with East. So how come you didn't tell me? Annie says. There I was, trying to organize those files and get the right forms in the right ones and all the time Annie's talking away. So how come, Barbara? she says looking so worried suddenly. It was supposed to be confidential, I tell her. She's looking at the files and each one has that confidential stamp on it. She just stares down at all those red confidentials on my desk.

Then Annie heaves one of her big sighs and goes and wanders off to look out the window. I'm sorry but I used to like talking to Annie but she wore me out. Now I can always tell five things ahead what she's going to say and it's always the same old thing. And this week it's too hard on me to be worrying about her on top of it all. Now Mrs. Guimond I don't feel that way about. Later she was just coming out from seeing Alice all in tears and I still remember when you could see those scars clearer and when her cheeks got wet from crying they showed more. Barbara, I miss you, she says, already I miss you, please, she says. I give her hand a squeeze when she holds it out to me. She can't even keep talking and just has to almost run for the stairs to leave. What's with her? says Mrs. Montagnoli. Mrs. Montagnoli might as well tell about her husband across the fence to whoesever's passing by for all the good coming here does her. But she keeps coming and Alice was finally going to make her stop except with the closing of the Center she figured she'd just wait her out. I'd like to see that Montagnoli husband, he can't be as bad as her. But then I'm thinking well he probably is. How come people seem like they have more problems since I been at the Center? I see problems being everywhere in people's lives. I don't know how Alice still can keep on her neutral sober look always and go helping everybody the same and always being patient. Maybe I should be glad I'm getting out. And with Alice not even having any boyfriend at all she says she feels sometimes like she's somehow drying up these days, just drying up, she says, and holding onto these people falling apart around her. Alice, don't take it so hard, I told her after work last Friday, at least Lou Ann is working over at East now too so you'll have one old friend to see there.

But what are we going to do about you, Barbara? she says. I'm going to tell them I just can't deal without you, Alice said, I'm going to be really adamant about it. What's that exactly? I asked. Like stone, she says, adamant. And of course anyway it's true, Alice says, she can't deal without me. She goes off walking her way to Sugar Hill and I wait for my bus. I wasn't writing anything for so long there but I did write on that Friday with my good old marker in my pocket. Be really adamant, I wrote like somehow it was in honor of Alice and yesterday I saw it there when I was waiting again. It made me have a little shiver inside.

I V

Paul and me went over to Ma's for dinner last night. You're not looking good, Barbara, Ma says when we're dishing up in the kitchen. You're worried, aren't you, she says. I just frown at her. I can see by looking at you, Ma says. Look at you, she says and she puts her fingers under my chin to look in my eyes. Look at you, she says again.

Well what do you expect? I say. That Center was wearing you out anyways, says Ma.

I'm getting the bread basket out and putting in the napkin and then I get such a great blast of bread smell when I open the oven door. I don't really want to talk about my job with Ma, she wants to make it seem better somehow I'm going on unemployment.

At the table Pa decides it's his time to say something. He's going to get me another job, he says, he's talking to his friends at Totney's and asking around and he's sure with my experience I can get something I'll like. Paul eats quietly not wanting to say the wrong thing but he knows it's my own job I want not some new job. I didn't realize till now how I want it so much what with Annie driving me crazy or some of the types that come in there but I really do. Thanks, Pa, for asking around, I say but anyways Alice says there's still a chance, I tell him, that she can get me my job back.

But you don't want to go working in East Common, Ma says. What's the big difference, I'm wondering. It's such a long bus ride from your new place, Ma says. So Catherine's bus ride's long too, I say. I know it isn't the bus ride Ma worries about, it's what she reads about the Puerto Rican teenagers down there.

Paul finally decides to say, You know, Mrs. Orsini, it's Barbara's special gift, I think, and it's such a pity she can't exercise it. The way Paul puts things my parents don't really know how to argue back, they just stare at him like how did those words come out of those big black lips. It gets me almost laughing to see them look so amazed always at Paul.

I appreciate what you say, Paul, says Pa. If we all could use our own skills, he says, everyone has a special skill probably for something. Except maybe a certain let's hope ex-son-in-law of yours, God forgive me, you might know who I mean, says Ma. Oh cut it out, Ma, I say. Well you know what kind of special skill he's got, she says and she's not joking about it. After the way William got at the end of the summer she's never forgiving him again, that's for sure. So then we're quiet and eat for a while Ma's good manicotti and I'm thinking Pa still wishes he was working too even if he likes being able to just read and go talk with his old buddies all day too.

Well at least your brother's in a good mood, Ma says. Who? I say. Who! says Ma, who do you think! I know she means Peter because it's Peter who always lets her know one way or other and Gregory instead keeps it to himself. But Gregory's usually sort of happy pretty much without getting as happy as Peter gets when he really gets happy. Like when Peter gets going on something like this Masked Ball thing, you can't stop him.

He should come home to Camilla and sit for a bit first, says Pa, but not him, he picks up a sub and he's off to the Atherton every single night. Of course I'm thinking Camilla really likes it because get-them-all-out-of-the-house-and-stop-making-a-mess is her philosophy. I worry about Lucius now school's starting up again, Ma says, him working with Peter, he's going to fall behind in his studies and he'll never get in Boys' Catholic next year. But look how he's learning things, Margaret, says Pa. But I don't want him falling behind in his studies, Ma says again.

When did she ever worry Ursula was falling behind from always going out with Ryan or Celia from being just the usual crazy teenager? Of course she always got the idea Stephen was studying hard, she just didn't notice mostly he was sitting and staring and turning a page once in a while. Lucius seems quite capable of keeping himself afloat, Paul says to reassure Ma. I love it when him and my parents talk. I don't know why it makes me feel so good to see him and them talk about anything even, just to hear them talk.

Ma never lets Paul do the dishes with us and now it's his regular joke. Am I banished once again? he says. Get out, get out! Ma's saying shooing him with her hands in the same way she shoos Gregory. Pa's off to some neighborhood meeting about the vacant lot where they been dumping stuff next to the body shop so when I go find Paul he's actually out on the steps and who's he talking to but Celia.

But being nosy I first listen by the door a minute. But all the guys are like, well excuse my language but—she's saying and then Paul comes in with I know it's not easy for you, Celia. So why Ursula gets all the luck, she's saying. But I believe, Paul says, as sure as rain, he says, that there's someone for you, waiting but not knowing it yet. I can't believe Celia talking to Paul, she'd only be flip with me or be her real most bitchiest self. But here's the question to ask yourself, Paul's saying: Are you going to recognize him, Celia? If he's real real cute, Celia says. Paul's making his friendly laugh so that's a good time to open the door.

What're you two going on about? I say. Hey Barbara, I heard about your job, Celia says. Typical her, she heard about it a month ago but she finally gets around to saying something. Yeah, I say sitting down on Paul's other side. I can see the old man moving around behind his shade on the second floor over there. So how come you aren't over to the Atherton like everyone else in your family? I ask Celia. Give me a break, she says, it's bad enough I have to listen to them talking about making scenery all the time.

Celia didn't have much of a happy summer I fear, Paul says. I look at Celia with the street light on her face to see if I can see her not wanting Paul to tell me that. I'm expecting her to come out with something bitchy but she doesn't. Herbie's Slush, some summer! is all she says. She looks sort of younger somehow like a little girl still in the warm yellow light from above the door.

V

Sometimes I don't give Gregory credit enough. Yesterday he came in to meet for lunch and try and cheer me up about it being my last week on the job. He says he's treating and we're not just going to the sandwich shop but someplace nice like the Post Road House just opened over in Pollard Square. We have big spinach calzones and Gregory orders us wine. So how am I getting any work done after all this? I ask him. Well they don't exactly give you job security so tough for them, says Gregory and he lifts his glass and gets me to clink mine on his. But Alice is still trying to get me transferred to East, I tell him but he doesn't think much of that. Oh they'll string you along of course, he says, what's in it for them to lose?

That made me think about Paul's opera him and me were listening to on his cassette all summer because he never got any other tapes. So I say that's like how in Utopia Limited, you know, Gregory, where it goes you don't have anything to lose when you're running a company? Where it goes what? says Gregory. Don't tell me Gregory the Great doesn't know that one! I say planning on stumping him. I thought you know the names of all the operas and you never heard of Utopia Limited! I say. Well who's the composer, give me a hint, he says. Sullivan, I tell him. Oh sure, you mean Gilbert and Sullivan, they do it on Channel Two, he says. Well, I say then, I bet you didn't know it's anticapitalist and anti-imperialist. He looks across at me like he's already thinking he shouldn't have given me that wine. Barbara, Gilbert and Sullivan is like old English, he says, what's this about antiimperialist? I tell him Paul and me studied this opera, Utopia Limited, and we always had it going on the cassette because he was in it once but now finally Paul went and spent twenty dollars on the Masked Ball cassette so we can study it too before November.

Hey, Gregory says, does Ma and Pa know yet about Paul moving in with you? Are you kidding! I say. But they know Stephen's living over there now, he says. I explain they all think I'm just letting Stephen share my place. So then what happens when Ma and Pa come by sometime? Gregory says. Them come by! I say. Pa came over once but Ma hasn't been ever. I bet they already know about Paul and you sharing, Gregory says, but they don't want to have to actually see it. That's their problem, I say and I'm thinking how back the first time when Paul and me didn't do anything, except to hold each other all night, I decided I was never telling anybody about it. But now so what if Ma and Pa know, I wouldn't care one bit.

I know Catherine does know, Gregory goes on. Sure, what would she care, but William doesn't, I say, he doesn't even know where Stephen went after that big fight so don't you tell on him, Gregory. Oh yeah sure, Gregory says, me and William going out for a friendly beer and talking about the family! You won't catch me talking to that crazy Albanian! And you make sure Tessa and Tommy don't say anything in front of Ma, I say. Don't worry, don't worry, hey, but Gwen loves all this though, he says, it's just like in her family now, what you can say to this one and you can't say to that. And don't talk about it to Peter's kids either, I say, Peter doesn't want them knowing. Yeah, yeah, says Gregory wiping off a spinach bit from his mustache, but so what was that you were going on about antiimperialist, Barbara? Then I realize it's too hard to explain to him.

But later when we order cannoli and coffee I try again to explain it better. Paul was in this opera Utopia Limited down there at his school, I say. His part was to be the Public Exploder who's always setting firecrackers off. It's a satire of politics is what it is. And Utopia's an island, I explain to Gregory, where the English come in and take over their government. Then I have to explain about the music master at Paul's school and how he's what you'd call left-leaning and he put this opera on to show capitalism is really an unfair thing. Gregory's shaking his head but he can just shut up and listen for once. I'm not saying I agree, Gregory, but it's true when you see capitalism in countries where there's real poor people, I mean real real poor. And it's not just from Paul I get it either, I believe it myself even if I didn't hear it from him, I have a right to my own opinion. I didn't say you didn't, Gregory says looking miffed at me.

Well do you know about the Limited Liability Act? I ask. Gregory's just going to listen now with that look still on his face. Well when you have a company you're not personally liable, I say, because you can just go broke and then start another company instead and go and make more money. So with these English taking over, I say, they give the king that idea and he turns it into Utopia Limited like the island's one big company. And then he kicks out the Public Exploder and all these black people down there are suppose to start acting like they're English. There's the scene where they get all dressed up in English style and the English are telling them how back in England they don't have slums, everything's perfect there, and those poor people believe them. But finally the Public Exploder, namely Paul, gets a conspiracy going to get people to put back on their native-style clothes.

There's some bald man at the table next to us listening and bugging his eyes over at me like I'm crazy. Then the king remembers about having political parties, I say finally, because one party always goes against the other one so things never really get any better. So that's the happy end? says Gregory. That's what they call irony, I say remembering how Paul explained it to me one time. That's not so hard to get, Gregory, is it? It's like they always got a way around you, the people running things, I say and I give that bald man his own look back when I'm saying it.

Gregory leans forward to tap at a few cannoli crumbs on his place mat. He's just thinking a bit and I'm thinking so what if Gregory thinks I'm left-leaning too, but what kind of a plan does he have to help matters along? He only said when he drove me back to work how I better not start getting in now with Gwen and her Irish politics, it's bad enough to have his wife acting that way, he doesn't need his little sister too. And I was thinking when we drove by the police station about something that happened there once and suddenly I remember it's that silent woman that sat on the bench and didn't talk all day. Everyone's got different ways of having ideas, I said to Gregory before I slammed that old Buick's door hard enough to close it and Gregory yells out the window: Hey I love you, little sister, and he's driving off before I think to say thanks again for the lunch. I can tell he wasn't really mad at me, he was more just surprised I knew all that. Before he was the only one of us who thought about politics or whatever and I could tell he's glad I do too now.

Then at work all we had to do still was driving me crazy. How was I getting all the files in the right boxes for the movers and cleaning out the drawers and at the same time people are having their appointments as usual. Since everybody knows now it's not so upset around here like earlier with Mrs. Guimond crying. Now it's just quieter and sort of depressed. There's not many of the people still coming who came when I first was there, like Mrs. Velis stopped, so you realize there's always going to be people stopping and pretty soon no one's going to remember this wasn't the unisex hair salon that's moving in Monday.

But all the time I'm organizing, people are saying good-bye and taking a last look around and it's making me get madder now, like what I said to Gregory about who is it really with something to lose. Well so I'm losing my job, that's one thing but that's not so much why I'm mad as thinking how we were driving out to Concord that day and seeing all those big houses, so why can't there be just this one crummy little Autumn Hill Center for all these people?

What're we doing about the illegals? I ask Alice next. There's these files all with the same name because they only got one legal card and they pass it around to each other so they won't get caught. We know they don't all have that same name but Bill and Alice told me just to write it down that way. So there's a pile of Clementine Levesques from Haiti and a pile of Maria Almeidas from Cape Verde. They usually only came in once anyway. I'm holding that stack out for Alice to look through and she thinks about it a second and then says, Oh just chuck them. We're supposed to keep everything, Alice, I tell her. No just chuck them, she says, I don't want trouble about it if they have different policies at East.

It's quieter later and nobody's coming in much. Then Alice takes a load over to her new office to get a head start and Bill's got a meeting at City Hall so it's just me sitting there almost too tired even to close up at the end of the day. I'm looking at the thing on my desk Julia made for me in crafts this summer. It's a plastic Pepsi bottle she melted somehow and stretched and it's filled up with different-colored sand to make a striped body and there's feathers glued on its head and one of those golf tees glued on for a nose. I wasn't going to bring it in for my desk because I'd just have to take it home in a couple weeks but then I brought it after all since she made it to cheer me up, she said, about losing my job.

VI

Did we ever get roaring last night after work. Forget this last mess, says Bill, I'll come in tomorrow and do a quick once-over but now we're going out us three and getting wasted. For lunch I brought in a chocolate cake I made for a little farewell party after the movers took the desks and files and I figured that was that. Well you got any other plans now? Bill says. Call up Paul, bring him along, says Alice. So I did but he's not back yet so they say let's go to Clooney's and get started. What about Polly and Sarah? I say. Bill looks at me sort of waggling his head and he says, I told Polly not to expect me home too early and definitely not to expect me sober. I never saw Bill act like this, he's usually so planned out. Alice goes back in her office to check the window then Bill squeezes my arm and whispers so she doesn't hear: Alice really needs a drink, Barbara. I look at him and he's raising his eyebrows so I'll get the idea.

I'm not much one for going drinking except maybe just one beer. Bill says we'll start off with a fancy one. He orders something called zombies for all three which when it comes you'd think was Hawaiian Punch till you had a sip. There's a lot of people jamming in but we did get a little round table in the corner so we're just crammed in there, me and Alice with Bill stealing a chair from someone else's table when they're not looking. Hey, he says, it's Happy Hour, every man for himself!

There's still no Paul each time I go call home but finally after I'm acting way too silly I get him and he says he was out getting the groceries for something special for us tonight. You better come to Clooney's first, I tell him, remember out in Endicott Square, because I'm feeling a little, you know, Paul? My, my, says Paul and I can imagine the teeth in his smile then. Then a song comes on and it's hard to hear. You coming? I say. I think he says he is. I'm not staying too long, I yell into the phone, so just come then we'll go back and eat. I'm not too hungry anyways, I yell. Not yet I mean! I yell. I think he's saying I'm his real sweet one. We're way over in the corner! I yell to him before I hang up. Maybe he was mad at me for going out like this.

Is it ever hard squeezing back through that after-work crowd and I keep expecting I'm going to see Horst but he probably only comes in later when it's more collegiate. Here's our baby, says Bill when I cram back in the corner. Alice grabs my shoulder and points to some well-dressed guy over there and says, Barbara, get me that man, will you please? Oh yeah sure, I say. I want him, says Alice, right now, put him on my bill. Isn't he a little slick for your taste? Bill says. I'm coming to like them slick, says Alice. Who knows if she's serious but I know one thing, she's still not feeling so great after two zombies. I mean what would you prefer, Barbara, she says, when you can't get what you want, you might as well get them slick, huh? There's no harm in looking anyway, she says. No, she says, there's definitely plenty to look at here anyway, gets my juices flowing, should've come in here years ago, she says leaning into my shoulder. Bill's catching my eye again. And you can just imagine all the other nice horny Irish-Catholic divorcées that come here too, says Alice, look at them all. Well probably not divorcées actually, she says.

Wait a minute, I tell her because I'm feeling drunk enough now. Bill looks like he can't believe it but Alice doesn't know what I'm doing. I squeeze out over to that guy she thought was so slick, I actually do it, since he was just standing along the wall there anyway and looking at some poster of old-time mustache styles. I look back and Alice is covering her eyes now like she can't believe it either.

Thinking of growing one? I say to the guy. I was thinking maybe this one, he says, pointing to the kind that droops way over the corners of your mouth. I got so good at talking to people at the Center who cares what this guy is thinking and besides he's talking back, I'm telling myself, so why not? Or how about one like that? I say pointing to one more like Gregory's. Yeah but I need something a little more like, you know, distinctive, he says. He isn't so slick up close, he's even a little pimply and I think he's definitely too young for Alice. I'm here with my friends and we all three lost our jobs, I say anyways. You wouldn't want to come have a zombie with us? That's a killer drink, he says, the last time I started in on zombies I don't remember where I ended up. I see he's just having a beer. You mean you all three lost your jobs? he asks. Well I did, I say and I'm pointing out Bill and Alice, and he quit and she got transferred. Hey sure, I'll come over, he says, so I'm leading him back and I can see Alice's face changing when she sees he's young with the pimples.

He tells us his name's Danny and we tell him who we all are. So he squeezes in on the corner seat first and Alice nudges over and then I sit down and suddenly I feel like we just trapped him. But he looks happy enough. Here's to you guys, he says raising his beer glass. So we all clink our glasses and I'm thinking now there's no room to squeeze Paul in and I'm having a hard time even hearing except that Alice is trying to do her sober neutral number on this Danny and it's coming out funny. I can tell she's wanting to make him feel we like him because she sees he's sort of a lonely loser type, just the way she does at the Center with those kind of people. So why isn't somebody doing that for Alice, I'm thinking, why is she always doing it for somebody else? And why did I ever get her into this, going and asking over this Danny?

Bill looks at me like oh well what can you do! So we look around the place and make some rude comments on people. See we're just observers, says Alice. This corner's the ideal spot to observe from, Danny, she says, people look better from a distance, did you ever notice? So for a while we're just looking and there comes a chubby black man nudging through by the bar and of course it's Paul.

I think we should just go but Bill says sit down and have a drink too and Danny thinks he should maybe go but Alice tells him to stay put and Bill steals another chair and now we're really all squashed in there. Good to see you again, Paul, says Alice. They only met that once when he came to see me at the Center. My profound sympathies to you all, Paul says. Except you I presume, he says to Danny who starts explaining he's just on his way home to the Heights and he just sometimes stops in here on Fridays. Then he gets telling us about his work to do with marketing pet foods. I'm only at an entry-level position, he says because first he went in the service then he went to Northeastern and he's still living with his parents. This might as well be the Center, I'm thinking, and now we're going to hear his whole life story. But the funny thing was we all started having fun after that, sort of kidding Danny like he didn't get our private jokes, like when I said, Hey Alice, you got your file on Danny for me yet? He says, You don't usually see people from work having this much fun together like you guys. We're a barrel of fun, says Bill. Even Paul's joking around. He's saying to Danny funny things like: In my country we have people like you for breakfast, pretending he's from some cannibal island with a funny accent. Danny doesn't know what to think but he's laughing and when Paul and me finally get up to go he's saying, Hey, see you guys next Friday, no really, I mean it, he's saying, and I'm waving good-bye to my two wonderful bosses for the last time. They're staying for one more round.

VII

I had the wildest dreams and Paul had to talk to me in the middle of the night when I was saying things that didn't make sense. Look out there's lions after you, I said to him he told me. He said that's just what happens when you have too much and you pass out after dinner and then sometime in the night you wake up and you don't know where you are.

But then I felt better after eggs and French toast and plenty of coffee. He had to go out to the library because part of this next year is he's got to teach the undergraduate students for his scholarship or whatever. I wish Paul wasn't always preparing things or studying things or at least he could do it more at home. But then I'm tidying up and Alice calls. She said she got home all right and maybe I even had a little companionship, Barbara, she says. Not that Danny! I say. Well we won't jump to any conclusions, says Alice. But she didn't call to tell me that, she says. Then for a second she doesn't say anything.

But it turns out she first called the Center to see if Bill wanted help cleaning and Bill told her the Saturday mail just came and there was a letter from the governor's secretary. They're such cowards, she says, you can go right to the top and still no one takes the blame. I got the letter now stuck on my fridge with one of the Smurf magnets: The governor is sorry to learn of Ms. Orsini's situation but, with current necessities as they are, he must allow the Neighborhood Centers Program to determine its own policies regarding staffing.

I knew it anyway, I tell Alice and somehow I don't feel any more worse than I did all week. So then what else about last night, Alice? I say just not to talk about it. Well don't say anything to Bill, Barbara, please, she says and then she tells me about yes it was Danny and he turned out to be nice enough for a one-time thing anyway. Well maybe that's good for her, I'm thinking, it couldn't hurt really. There's lots of women go with guys that way, just because I never did it.

Later when I'm sitting on my window seat looking down Milk Street I'm having strange ideas though. I don't know if maybe I'm not still wasted a little from Clooney's. Then there's something crazy I just suddenly decide I'm going to have to do.

I get on my phone to Horst and it wakes him up. It's not already so late yet, he says like he's about halfway there. I don't want to tell him for what I need the help but just to come over with his Volkswagen. I sound like it's a big important thing so he says he's coming and I'll meet him on the corner. So I'm down there with the ropes I saved from tying up my stuff moving in. Don't you ever wear something else except that sweat suit? I ask him when he rattles his car over and I get in. Barbara, when I'm rolling out of the bed to help ladies in distress, he says, I'm grabbing the first thing. He squints like it's still too bright for him in the mornings.

We're going to the Center. It's so bare in there now. Bill's mopping the floor and Polly's dusting and Sarah's crawling in and out of the beat-up fridge box. Luckily they left it. Polly says, So you went along on this famous bar crawl, Barbara. What time did he get home? I ask her. I was in bed by ten! Bill says mopping along past me and Horst. And that entry-level-position guy dropped Alice off, boy, was she roaring, Barbara, says Bill. Horst is standing there scratching at his beard so I explain I'm here with Paul's friend's car and I was wondering since they're going to leave it if maybe we could have the old lopsided box the fridge came in. Well the fridge itself is staying for the unisex people but I suppose they'll just throw the box out, Bill says. Good then I want it, I say.

And Barbara, says Bill, you probably want this too. He gives me that letter from the governor's office. For your scrapbook, he says. I know already, Alice called, I tell him. Polly says she's so sorry about it but what can anybody really say by now? I just fold the letter in my pocket and we all give a little sigh. We're going to New Hampshire now, says Sarah. I know, I tell her giving her curls a tug, you have a nice vacation, okay? But she gets into a screaming fit when we start to take away her playhouse.

Horst and me finally carry it down the stairs and get it tied on top of his Volkswagen and then slowly we're driving up Milk Street and he helps me with it in the front door. I love to make a secret mission with you, Barbara, he says. You plan perhaps to put Paul inside and ship him home? Just don't tell him anything about helping me, Horst, I say. And then I ask if he could come over Monday morning again after Paul's at the library and then he'll find out what I'm up to. Unless you have to study, I say. Me study? he says. He's looking awake more now scratching at his beard and he says, Comrade, count upon me! and off he goes to his car with his pants so loose they're almost showing the top of his pink bottom.

Then I'm knocking on Stephen's door. He comes out in his too-short pajamas sound asleep still with a big yawn and his hairy chest peeking out. I say I need to leave this box here for the weekend, okay? But don't tell Paul. He's just blinking at me waking up and there's empty beer bottles on the sink and on his windowsill. He was there all night drinking alone after getting off work, I'm sure he was.

VIII

It rained yesterday and Paul had the Sunday paper all over the apartment when Catherine came up. So you're already looking in the employment pages? she says. I'm not looking yet because Pa's got some contacts instead maybe, I tell her. So you're hitting unemployment then? Catherine says. Maybe I'll go over there tomorrow, I say but of course I'm really planning to do something else crazy instead.

Coffee, Catherine? says Paul. He's warming up some treat in the oven too. Catherine takes some coffee and I have another cup and then out comes Paul's special coffee cake. I knew he was hiding something when he came in with the paper. Then later he says he's off for a stroll now with his umbrella. I figure he wants us to get our chance to talk like sisters. Paul likes the cold rain, I tell Catherine, it's like he likes cold showers in the morning. You must know, says Paul putting on his fold-up plastic raincoat, what a nice cold rain means to someone from my parched little island.

He's nice, Catherine whispers after he goes. So you just noticed, I say. She's got her feet tucked up under her on the Danish chair. Mmm that was something, she says putting down her empty plate, you guys know how to eat. So how's it going without William these days? I ask her. Oh he's back, she says.

If that isn't Catherine. She goes through some kind of hell building up all summer till she finally kicks him out and then it lasts hardly two weeks. But she says it like it's just casual, oh yeah he's back, big deal. Well I can't get you your next appointment, I let her know, but I'll get you the number for East and you can call. Who said anything about appointments? says Catherine. You're going to in another week, I tell her.

Barbara, you're not going to listen to this I know, she says, but William's in a good mood now with this new job he got supering that elderly complex up the Heights. Tell Stephen that, I say. Well look, William just managed to get this job on his own last week, Catherine says. All the time she wouldn't let him back he was up there sponging off his aunt and it turns out they needed another super so the aunt puts in a word for him. Good for her, I say, so she's got family feeling, that's what William always wanted.

Well how is Stephen lately? Catherine says. I suppose he knows William's back so now he's not coming around again, is that it? I ask. Barbara, will you stop always getting on my case! Catherine says. I'm not on your case, I'm on Stephen's case, I say. Look it's not I don't appreciate you helping Stephen, she says, but I think you could maybe let me and William iron out our problems and not get on me about it always. Go ahead, iron them out, I say, I got my own things to think about like did you notice I'm out of a job, Catherine? Isn't that the first thing I asked you about? she says. Well good for you, I say. Paul should've stayed in, we wouldn't be scratching at each other. Thanks, Barbara, I was in a great mood till I came over, Catherine says.

I'm thinking how she comes over when she's in great moods or she comes over when she's in terrible moods but when does she come over when she ever just wants to talk normal? Her own kid gets beat on and cut up and everything so he won't even come home and who knows what maybe she's not telling me William did to her then too. And then she's got us all running around and Gregory and Peter taking turns hanging out there for a while in case William tries to come back and Ma's in a state. And I'm taking in Stephen for her and risking it with my landlord and all the time I'm probably losing my job but what does she care about any of that? So now we're all supposed to act happy William's back and working again like nothing ever happened? And we're not supposed even to talk reasonable about it to her!

Well maybe I wasn't in a great mood, I decide to tell her. All right so I'm sorry I wasn't thinking more about you, Barbara, Catherine says still sitting with her feet up under her and not coming to give me a hug or even look my way. When she's mad she doesn't soften up for a while usually.

You got to wake up and realize, Catherine, that the bad things keep happening over again, I tell her. You can't just go on thinking things get better. It doesn't get better, it just stops for a while and then you forget. You don't want to think about it when it stops. The only way you'd ever want to think about it is if it didn't ever stop and then you couldn't help thinking about it all the time. But see William's too smart for that and he knows how to stop. I'm not saying he can help it either. I mean I can feel sorry for him too if I think about it, I guess. You know what's funny though? I say. And then I tell her Stephen told me how he's really close to his father. Do you understand what I'm saying, Catherine? He really can't help it to love him anyway. That's what I mean, it's all messed up. So why don't you realize, Catherine? Go call Alice next week at the East Common Center and talk to her because now you could talk and it's not a big tragedy right now.

Catherine just looks at her blue-jean knees. Where's William today? I ask. Oh he's up to the Heights, she says. You want me to go down and wake Stephen up? I ask. I'll bring him up for coffee cake and you can talk. She frowns like she doesn't really care but when I go down and knock on Stephen's door there's no one there anyway.

So upstairs I tell Catherine one more thing. See I'm real mad right now, Catherine, I say and show her the letter on the fridge. And these people think they got nothing to lose,

I say. Well maybe I got nothing to lose really either now so maybe I'm going to do something. Like you should do, Catherine. Because there's other people who do got plenty to lose still, they got plenty to lose and who's ever helping them?

IX

The day came and I wasn't nervous either. When Paul went I got into Gwen's magenta running suit since it's the most comfortable thing to wear. I didn't get around to washing it yet after soccer though but that would be all right. Then I went down and woke up Stephen. You get dressed, I said, because you're coming with me. What you want now, Barbara? he says. Get dressed, ask questions after, I say. I was up all night, he says. So you can sleep later, get dressed. He goes down the hall with his bathroom key. So then I take out my marker and figure which side of the box is best and I start writing on it. The Autumn Hill Neighborhood Center, I write with big letters above where it says Frost-Free. Then I write smaller: Our motto is to be really adamant. Upstairs I looked it up in Paul's dictionary to be sure I spelled it right. Then I think for a while and they start coming, things I wrote from before. Mothers don't hurt children, then who does? I write across one side. And I write by the arrows on the this-way-up side: New children coming along every day. On top I write: It helps matters along, and from the paper that headline about Italian Opera Night: Stinted Common did itself proud. Stephen comes back with his hair still not combed and I'm writing on the back from what that stupid letter from the governor's secretary said: With current necessities as they are.

What's this junky old box anyways messing up my room? Stephen asks. It's my new office I'm opening and you're helping, I say. He doesn't have any idea what I'm getting him into. Comb your hair and look nice, I say, I'll treat you for coffee and doughnuts. I opened the shade so I could be keeping my eye out for Horst. Stephen sat down and looks at me funny when he's putting on his Nikes. After a while I hear that rattly Volkswagen coming.

So Stephen and me get the box out the door and I tell Horst my nephew's coming along and us three tie the box again on top. Off to the doughnut shop, I say. Yes comrade, says Horst. He's wide awake it looks like but as usual the same old sweats. When we're through eating then he says, Where now, comrade? Over to Boston, I say. What is this, some kind of crazy demonstration march you're getting me into? says Stephen in the back seat. I pretend to zip up my lips. So then they figure this is some kind of joke I'm having them help me pull.

We're going over by Neck Village and the back way so the box doesn't get blown off on the interstate. But my heart inside is thundering almost. You mean actually the State House, Horst says after I tell him where next. Right by the front steps, I say. It's a sunny morning that's not even really fall yet and rush hour's over but lunch crowds aren't out so we can pull right up. I am going to ask one question, says Horst: Now what is happening? You don't have to stay but just don't go tell Paul and make him worry, I say. I had to drag Stephen out and make him help me untie the box. But Horst says whatever it is he's paying for a parking garage, he doesn't care, he's just not leaving me and Stephen there to get in trouble.

So he goes to park and Stephen and me carry the box up the State House steps to where it levels off then I say, Okay

Stephen, put it over me. But you can't see out, he says, but I explain I don't want to see out and he should just sit over on some bench and make sure no one does something funny.

It's strange in the box. There's almost a brown glow at where the edges are. It's steady enough even after all those kids at the Center playing in it and now it's so quiet. First thing I hear after five minutes is Horst tapping on top. Comrade, he's saying. You see Stephen? I say out to him. You sit somewhere you can watch him and the box too and make sure no one does something funny. I have my orders, Horst says.

Sometimes I can hear footsteps going by but it's not scary. Someone taps once then goes along. I hear some people reading my sayings and mumbling things. It feels like all around the box it's cold and moving but in here it's almost peaceful. The box has sort of veins I can almost see on the side the sun shines on strongest. It's not all dark. There's funny threads of light in the air.

Did you put this here? says a policeman-type voice and it must be that Horst and Stephen are out there talking to him. My aunt's inside, says Stephen. Has she got clothes on? says the policeman. Then he tips up the bottom of the box and I see his big trooper boots and he sees my sneakers. What are you protesting? he asked. She's not protesting, Stephen says. We're only looking out for her, says Horst. The trooper lets down the box and then whispers but I can hear what he says: Is she nuts? Horst thinks it's funny but he's trying not to laugh too much. But Stephen's sounding like I bet he sounds when the police come around the project and tell the kids to move along. He's had practice.

She lost her state job, Stephen says, and they closed her Center where she worked. See here it says Autumn Hill

Neighborhood Center, he says. So she's protesting like I said, the policeman-voice says. You boys just hang on here a minute, and off he goes. I'm not scared at all inside, I feel it tingling all in my forehead and my heart going and I just think about Paul, Paul, Paul and I feel how sure I am doing this, I really am sure doing this.

What are we doing next? Horst is whispering down into the box and that was still the most exciting time, before the State House reporter came and the trooper made us take away the box unless we got a permit. That was more exciting just sitting inside the box and waiting, feeling I never before did a thing like this in my life.

So what then when Ma called up later all choked up and she's saying she was so ashamed when she was cooking there in the kitchen and on comes my name on the radio, she's so ashamed to think what if people would hear her own daughter talking on the radio about welfare. It's bad enough your sister can't get out of the project, she's saying. So how do you think it makes me feel hearing your own voice coming out at me from over my sink? She's almost yelling at me in the phone and then she sounds like crying. And before she called I was already crying anyway myself because when I told Paul what I did he was real upset too and saying why didn't I tell him I was doing it, why didn't I let him in on it? But then after Ma called he said it doesn't matter I didn't tell him but from now on please to tell him because he won't ever try to stop me doing something I really want to do. So then next we're turning on his radio to see if it comes on the news at six again but it doesn't, it must've been just on once in the afternoon.

X

Yesterday it did have to go back to raining. That meant the box would get soggy and maybe my sayings would get blurred but we were doing it again and Paul was coming too with his umbrella. Since there was something in the paper about it that morning the State House police decided to let me stay there and not make a big deal out of it, anyway they didn't expect me in the rain. But I was planning to keep going every day and get kicked off the steps, I didn't care. What I don't see, Barbara, is why you'd keep doing it though, Stephen says when he brings me coffee and a Danish. You're just going to get wet and too tired, he says. I take in the cup and the bag and let the box down again. I put down some plastic and a pillow for today. Don't you have difficulty breathing in there, sweet? Paul says.

For that weather I added some new sayings for laughs, like what Paul said once: It's not likely to be a terribly pleasant day I fear. And then I also wrote on one side: We're a very mixed lot, and on the other: I feel very luxurious! Might's well keep them wondering, I was thinking. I'm breathing just fine, I say, you guys take turns with the umbrella. That same trooper's up under the entryway keeping dry, they tell me and then Stephen goes up there and hangs out with him.

Sometimes people splashing along stop and say am I open for business. I tell them the governor cut our funds, he can pass the blame to someone else but it's him that cut it and he knows it. It's what I said to the radio and what it said I said in the morning paper. Can we see you? they want to know but I say I'm staying inside. It's amazing how polite people are about this, Paul's voice says up there in the air above my head.

More reporters came than before, even the TV Minicam did, but all I say is no interviews, I'm only talking to the governor. But then later Paul says there's someone else here, Barbara, and she knows you. Can I come in? says Annie Randall's peepy voice. So I say, You come right in, after all she was such a regular at the Center and for once I don't mind seeing her again. Paul tips the box and in crawls Annie in her raincoat and rubber boots and hat. Then it's dark again. There's just room for us two squashed in there.

You here for your appointment, Annie? I say and laugh. You bet, she says. You're early an hour, I say. So I always am, Annie says. I even give her a hug and her cheek a kiss. I can just see her skinny shape in there up against me. Why are you so brave, Barbara? she says. Did you hear me on the radio? I ask her. Yes and Mother heard you too, she says and Annie even called Alice to see if she heard too but she didn't so she told her all about it. Alice thought I was making it all up, Annie said. I didn't even think it'd be actually you when I got over here, she says. Then she tells me all the bus changes she made and how she didn't know if she should come out like this, she never came into Boston before and Mother was worried but she had to go see Barbara, she said.

I get asking her what did Alice use to tell her when she had her appointment all those times, I'm curious about it now. We just talked, says Annie, I was supposed to eat more and do more things outside like be in choir. We always talked about you too, Barbara, she says but that I knew already. So you want some free tips from me today? I ask. She's still leaning on me and our plastic raincoats are crinkling together with us mashed in. Why don't you sign up for the chorus for the Masked Ball thing at the Atherton? I say. I can't sing opera-type music, she says, I just can sing hymns. But they're desperate, I tell her, my brother Peter's telling me how Dom's going to have to start raiding the church choirs, look, I'll go over with you for the tryouts. Annie still doesn't think she could but I say that's her one tip from the Autumn Hill Center for today and she has to do it or she doesn't get to come back. I keep having to remember Annie's in her forties probably and here I am twenty-nine and telling her what to do. But she has this voice like she's a little girl still. Then I make her get out of the box and say she better get back to Stinted Common before rush hour gets her all confused.

The box is leaning pretty bad when we're driving it home last night but me and Paul and Horst go drop off Stephen first at Veracini's and go out for pizzas before we bring it home and watch the TV news. Just for a minute there's a picture of the box in the rain and Paul holding the umbrella over it. You can just see the line about it not being a pleasant day but that didn't stop Barbara Orsini of Stinted Common, the news lady says. And then they told how I'd only talk to the governor. Paul, I thought you were holding the umbrella over you not the box, I say.

Well will you come over and talk to your mother at least? says Pa making a joke when he gets on the phone to me right away. He says Ma won't come to the phone and she's crying but he's not saying what he thinks one way or another. But I don't understand why you're doing this, Barbara, he says since he's looking to get me a good job. I talked to George Ippolito today, he says but I don't even want to try to tell Pa why I don't want to hear about George Ippolito. So I say, Tell Ma to take it easy, tell her I'll come talk to her tomorrow afternoon I promise but I'm too tired and wet now. What I need is a good soak, Pa, does she want me coming down with pneumonia?

XI

So it was a sunny day and the governor came. Who does he really think he is? I'm thinking. Stephen just whispered into the box: He's coming! and I'm sitting in there saying one more day of this is all I could take anyways. I got so used to it in there though. There's times I wouldn't mind going back in some box to get the quiet and think. I take out my old marker and just barely I can see enough to write only for me my most favorite saying of all: A feeling of it moving inside.

There's sounds of lots of feet out there and Paul says the TV and radio people are wheeling up too but I don't care about looking. I'm thinking what I have to say. There's lots of mumbling then a deep voice that says first: In here? She's not coming out though, I hear Stephen say. One simply speaks to the box, says Paul to the governor.

Ms. Orsini, is that you? says the governor sounding like on TV with his grinning sort of voice. Autumn Hill Neighborhood Center open for business, I say. I'm sure they're all of them grinning out there. Would you like an appointment? I say figuring it's just as good to keep them laughing and wondering what next. It makes me be able to say things more.

I've learned of your situation, says the governor's voice, and my secretary has shown me the letter written in your support by Ms. McKeever. I'll let him just talk, I'm not saying anything. And we feel that someone as dedicated as you have proven yourself to be should not be let go—Ms.

Orsini? he says. I can hear you, I tell him. I wanted to let you know personally that I feel sure we can work something out for you in our Neighborhood Centers Program, he says.

Some people out there started applause and the reporters want to say something but the governor says this is just between him and Ms. Orsini. Like he doesn't even know there's cameras going! I know what he's looking like on TV too, so smooth no matter what. I'll tell you something, I say with my eyes closed in the box so I don't even see where the edges are but just can think of what to say. You still there? I say. Yes I am, the governor chuckles away.

You don't understand what I want, I say to him. I don't want some other job in the Neighborhood Centers Program. I don't need a job, I'm okay, my father can help me get a job. But I just want you to get that unisex hair parlor out of there and get back Alice and Bill and let those people keep coming there.

Now there's mumbling again outside all around me. Paul says Horst and Stephen were just standing there like proud bodyguards and Horst even had on his beret he wore in the Namibian desert, he says, and Stephen had on his uniform from Veracini's with the Stephen nameplate on the pocket.

We're unable to keep your old center open but that doesn't mean the people of your neighborhood won't be well served is the last thing I hear the governor say. Then I start just saying what I think and I don't care if he hears me: You know what this box is, Governor? I say. You think this box is just something funny I'm sitting in for TV or something? Well listen, this box is somebody's house down in Haiti in case you didn't realize. Do you even know how bad off some people can get? This box is a house for some people. Put a little plastic over it and they could live here months. That's how they do it, you know. Don't you know things like that?

Then somebody knocks it over and Horst is pushing at him to get him off and there I am in Gwen's running suit blinking from all the concrete around that's so bright white suddenly. The trooper is coming down saying, That's the end of the show, people, let's move this on, and there's the back of the governor and his bunch going in the State House door. Some guy with the Minicam says to me: Lady, there's nothing in it for him talking to nuts, can't you tell?

Stephen's standing there looking sad at me. Then he tries to straighten out the box which is still leaning funny after it got so wet the day before. His trooper friend is helping with it and saying, Here Steve, let's get it folded up, you can dispose of it better flat. Then Paul's kneeling down beside me giving me squeezes. I understand about the box now, Barbara, he's saying, Barbara, I love you so much. Did he hear me? I ask. His Excellency? says Paul. I'm feeling like I'm already crying. He couldn't help but hear you even as he walked away, you spoke out so strong and bright, says Paul with his cheek on my cheek.

And then soon we're gone. First Horst drops Stephen at Veracini's and Stephen was going to put the old box in their dumpster. I didn't want to see it go, it made me too sad. Then Horst drives us by Ma's because I did promise we'd go. There's all the little kids out front of Peter's and there's Gregory's Buick and Tommy and Tessa holding up a sign they made saying Have You Hugged Your Receptionist Today? That was Gwen's corny idea, she had her kids working on it right after school. My running suit is famous now! she's yelling. It was just on the radio how I was a large woman clad in a magenta running suit apparently.

Julia and Quintus are jumping all over me when I get out and then Paul squeezes out the back and they're jumping on him too. All the kids on the street are there looking or whistling and carrying on too. I'm off, comrades, says Horst because it's too much for him and some kid even is bouncing on his bumper when he drives up the street. Gregory and Gwen are up on Peter's steps and hugging me when I get that far and Camilla comes out. Then I see Pa also coming over from next door and even Ma's back standing in the door looking like she isn't sure what she's going to do.

Gregory heard the radio when he was on break and called me at home! Gwen is yelling. What's he look like up close, the governor? she wants to know. Wait a minute, wait, I'm telling the kids. It said on the radio how he actually talked to you, Gwen keeps yapping. But I didn't see him, I stayed in my box and told him off from inside, I say. You told him off? says Gwen and everybody's saying: What, you told him off? But the radio said he offered you back your job, says Camilla. What did it say, who heard it? I'm asking. Only Gregory heard it, Gwen says, when he was on break. So Gregory tells it. It just said there's a resolution to that story they reported about the woman from Stinted Common on the State House steps. And they described you and said how the governor met with you today and offered you another job in the Neighborhood Centers Program, Gregory said.

It was even worse on the news at six. The older kids had got home and then Peter and we all were crowding around in Peter's family room that he just paneled, Pa and Ma too. There wasn't anything for a while and we kept switching the channels, then we caught one: A footnote, says the news lady, that disgruntled Stinted Common woman camping out on the State House steps has been offered another position in the Neighborhood Centers Program by the governor himself. And then off she goes to the sports. Camping out! yells Lucius looking like he's going to slam the set. Wait, leave it on, yells Quintus for the baseball scores.

Then Ma says thank God they didn't use my name again. And Julia's nudging over to me and saying me and Paul have to stay for dinner too, Peter's already ordered in pizza for the whole family. Ryan's there hugging onto Ursula on the couch next to Ma. I suppose you're staying too, Ryan? says Camilla.

XII

Finally I got ahold of Alice yesterday and when I tell her she says I did the right thing to not take the job offer, I'd hate it down at East anyways. She hates it already, she says. There's so many people and you don't see them more than once usually and she doesn't know Spanish so she just gets all those Clementine Levesque types always. I think she almost doesn't believe I really did go over to the State House. Annie told her about going over but she didn't get to see it on the news that time they showed the box in the rain and then of course they didn't actually show anything the next night when she could finally watch.

Dom told Camilla there's maybe going to be an article in the Stinted Commoner next week but so far there was only those two little ones in the Boston papers and no pictures. The second one said disgruntled too. That's one thing I'm not. Paul thinks the TV gets embarrassed to show when someone says something mad like that unless it's when they just had their house hit by a tornado and they lost everything they ever had. But people sounding off they don't like. They probably figure they're just crazies.

Last night late Paul started telling me about him talking to Horst at the college that day. Horst thinks you're an angel, Paul says when we're cuddled up in bed under Nonna's spread. But then Horst also said a thing that got Paul to worry. He told Paul he always had need of an adversary is what Paul said. When he was standing there in his beret, he told Paul, he looked at the governor and then he knew he had to go back over and be with them blowing up things, Paul said, not here studying the way his father wants him to. It's rather more desperate over there, Paul said. Horst never did really blow anything up though, Paul doesn't think. He can tell by the way Horst talks about it like it's more he just wishes he could. But he probably knows the people in this SWAPO organization, it's called, and who knows what he might go and do. He's a strange fellow, Paul says then, I never quite get his story straight, I don't really know him I fear, it's usually bumping into each other at the cafeteria that we get to talking. He seems a lonely soul, Paul says. And I was thinking of when Horst drove away after taking us to Ma's. He didn't want to come in and meet the family.

I hugged onto Paul in the soft darkness of our bed feeling lucky all over. We international students are a funny crew, Paul said then, some of our families own banks and oil wells and even whole countries and some are penniless refugees, some yearn to go home, some not ever again. But I'm thinking I can't even think of Paul being foreign or Horst or any of them. I know there's all these countries in the world besides the ones I knew about but it's hard to think you'd know people who really came from there and sometimes they seem to me just like Americans too.

We don't always know what to do when we think of

home, Paul said then, especially if we can only look back on strife, and it's quite complicated with Horst because his family wants him to stay away. He's a good deal younger than we are, Barbara, said Paul, and what worries me about this need of his for an adversary, well, I think it's partially a need for some kind of a cruel father, isn't it? That is, can you imagine what his own father must be like? Paul says.

What if you ever had to go back to your father, Paul? I suddenly asked. This is what we never talked about yet. But I think you and I will always be together, sweet, Paul tells me, both here and there. But Paul, how? I ask and then I ask him why didn't we ever talk before about the future? He says he was afraid I didn't know if I'd want to spend my life with him yet. But I'm wondering why didn't I even think about it. Why did I just keep on day by day not thinking what would ever happen to Paul and me together? I'm afraid too, suddenly I feel it. We could go someday to my island, he says, and then we would begin to think about it. But how could I live there without seeing my family ever? I say. No, only for a visit there, says Paul, and then we will both know more. I don't know either yet, he says, I'm afraid like you, sweet one.

We don't talk now but the feeling of wanting to make love is moving inside me and I can tell just by the way he's leaning now and nudging that he's feeling it too. But I ask him first: Your father isn't cruel though? My father is quite a kind man, says Paul, I miss him every day, Barbara, and he will love you, I have no fear.

Why don't I know more about Paul yet? All I know is his mother died and he went to college in the West Indies not England and then he came here and his father's a minister. I want to know Paul but it's all so far away. Hold me, Paul, I tell him. Before I never felt sad when we made love.

A Masked Ball

I

Mornings are all right because first we have breakfast, eggs with cheese melted in with them and toast or those crumpets Gregory got us hooked on, and then when Paul's gone I clean up and have my soak and do a little shopping. Sometimes I go meet Catherine on her lunch hour or once even I met Alice down in East but then there's the whole afternoon left. I'd feel funny going out to find Paul and hang around there though he said why didn't I. I took to going to Ma's instead but that's not good except I can see Peter's kids when they get home from school. Lucius has to go right over to the Atherton always and Ursula's practicing for her dance part or out with Ryan but the others are there.

Yesterday when I was in Camilla's pink kitchen watching her do ironing and yapping along about Peter working too hard these days it's Dom that comes by. He's on his way to the airport to pick up Marianna Antonelli and he's got to check with Camilla about putting up this other singer that's coming over too. Joan Ippolito was going to take her but she decided then she couldn't handle more than the one she already has, the one who in the opera's supposed to be the Witch of Salem.

Dom's pacing around Camilla's kitchen like it's a real tragedy he's in. For somebody short he takes up more room than most guys. He's pounding his fists together trying to think what we can do like he's just waiting for Camilla to say let this extra singer stay there. But Camilla knows to say right off: Too bad we don't have room ourselves, Dom. Hey, what about your mother-in-law's! says Dom like he just thought of it. Camilla heaves out a big sigh. I don't think I could ask her that, that's a lot to ask, she says. Or maybe she could take in some of your kids, Camilla, and then Giuseppina could stay here, Dom figures. My kids drive her too crazy these days except when it's one at a time, Camilla says. Barbara, you got any room? Dom doesn't lose a second and he's shaking his hands like what is he ever going to do.

You're picking up them both right now? I ask. See it's Marianna's best student she's bringing along, she's a wonderful girl, Giuseppina, practically still a teenager, says Dom. So why doesn't she stay with you and Gina too? But he explains Marianna being the big star has to have her privacy. I mean it's her American stage debut, Barbara, says Dom. And then he's pacing into the family room and poking around out there. Maybe Ma would even like it having a singer stay over, I say to Camilla. You ask her then, says Camilla.

Well what with Ma always complaining about Ursula and them not being musical or taking up instruments she ought to take in this Giuseppina or shut her mouth, I'm thinking. Dom's looking at his watch, he's got to go. So how come you didn't take that job from George? he asked me. I'm taking my time, I tell him, I'm not into real estate things anyways, I want something more with people. What's more with people than real estate! Dom says, all hyper like he was ever since this whole opera thing got going. So do you think you'll ask her, Barbara, your ma I mean, it'd be really sincerely appreciated, he says. Sure I'll ask, I tell him but I don't promise anything. Giuseppina's a real cutie, he says, wait'll you see her in that page boy outfit, will she ever be cute! Dom's winking at me. And can you girls believe this is really happening? he says grabbing my elbows and shaking them. My opera's actually happening! You're really doing a great job, Dom, Camilla says going back to ironing which she couldn't do with him jumping around her kitchen.

When he goes out he's still saying how he really sincerely appreciates it about Ma maybe putting up Giuseppina even though she doesn't speak English yet but that won't be a problem, she's so cute and talented, says Dom.

II

We had to reserve a table for ten a week ahead and plan what we'd have and get Pa thinking him and Ma were going out for a quiet birthday dinner to where Stephen's a waiter. Then they get to Veracini's back room and there's all of us standing around having a drink yelling surprise. No kids for once though, just their own grown-up kids if you can call us that and Paul's there with me. He wasn't sure he should come too but Gregory said was he kidding, of course he should. Gregory thinks Pa prefers Paul to him and Peter anyways.

So Pa really was surprised like he never thought we'd do

it again so soon after his retirement party from work last winter. Well just don't let it get to be a habit, he's telling us. He takes one end and Ma takes the other and me and Catherine are on Pa's end and our brothers are down on Ma's but just when Paul's sitting next to me Ma says couples have to sit opposite so that means I get William and Paul's between Catherine and Camilla. Paul can handle that but me next to William I could do without. Luckily Gwen's starting right in to him on the other side so I turn mostly Pa's way.

Since it's all ordered ahead we just wait for it to come. Around the corner from the kitchen comes Stephen, he's already smiling and blushing. Hi, I'm Stephen, I'll be your waiter this evening, he gets out except he starts laughing and you couldn't tell what he's saying unless you heard him do his routine before. Give me a big kiss, says Ma grabbing onto him. Oh Grandma! he's going. Ma's in a happy mood.

Actually Stephen's not our only waiter, there's a couple others too coming back and forth with all the food. Paul keeps privately looking across at me and smacking his lips at every dish. We're fighting over who gets which antipastos and everyone makes like they want to be sure Paul gets a taste of each kind. Pa doesn't know anything about Italian cooking but he's telling Paul what's in each anyway and Ma's letting Pa talk since it's his birthday. I'm thinking it's good to have Paul along, gets them all behaving better.

Stephen's trying to act like he's just a waiter but of course we give him a hard time, especially Gregory and Peter. This wine's no good, take it back, cameriere, says Gregory after they go through the whole tasting routine. Don't give me that, says Stephen. Then Gregory pokes at his skinny ribs. Lay off him, Ma's saying.

William doesn't talk to his own son except for like: Here, take this, when he passes him his empty plate. Ma and Pa are acting now like they forgot last summer already. It's for Catherine's sake is what they'd say. William's looking good though and you can see, with him and Stephen dressed up, how Stephen's getting to look more like him if now he just filled out more. It's my favorite Chicken Marsala alla Veracini we're having with fettucine too and I'm beginning to feel full already before dessert even gets there.

The big thing Pa and Ma are going on about is their new neighbors, it's all they talk about these days. It took awhile after Marjorie died even before anyone cleaned that place out but finally it was some nephew that came from California to do it. Then the place sat empty the rest of the summer with the For Sale sign up but not too many people came. Ma was going crazy with nerves especially when people were looking with kids. All summer Pa's talking about getting our half of the house aluminum-sided because now was the time when there wasn't neighbors to argue about the color he wanted. But Peter was saying wait till someone moves in and you can get a better job done getting them to go in on it for the whole house at once. Gregory was asking what does Pa want to aluminum-side it for, he's going to ruin the authentic looks. So you come paint it for me every five years, Gregory, is what Pa told him.

But that's not the big deal now these people are actually moved in. These people wouldn't care what color it is, that's one thing, they got enough other problems. I knew right off they were some more of those East Timor people, they looked just like the bunch that came in the Center. I keep expecting to see my buddy Mikey from soccer coming over but so far not. They must not be doing too bad themselves because Armindo, the man who actually bought it, has a new Reliant with a letter license plate that we can't figure out. It goes: OCUSSI. Someday I'm going to knock and ask him what they mean by that. They come and go very quiet but sometimes there's other families staying there too, new ones, maybe just getting to America and they need a place to stay. Ma keeps peeking out back at who's out there or if they sit on their side of the front steps she's peeking out the shade.

At the birthday if Paul wasn't there Ma would be telling us one more time about how really dark their skin is even though they're not blacks, they're Orientals, but she doesn't say anything about skin with Paul around except she's whispering something to Peter and that may be it. So what should I do, Peter, says Pa all the way down the table from our end, go ahead now and side it on my own or discuss it with these people? Pa, if it was me I'd talk to them, says Peter, but why don't you just do what you want? It's a big investment and I want it done right, Pa says. Too bad Common Lumber doesn't do siding jobs, he'd get it with a discount then, says Camilla, we got our paneling cheap. I'm staying out of this round, says Gregory but then he can't help saying, Don't you realize, Pa, in my neighborhood there's people like Frank Bartlette paying good money to take their siding off? He's getting his properties all back to nice trim paint jobs, attracts a whole different renter, then he deducts it from his taxes and ups the rent, you can't beat it. Well we don't need that around us, says Peter, I was telling George Ippolito no way is he putting in that new fence he wants, I don't care if our old one leans, you know how much that'd end up costing me when he uses it for an excuse to jack up the rent?

Barbara, now don't you wish you got into real estate? says Camilla. Oh yeah sure, Camilla, I say and Paul's listening right and left and smiling at everything and still trying to hear what Gwen is going on about to William too, probably some crisis of her family in New Hampshire.

So what would you advise, Paul? says Pa. See, I told you Paul's got clout, says Gregory, you got Pa under your thumb, Paul, he'll do whatever you say, just you watch. I respect his educated opinions, says Pa. So who's not educated! Gregory comes back with. Stephen's trying to clear off but he keeps ducking Gregory and Peter when they're waving their hands around.

If only, Mr. Orsini, you could claim that Italian singing girl you're housing as a renter who required aluminum siding! says Paul. One of his fellow students, Paul explains to Pa, bought a house with his father that on paper they rent to somebody they know but actually this student lives there too, and it ends up costing him less to own than renting would because of his father's tax bracket however that works. Then Gregory tells about some guy he works for who bought a new BMW because he couldn't afford not to, says Gregory. He's got properties out in the burbs, he says, and he can claim this car as a business expense for going to look after his properties. So when you see a guy driving around in some slick car and you're thinking what he must've shelled out for it, that's only what we would've had to, Gregory says, because you or I don't get these deductions like in the fifty-percent bracket but these guys are driving around in BMW's for less money than my old Buick! Gregory, that Buick's not worth two hundred dollars, says Gwen over to him. Wait a minute, I'm saying but I'm counting on Paul explaining it to me later. Now he just says to Pa: It's the wonder of capitalism, Mr. Orsini. I know he knows how to not say any more that might get them thinking he's a communist. Paul wouldn't do that.

It really bites it, doesn't it! says Gregory. Myself I'm not complaining, Peter says, look at all we got, look at this meal. I don't know, Ma's saying to herself till she knows she's got us all listening, I don't know, with these new people moving in and you can just think all the children they're going to have and where are they getting jobs when they come along? I know I don't know anything about these things, she says, but I just don't know what's going to happen with all them.

Hey, we'll all move to Arizona and move in on Aunt Anna! Peter says because he knows that's how to get a dig in at Ma. She flicks her hand at him making her disgusted frown-face. I don't even remember Aunt Anna but I remember Ma saying how she was always coming around the house complaining how Ma was changing things. Anna did call up her brother today for his birthday long distance, I'll give her that, Ma says.

Then in comes Stephen with the cake and everyone sitting in the main part of Veracini's is looking around back and they sing along but wait to see what name to come in with. It comes out Dear Frederick and Dear Pa and Dear Grandpa from Stephen. I think Paul's lips are going Dear Pa-aa.

William leans over to me and he says, Notice I'm keeping my mouth shut, Barbara? If I wanted I could tell them plenty about tax deductions but you don't see me horning in on one of these family confabs, you notice? You're doing good, William, I tell him. Yeah but, and then he leans in closer to my ear, if I have to keep hearing about those nuts in Gwen's family— then he stops and looks at me like he's had it up to here. I smile like I sympathize.

It's true William's keeping it in pretty good for once. He kind of likes me more after the box thing too, he thinks I'm more like him now, like I finally saw the light how bad things really are, he apparently told Catherine. But you never know what his next idea's going to be so it's better to shut up around him still. How do you like the unemployment lines? he asks but I just smile and give a shrug. I wouldn't tell him how I'm not going. If the governor would've given me a job I shouldn't go on unemployment just because I didn't take his offer. William would say don't be such a sucker probably but Ma and Pa think I did right and so does Paul.

Now Stephen's passing the pieces of cake around and Paul's smacking his lips again at me when we see it's also chocolate inside. William leans over again and I'm thinking I knew I was getting stuck with William sooner or later, Gwen did her share but now mine's starting. You see what I was telling you once about that kid? he says looking at Stephen balancing the plates. What's he going to be, Barbara, a waiter all his life?

III

And you never thought they'd get fund-raisers in Stinted Common, I'm telling Alice at lunch when I go to see her another time. You're coming, aren't you? I want to know. But do you really have to wear a costume? she wonders and I tell her didn't she read in the Commoner how it's not costumes, it's a Masked Ball, you wear a regular party dress but then they give you a mask at the door just for your eyes, I say, it's the old tradition. Call up and ask Danny to go, I suggest to her. Alice looks across at me like old times when we had lunch at the sandwich shop but now we're in some greasy joint I would never go in otherwise down almost as far as Neck Village. Barbara, says Alice, that man is turning out to be a little more difficult to discourage than I thought. So why discourage him, Alice? I say.

But I should know by now Alice isn't going to find the right guy for her easy as that. It goes from her thinking she shouldn't see anybody so as not to get disappointed to then thinking she should see as many guys as she can because how else would she cover all the possibilities. And she keeps changing her hair. At Autumn Hill for months she looked the same but already at East she had three different looks in not even two months. Alice, sometime I'm passing you by, not knowing it's you anymore, I told her. But then I said I really like this latest pixie look and she should keep it.

You and Lou Ann have lunch together much? I asked but it turns out Lou Ann has to cover for Alice during her lunch hour. You ever see Bill Potts now? I asked. She tells me about him and Polly and Sarah, how they're getting a house Polly's parents are helping them buy but not in Stinted Common. They figure with Sarah coming along they want to be out where there's better schools. That's when I think to tell Alice how I'm maybe going on to school myself. I say I don't see why I couldn't especially if Paul helped me out writing the papers at first. Paul's really for it. Of course it means we got to economize but I could go back to working at the doughnut shop to make enough for starting after New Year's. Bunker Hill Community College is what I'm thinking. I wouldn't tell anybody in my family yet but I could tell Alice.

But Barbara, she says, is that old manager still at that doughnut shop? It's not the same branch I'd be applying to, I tell her, it's the new one opening up Quarry Hill, they're starting to hire in a couple weeks. Well, Alice says, it sounds right to me, your going on to school. See what if ever I wanted to go with Paul to his island, I say, maybe I should have a skill, you know, something I'd be more useful at. There's so much you'd be good at, Barbara, did I ever tell you how smart I always thought you were? Alice asks. I tell her she didn't. Well I'm telling you now, she says, and you know why I think so? Because you really figure people out, she says. You get them just like that, she says snapping her fingers. Well I got good common sense, I tell her. I always knew that.

I got this idea about going on to school when that article about the box didn't come out in the Commoner. Camilla told Ma how Dom said there was definitely going to be one and I bet Ma called up her old friend Marietta who works at the paper and got her to make them leave it out. I didn't want to fight with Ma over it because I'm not sure what she exactly did. But then I started writing my own letter to the editor, I decided, and it was going to explain how those State House reporters got it wrong, I wasn't disgruntled like they said. I wanted to explain how I'm a happy person and how I feel lucky for myself. I tried writing it different ways but it came out sounding too stupid. I'm better just at those sayings I wrote on bus stop shelters when I didn't have to think about them. I could've got Paul to help me but there I was, thinking how come I didn't go on to college like Gregory and know how to write out something like this for myself? I'm as smart as him, I'm thinking, and I got things I want to say to people now. I didn't have anything to say yet back when I graduated high school.

I V

I fear our shapes and skins make us an undisguisable pair, Paul said when we're putting on our masks at the gym door. Did you figure out who was that taking donations? I asked him and he said he couldn't help recognize Celia's cute dimpled chin. And her new pimples, I whisper back.

I didn't go in the gym since my awful high school gym class or those dances that weren't as bad only thanks to boys like Robert Santangelo. For this fund-raiser they put streamers up like in high school and the same songs are playing that were oldies already back then. These kids now don't have oldies, all they're into is what's just coming out, but Dom figured the crowd he was attracting to this event though would be likely to go more for the way it used to be.

It's a pretty good crowd but I never went to a dance where everyone's got masks on before. It looks strange walking in, like it's some big conspiracy. You could choose a color to go with your clothes but they were out of the apricot shade Celia had on so I had to take yellow and Paul took the plain black one like most guys did.

I wonder if Alice got that Danny to lay off and would be coming by herself but I don't see her. You have to judge from people's shape and their hair or if you ever saw them in that dress before. I can see one of Gwen's dresses over there so that's her, I guess, but I think it's Joe Donnell she's dancing with not Gregory. I'm saving my dress Gwen picked out for going to the actual opera in so I got out my plum and gray dress from two years back though it's not as good for my figure. I never did dance with Paul before except up in our apartment we pretended to do sort of a waltz to his opera cassettes, the part in Utopia Limited where the black people dress up like English, but the dancing part in The Masked Ball was too fast for us chubbies to try bouncing around to, at least with old lady neighbors below. We been studying it though the same way we studied Utopia Limited and I didn't realize before how The Masked Ball was supposed to be happening in colonial times in Boston, Massachusetts. I never thought they'd have an Italian opera happening over here but of course that was why Dom chose this particular one to put on. My life's dream comes true, my old home Italy comes to my new one Boston! he was going on to Ma when he came over once checking how Giuseppina's doing. He's definitely got his eye out for that girl but she keeps him off like a pro.

I bet that was her over dancing with Lucius on the other side of the gym. I knew it was Lucius with his curly hair he lets go so long now even though other kids are going back to almost crew cuts. The girl was so short she could've been Julia dancing with him but I doubted it because Camilla was making her stay home and watch Quintus. But it was definitely Lucius, he'd be the only boy to choose a red mask.

Paul doesn't really know how to dance to songs like I Can't Help Myself or Everlasting Love but he stands there and jiggles and flops his arms around to the beat. When they play a slower song like from a Dionne Warwick album we do hold on to each other and first I thought we were the only couple there that was white and black till then I saw a huge tall black woman with a black mask dancing close with a short guy who had to be Dom. Later I found out she was the singer from New York who's supposed to be black anyway in the story of the opera. That must've been Joan Ippolito sitting there watching them.

You wouldn't catch Joan on the dance floor, that's one thing, she's too big a deal.

Since Marianna Antonelli wasn't going to be there for the intermission feature like they advertised, Dom had to get up and make an announcement about her saving her voice and so instead we'd like to introduce you, he says shifting on his feet, to three of our other stars that are already here working with us preparing for opening night. His wife Gina was serving Paul and me at the refreshment table when Dom started so we stocked up and went to get a seat.

First comes Giuseppina and Dom explains how she studies in Rome with Signora Antonelli and she'll be the part of Oscar the page boy. When she comes up I see it was her like I thought dancing with Lucius before. I guess it doesn't matter she's supposed to be a boy because you shouldn't expect it to be too realistic in operas. After all, what people go around always singing anyway and they certainly didn't all sing Italian around here back in seventeen something. It's the emotion of the drama that counts is how Gregory explained it after Pa's birthday when I was complaining about this crazy story of The Masked Ball that me and Paul were trying to study.

But it did make a difference I already knew the songs they sang at the fund-raiser. It wasn't like the concert last spring when I didn't know what was coming next. Giuseppina sang the bouncy song about how the witch turns her black face to the stars and she got a big hand. Then on comes the huge black woman herself. Dom introduces her, Wilba Suggs, a discovery of our own School Board President Joan Ippolito, making her New England debut in the role of Ulrica, the Witch of Salem. The lights went dim and she wrapped a black robe around her to sing one of my favorite songs. King of the Abyss! it goes. She knocked them out with the low notes that sounded like they came out of a man. Wilba Suggs isn't round like Dom's sister Marianna but she's so tall and broad she was almost scary when they dimmed the lights and there she stood singing so loud it echoed.

We were sitting back on the bleachers. Paul was squeezing my hand he was so excited hearing those voices sounding like they were right in your ear, not tinny coming out of his cassette. And then up pops this gray-haired man with no mask on, Mr. Procopio who used to live in Stinted Common and sing sometimes at Saint Vin's if it wasn't the usual wobbly lady singing but now he's retired down the Cape. His voice is still the radiant tenor you all remember, says Dom. So the old guy sings the part where Riccardo pretends he's a sailor to find out his fortune from the witch. At the end Procopio really belts it out but his face is turning red and his arms look so short when he holds them out in front. Then all the lights come back on and everyone is going wild clapping and Dom makes the singers come back up and bow including the piano player who's Mr. Allison again, that new music teacher from the high school. Even the girl who turned the music pages bows and everyone whistles and stomps. Sounds like some basketball game, I tell Paul. Then it goes back to dancing after the concert part of the evening.

Once Gregory and Gwen cut in on me and Paul. I couldn't believe it to see Gwen dancing with Paul but she's letting him shake and wiggle and trying to do it sort of like him not to make him feel he's no good. Her and Gregory still go dancing sometimes at Clooney's when there's a good band, they like showing off their style. But Peter and Camilla I bet didn't dance since high school.

Peter's so hyper lately since he's got still more renovating to do in the Atherton lobby before the opening. Why Camilla ever got him paneling their family room last summer too I don't know. How did you guess it was me and Paul in these masks? I joke at Peter when he comes over to talk to us. Well hey that was a rough one, Stuffs, he says. I love dancing with my brothers. We always danced around home when we were little to drive Ma and Pa crazy. But of course Peter wouldn't have Camilla dance with Paul when he dances with me. She's off clearing up the refreshment table with Gina.

Looks like Lucius has got a crush on that little Italian import, I say. Peter says how she's hanging around the theater all the time now helping out Lucius and he's teaching her English. He's a real mover, says Peter. Maybe she figures she's safer hanging around with a kid instead of some of the boys Ursula's age or those guys down at the body shop. I'm sure Ma warned her to stay away from all of them.

Peter says he keeps telling Ursula she should go over to Ma's and make friends with Giuseppina but she's got to be with Ryan all the time. He'll do anything she wants, right? She's even got him signed up for being an extra in the opera, Peter says like he can't believe how Ursula does it. Dom needs boys to stand behind while the girls do their dance routine, he explains. Oh it's all so romantic! I say like I'm sighing in a sexy way on some commercial. The best thing about these masks is you feel different talking to someone even when it's your own brother. It makes you think you can say whatever you want and be almost mysterious.

Later I go out to find Celia who's still sitting at the front desk though nobody's arriving by now. How come you're not in dancing, Miss Apricot Mask? I say. Well because, Miss Yellow Mask, who's going to dance with me anyways? There's all these mysterious men out there you never saw before, I tell her. Yeah like my horny brother Lucius, says Celia. I'll take over the desk, I tell her since Paul's dancing with Gwen again anyways. Celia says she doesn't want to go in there though, it makes her think of the dance last week when she didn't get anywhere with anybody.

You're changing a lot this year, Celia, I say, maybe you scared off some guys when you were being so tough-acting last year, maybe it takes a little time for them to see how you changed. I changed a lot all right, Celia tells me, I'm really losing it. So why don't I just give up? She leans over on me. Give them time, I say but that's not it I find out. See something happened once, Barbara, she's saying now, and I just didn't want to do it then, I just didn't want to do it, Barbara. Her mask is getting wet around the eyeholes. It's funny to see her crying in a mask but she leaves it on and I leave on mine too because we can talk better to each other with them maybe. Celia, Celia, I'm saying to her.

V

I should've thought something was funny when me and Paul were coming back after the fund-raiser and we hear noises in Stephen's room but then no one answered when we knocked. Then yesterday morning we were just having breakfast and there comes the landlord pounding on our door. It's Mr. Felice he wants. He says it the Italian way, Faleechee. He's your typical landlord like some small-time George Ippolito. He thinks he's got power like George too but he only owns a couple medium-size buildings. Paul's in his bathrobe and slipper socks with his black shins showing and I'm in my old bathrobe too. Paul's lips and his fingers looked all buttery from eating our crumpets. We didn't know what to do so we stood there just looking at him when we opened up.

Mr. DiNapoli says it all real quick. No sublet, no sublet, I already tell you! He's shaking his finger out at the stairs. No, Mr. DiNapoli, it was only my nephew spending a few nights what with his parents away, I try to explain real fast. Your nephew and some whore then, he says. Oh my God, I'm thinking, no wonder Stephen didn't answer the door. I throw out both of them, says Mr. DiNapoli. The old lady, nice old Greek lady down your hall, she's coming down the steps this morning, he says, and you know what she has to hear out loud under there! She call my number, I come right over, he says waving his set of keys at us, and there's some cheap Italian girl, I don't believe it, he says. I'm not calling police, only my old ladies don't like these noises, I don't like these noises, you know what I'm talking about? No sublet, never, he says, no young kids in here ever. You and Miss Orisini, you stay in your own places, okay, he says to Paul, or if you want stay together instead, you think I'm prejudiced? I don't care, you tell them you married, black, white, not my business, but no kids, no whores in my properties, you hear what I'm saying? You want to stay together, okay by me, I rent out the little room to my cousin instead, no kids! he says.

When he's gone we sit on our window seat and I don't know what to say to Paul for once. We told Stephen not to make noise, finally I say. But I'm rather glad in a way, says Paul, to know he was with someone. Not a whore though, I say but Paul thinks it was just what Mr. DiNapoli called

her, he'd call any girl that. But what can we do, Paul, now?
I wonder.

We haven't figured it out before there's another person
knocking and it's Stephen who looks like he didn't sleep
much. He comes in and slumps down on the chair and I'm
expecting him to tell us about it but he doesn't, he tells us
how he was out all night. Please tell us the truth, Stephen,
Paul says and suddenly Stephen looks at Paul like he hated
him. That's the truth! he says. We know what happened
though, Stephen, I say. You mean you saw them sneaking
out? he asks us looking afraid.

So it came out it wasn't Stephen at all but Lucius who's
just turning fourteen coming over here with that Giuseppina. I was sitting there with my mouth open and Paul too.
He brought her over from the fund-raiser and they had
some of Stephen's beer and got him to let them stay there
the night. Camilla thought Lucius was over to a friend's
and Ma thought Giuseppina was staying with Marianna
Antonelli for some reason, who knows, maybe because she
was sick. Doesn't Giuseppina know better than to mess
with just a little kid like that? I ask Stephen. Oh they been
messing with each other all week I guess, says Stephen.
Then he wonders if he could have some breakfast with us
because there's nothing in his place after Lucius and her
made sandwiches in the middle of the night.

But where were you all night? Paul asks him. It wasn't so
cold so he slept out, Stephen tells us. There's that shack
the kids built on the vacant lot up our old street. Lucius
told him he could go there since that's where him and
Giuseppina snuck out the first time. Stephen said how he
was sleeping for a while till then he heard some neighbor
kid's radio coming real late so he slipped out and took a
long walk, he said. He walked all the way through the

western end and on to the college. He was thinking maybe of finding Horst because Horst told him to come out and visit sometime and gave him his address when they were guarding me in the box. That was so great down the State House, Barbara, Stephen says, I never did something great like that ever. Sometimes I feel like I'm not doing another thing ever after that, he says. Who cares if Lucius wants to mess around in my apartment, let him, says Stephen, he can do whatever he wants.

Paul's cooking up some eggs for him and puts more crumpets in the toaster. Stephen said he found the place Horst lived but it was so early he just sat out on the porch and some other graduate student comes out for jogging and asks him what he thinks he's doing there. But he's waiting for Horst he says and when the jogger guy comes back he says how Horst always sleeps late. Well tell him Stephen Konitza was here, Stephen told him and then he figured it was safe to come back home.

The trouble is, Stephen, Mr. DiNapoli came by, I say and then I tell him what happened.

VI

Yesterday we went out for Horst's Sunday soccer game but this time just to watch and we got Stephen to go along too. Horst wanted him playing for Albania but Stephen said he was no good, he only wanted to watch. It was a bright fall day with all the leaves turned red and gold around the field. That campus probably has got more fields and trees than all the parks in Stinted Common together.

When Mikey sees me taking a seat on the grass with Paul and Stephen he forgets the game and comes running over from the other side. Mees Barbara, how come I never

see you come play with me? he says like he missed me for
months. He sits down with us and his bare knees look
cold. I tell him how some of his people moved in next to
my Ma and when I say the address he knows who it is I
mean and says how Armindo got out a while back and he's
doing all right, he's helping the refugees keep coming over
since Stinted Common is the one place they know besides
Portugal to go to. I ask why Armindo's license plate says
that word I couldn't pronounce. I spelled it out and after a
while Mikey gets it. As if I didn't think it was strange
enough there was a place called East Timor it turns out
there's also this small other place called Ocussi that was
really part of East Timor but it was over on the West Timor
side of the island. I tried looking in Pa's almanac last night
but you can hardly even find Timor and it doesn't say
anything about East or West. You think you're just learning geography and then there's a whole other bunch of
places you can't even find!

But then Mikey starts telling us what is happening over
there and Paul and Stephen and me listen like we're not
sure he's telling us for real or not. Is hundred thousand
people slaughter, Mikey says, American guns, American
guns, he says. Yes American! he says with his black eyes
looking at us like he's still seeing guns pointing right at
him. It's true America supplies the Indonesians, Paul says
to me. Yes, yes, Mikey says, hundred thousand people and
more more, he says, it is not how you could ever believe to
see slaughter, Mees Barbara. Then he holds up his hand to
me and it says like a tattoo on the brown back of his hand
FRETILIN.

I'm beginning to learn these names, like IRA and
SWAPO and now it's FRETILIN. He holds his hand
proudly at us and says: I be dead when they see thees! I

touch his hand where the tattoo is. Is it beautiful? says Mikey. Then Stephen says he wants a tattoo like that, where did Mikey get it? But I know it's something you don't just go get. It's something we don't even know what it's like to have on your hand.

We're going for ice cream after in Endicott Square with Horst and Stephen's telling him about Mikey's tattoo. There's a boy who is seeing everything in the world, says Horst, and now he comes here sweeping up in college dormitories and to play soccer with us! Such a world that never was! Horst says and shrugs his hands up in front of his face. But hey man, he says to Stephen, you come to my apartment again but next time not so early, then we go teach you how to kick a ball around.

When we finish our sundaes Stephen says this is like our reunion, you know, from when we were all taking the box over to Boston, that was so great, wasn't it, Horst? he says. But all I'm thinking to myself is how now Stephen's gone back to the project and I know William's not going to be so nice for too long. And then it's so crazy for Paul and me having two apartments now and if I'm going on to school we should move into just one by November first. If only we talked straight to DiNapoli about Stephen right off. He probably wouldn't mind a quiet kid like Stephen being there. He would've given him another chance maybe.

Last night in bed I tell Paul how much we have to save our money now and what if we moved down into his old room but Paul thinks it's worth the money to stay up in my apartment for features like the tub and the window seat I love to sit on. I want you feeling happy about all the work you're going to have to do, he says when we're propped up on all our pillows and the lights are off, just lights from traffic sometimes moving around in the dark.

But somehow I'm thinking only how bad things are in the whole world and I feel almost funny to have a window seat looking out over everything, like I was too lucky. We could save two hundred a month down under the stairs though, I tell Paul. He knows that's true and he wouldn't mind for him but he would mind for me, he says.

But I didn't do anything for almost two months now, I say, so I'm getting tired of my long soaks and sitting watching out at things. Still it's hard for us to decide. Finally I said it's what I called a sacrifice I wanted to make so's I can work very hard and not relax so much. If I'm always out working or studying it doesn't matter really to have a more expensive place, I tell him. But you love our little home up here, Paul says pulling up the spread over us to keep us warm in the night breeze. It's quiet and so light in the mornings and think of all you did to make it pretty, sweet one, he says. I try to explain it doesn't matter if only I'm with him, if I'm still with him I'm happy wherever, really, Paul, I say, it's true.

VII

Yesterday was Peter's afternoon off from Common Lumber so I knew he was at the Atherton already and I wanted to go see him. He's the one I decided to ask advice from. Catherine's got her own worries always and I know Gregory would be all for me going on to college so it's no use asking him, he'd be telling me already what courses I should sign up for and telling me books to start reading. Instead I want to find out what Peter would think.

Some other Italian cousin of Camilla's is there painting in the lobby. A whole bunch of them is over now like it's a real family operation and I began to wonder where the

Ippolitos are getting all the money to bring them over. This one doesn't know English so I'm pointing at things and asking how I can get backstage. It feels stupid I don't speak any Italian since all the people in our family that came before us kids could speak it but now that's the end of it except for what Gregory learned at Boston State.

Finally I just open the swinging door into the theater and on the stage suddenly I recognize there's Autumn Hill. It's exactly the shape of where the big rocks are back by the project which you see when you're walking out of Catherine's. There's blue light behind them like the sky but there's of course no houses on top, just those rocks, except there's a hangman's noose and what they called the stocks for putting prisoners back in colonial times. Peter Orsini! I'm calling.

His head pops up on top over the rocks. Is this suppose to be Autumn Hill or what! I yell to him. You got it, Stuffs, he yells down, isn't it dynamic! I go pull my bottom up on the stage and swing up my feet and then get up and climb back over these fake rocks up to where Peter is. Is this strong enough for me? I'm asking since it's shaky up there. Well you know who's responsible for the construction, says Peter.

Is this all for the opera? I ask and he tells me how Act Two is supposed to be on the desolate plain near Boston at the bottom of a steep cliff and Dom figured the desolate plain could've been what used to be the old clay flats in Stinted Common where the project now is. Why not! I mean this is definitely a local production, says Peter. And Dom's got the Governor's Palace to look like the original Old State House in Boston for that scene. Dom thinks it's great for publicity, you know, the authentic production, but the stupid thing is, says Peter, the only reason Verdi made it be in Boston was because they wouldn't let him have an opera about the real king of Sweden who really got killed at a masked ball. They figured if it's only the governor of Massachusetts it wasn't going to give anyone in Italy ideas, right? says Peter.

I tell him me and Paul read up on it too and I know it all backward and forward. So you been doing your homework, Camilla must be after you too, says Peter. It's funny to be sitting with my brother on rocks made to look like the edge of Autumn Hill where we actually did use to go sometimes and watch them building the project. And I'm thinking how back when Verdi put on The Masked Ball in Rome there was only those clay flats over here and the rangeways that are on that historical map and these rocks on top of Autumn Hill were bare like this and our great-great-grandparents or whatever were over there in Italy still.

Do you think I'm smart, Peter? I ask him like it's out of the blue. Well you're definitely getting smarter the longer you hang around with that black guy, he says, and you must be smart for him to like you anyways since he's so goddamn smart. I been able to tell all along Peter was feeling funny about me and Paul. I could see how it's hard for him even if he's the one who was always on me about getting a boyfriend. But he's just never knew black people much except in the service and them he didn't like.

Peter, I keep learning things, I say, and I keep wanting to learn about more things I didn't ever know before so I'm thinking I might have to go take some courses at Bunker Hill Community but that'd mean working at a doughnut shop again maybe and maybe me and Paul moving in down in his cheap room instead and I don't know what Pa would say.

I didn't think I could get it all out without Peter stopping me. But he sits there putting his elbows up on the stocks where you'd put your hands through. Hmmm, he just says. You got such a great apartment all your own, he says, why don't you just let him stay in his own place? I mean why do you really have to get so serious, Barbara? I mean he's going to go back to his island probably someday anyways.

Well but for now, I say. Well would you think it was stupid to be going on to college when I'm twenty-nine? I say. I want my kids to go so why shouldn't I want you going too? he says. Like Paul would help support you, right? he asks. I tell him Paul really wants me to go and he's going to help me out with my papers at first. When I say I didn't know how to tell Pa though, Peter says he's glad I talked to him first instead. I didn't talk to anyone else yet in the family, I tell him. So you still come to your old big brother, he says. It's because I trust you to say the truth, I say.

He doesn't say anything about that, just thinks a minute. You know it's sad, he says, to see my kids growing up already, I get the feeling it's almost all over before I even knew what was happening. But there's still Quintus and Julia got a long ways to go, I say. You just watch how fast they go, Barbara, Peter says, you just watch. Then he says, Yeah Barbara, you should go on to school, you should do anything you want, the things you do are good. It's not like Catherine not ever doing a thing for herself, you know? But you really do things for yourself like someone who likes living her life, you know? he says. And I don't mean you're not doing things for others of us because you're always doing that too, that's what's so different about you, Stuffs. I'll probably get used to Paul maybe, he says, he's different than most black guys. Ma's real upset though, you know, Peter says when he reaches his hand down off the stocks to touch my hair. She's praying about it, that's what she told me, because Pa tells her to shut up about it always. Then suddenly Peter says, But where do you get all this energy anyways?

Well look at you too, working what's like two jobs all fall, I say. Peter says it's funny how when he gets going on something he can't stop going, he gets all wrapped up in it. I never thought I'd be worrying all night about how to make something like these crazy fake rocks here, he says. Or see that gallows up there? He points to the noose that's hanging over us. I made that! says Peter.

Suddenly all the lights come on in our faces. Dammit Lucius! he yells. You're both under arrest! yells Lucius back somewhere behind those bright lights. And then I hear a girl giggling and I figure it's got to be Giuseppina. Aren't you supposed to be at school, kid? says Peter but Lucius yells back that he's cutting because he had to help Giuseppina go get some boots for her costume. Your mom's going to kill you, Peter yells back. So don't tell on me, Lucius yells. I'm already in enough trouble on my own, Peter says to me. Hey come on down here, he yells up to Lucius, you and me got work to do seeing as how you're here. Then to me he says: Another week and this opera's going to be all done and then what are we going to do, Stuffs? like he just suddenly realized it. He's bouncing down over those fake rocks to where he left his tool chest and there's Lucius walking down the aisle with Giuseppina in those supertight designers behind singing la-la-la-la-la up and down to practice her voice.

And then I wonder what it's going to be like when suddenly the curtain raises and this little Autumn Hill I'm sitting on is all made up like the steep cliff and the desolate plain, misty and dark like it says in the story of the opera. And that fat Marianna Antonelli comes out at midnight to find the poison plant growing there by the gallows that's supposed to stop her from being in love with Riccardo but instead it's Riccardo himself, that old retired guy Procopio stumbling along in the dark. And they can't help themselves being in love. It's funny to think her lover Riccardo is the governor of Massachusetts in some Italian opera.

Here comes Lucius climbing up beside me. What's up with you these days? I ask like I didn't have any idea. I'm so busy, says Lucius, or I would've been over, Barbara, but I never been so busy before. It's crazier than that survival course I did up in the wilderness, he's telling me. He's not really looking at me though. He's got a sort of smile on like he just came up to be polite but he's not calm with me anymore, I can tell. Well you get to work, Lucius, I say giving all his curls a tug like I was mad at him for a moment. Then I try working my way down those rocks so as not to fall.

VIII

Ma says we were ignoring Nonna too much with all this opera stuff going on so she gets me and Gregory to go over once on his lunch hour. Ma said I should maybe take Paul sometime too but I gave her a real look. If she's got her problems why does she start in getting me bothering Nonna like that? Gregory said it was just Ma playing games because she doesn't have enough real to worry about.

Nonna just had her lunch and she was in her usual chair by the window looking out but she was in an old yellow housedress of hers which she isn't usually. I hear you got a birthday coming up, old lady, says Gregory when he comes up behind her and gives her a careful hug. Nothing surprises Nonna, she just keeps looking out. After her last roommate died she's feeling pretty good how she keeps on lasting.

I get a couple other of those plastic chairs which remind me of high school lunch and I give Nonna a kiss on her forehead before I sit down. I hear you're coming out for your birthday over to Ma and Pa's, Gregory says. We haven't seen her out since Christmas. I know that, Nonna answers Gregory.

I don't feel like going on about things the way I usually do so I let Gregory talk. He's telling her about how Tessa and the Bartlette girls are making a puppet show for the neighborhood when Tessa got inspired by Gwen sewing costumes for the opera. And Tommy's in the fifth grade and all he does now is draw dinosaurs and he pretends he's the Brontosaurus around the house and he's got Tessa to be the Stegosaurus and they're driving him and Gwen crazy.

I'm looking at Nonna and thinking she must be the only one left who remembers when Pa was a little boy. I wish she could tell me. I start thinking of everything Pa's seen, first living as a kid in their place over Pollard Square and Nonno working long hours at the brickyards and then when Pa left school and was working there too before he went to Italy in the War. By then they were all living in the house and Ma was there with Catherine waiting for Pa to come home safe. And everything changed, Pa says about it now. The brickyards closed down and Nonno never got another job and Aunt Anna and Pa had their big fight and she went off to Arizona. Then the rest of us were coming along and Pa got working at Common Lumber in their brick and concrete department. By the time he retired

Peter was already working in floors and it was such a big company they were getting bought out by some chain for millions of dollars. I'm lucky how everything went just right for me, Pa said at his retirement dinner we gave him.

The black man who usually works nights comes over and asks Nonna if she wants to go in now to her room, it's nap time. No, she snaps at him, she doesn't want to go. Then she starts looking over her hands like there's something wrong with them. Do you see the bitterness of God? she says to us after that black man is going off down the hall. Gregory and I look at each other but don't dare to make a face. Do you see the bitterness of God? she says like she wants us to answer. What can you say but yes you see it. Then she smiles at us. She first got talking that way with her last roommate who always read from the Bible. She was some kind of Protestant and I don't know what she was doing in a Catholic home.

After Nonna's, Gregory and me got meatball subs at the corner to eat in the car on the way to drop me off. I wish Nonna could remember better, I say, because she could tell us things about the past then. Sometimes I wish she could just die, says Gregory because he doesn't think she's too happy hanging on there. But we're all sort of confused mostly, he says, sometimes I don't know where I am either.

IX

When me and Paul came into Clooney's I thought it was that same Danny standing by the mustache poster again. He looked over like he thought it was us and when he got closer I could tell for sure it was him. He said hi and wondered did we ever see Alice these days. Sometimes I see her, I said. Well could you maybe ask her to call me if you see her ever? Danny said. He didn't want to bother her really but he wanted her to be sure she knew he was there if she changed her mind. See I thought we got along real good but maybe I'm not really her type, I don't know, see she was married once and that can do funny things to you, he says and then he thanks us and wanders off back over to where there's more of a crowd. He's looking too sad for Alice ever to like him, that's one thing, and he never did grow that mustache like he was thinking of.

It's later than when we were in here before, more the time Horst likes to come. We're supposed to meet him because he told Paul at school he really had to talk to us both and it's serious. There's college students coming in by now but they hang out more in the video room. We go to our same table in the corner but this time we just order beers. Then in comes Horst dressed up in a floppy gray Irish sweater like I never saw him look.

It takes awhile to get down to what he wants to talk about which is Stephen. He came over to see Horst late after Veracini's a few nights back and he was drinking a little bottle of peppermint schnapps. He couldn't go home, he said, so Horst let him stay there on his floor. I suppose it's William again, I said but Horst didn't know much about that and I really couldn't get going again on explaining William. I get where I don't even want to think about how William can be.

So Horst was saying, That's a very lonely boy, because when I ask him what would he do in the daytimes he tells me for him there is nothing in Stinted Common, nowhere, maybe he wanted to go to an arcade but there wasn't one and if it's sunshine he goes to sit on his bench by the river but he's also doing nothing there. I wonder if even he is thinking, said Horst.

Paul was sure Stephen was so sad from losing Paul's old room we got him fixed up in. When we were there pulling the tape off the Def Leppard poster and rolling it up for Stephen he stood watching like he wasn't going to let himself cry over it. All his other things fit into his backpack. I realized for a kid who tries to look so sharp all he's got is a few clothes that he keeps washing all the time and his Members Only jacket. It's a good thing Veracini's supplies uniforms.

And he doesn't like to be a waiter, says Horst. I say I thought he did though. No and he doesn't like anything, that's all he was saying to me. Except he loves you I'm sure, Barbara, Horst tells me. But that gets me wondering why it's not their parents teenagers ever can love, why it's not William who ever could help him or Catherine he could go tell if he's sad. And even if he can't then why isn't it them that can see it and do something? They brought him into the world so they should worry more but what do they ever notice? I mean Catherine at least should notice more.

We moved Stephen back to the project that day and I made up a story so Catherine wouldn't find out about the mess with Lucius. She thought we decided we needed both places ourselves. Stephen was going to start paying them some rent so he could still feel on his own though. She tells him right off she doesn't want him coming back and hanging out with that bad crowd. Stephen says they're his friends. But you know what they been up to lately? Catherine says and apparently one kid slipped a knife into another kid's collarbone in some dumb fight they were having. They always carry knives and they're stealing radios from cars. I know those kids, they're my friends is all Stephen would say.

So it must've gone on from there and in a couple days William was back on his case I suppose and so now Stephen's just staying away. I tell you something, says Horst now leaning from his chair over to us two in the corner at Clooney's, Stephen came today again before my class when I was rushing and he had something I find strange, a black glove on one hand with knuckles of metal, I don't know what you would call it, I think it would be for fighting. Well it's to look tough anyways, I say, a lot of those project kids have a glove like that. And then he took it off, Horst goes on saying and Stephen showed him what he wrote there on his hand with ink like it was his own real tattoo. Horst leans closer to us and he looks almost afraid or like he'd cry. He wrote FRETILIN? I ask. No, says Horst, no, he wrote it for me only to know about, he wrote SWAPO instead. When Horst tells us I see gray tears squeezing out his eyes. Excuse me, he says. Then he drank from his beer a minute. You see, my friends Barbara and Paul, he says, I am afraid. Maybe I am too famous already in your Stephen's eyes.

Paul told me how you wanted to go back home to help out the people in the desert or wherever, I say but then Horst has those tears running on his cheeks where he didn't shave and he's holding onto his beard maybe to stop them. Paul and me are reaching over the tabletop to hold the thick wool on his elbows.

Thanks my friends, he says over and over. Then he looks up at me. Yes, Barbara, he says, to go home where my own people do wrong against the helpless ones. Paul's got Horst's elbow tight in his big brown hand and his lips are open like he wants to say something to make Horst feel good but he doesn't know what it is. But I must confess to you, my comrades, Horst says next blinking at us, to my shame I never was really with SWAPO, you know. I was pretending only. I wanted you to think it.

But that's all right, Horst, says Paul soft and friendly because he already figured it out anyway, and what would I know, so I'm not too surprised either.

My parents, you see, Paul and Barbara, my father, he still doesn't think about it right. The German South-West Africans, Namibians I mean, some of them aren't really so good. They go back to the Kaiser.

Horst, what people is ever so good? You are good, says Paul to him.

But Paul, I never did anything in Namibia that good, Horst says. I was only a boy there. My parents sent me to South Africa to school each year. I can speak English, you know, better than I like to do. I was very cautious down there. It's only here, my friends, where I write SWAPO on my notebooks. And I like to try to speak like my old grandfather did, my mother's father. He was doctor to the Ovambos. Horst takes his beer in his hand so I let go his elbow.

Who are the Ovambos? I ask but that's not important.

And Barbara, he says instead, who was I to talk to you about the American middle class? I'm sorry. I was making fun. But when your Stephen takes me so seriously then I have to feel ashamed.

Something was changing, he was looking different to me. Paul raised his beer glass then and said for me to raise mine too. There is no shame among friends, is there, Barbara?

No never, I say. And I think it doesn't matter that

Stephen still thinks Horst is with SWAPO. I wouldn't want Horst to tell him the truth anyways.

But no question Mikey really was with FRETILIN, Horst said next. Now he was drying up his cheeks and his voice sounded more English like Paul's but I didn't like it. You see, I cried when I thought of that SWAPO he wrote on his hand for me, Horst said. He shook his head once and blinked the tears gone and he looked over at us all tired out.

What did you say to Stephen? Paul asked him.

I only told him it was beautiful seeing that on his hand, Horst said. I told him it was something private between just us, I shook him by his hand very firm, you know, and I said with my grandfather's accent strong as could be that we were brothers now.

Horst, I told him, please keep talking in your accent to us, I miss accents now I don't work at the Center, I love hearing you talk your own way.

But my friend, he says. Then he touches my elbow right inside where it tickles and his fingers feel hot so I get goose bumps up my arm. He is a beautiful sad boy, he says. What if he wants to run away to me? Barbara, I cannot be father to him. I cannot be brother. I cannot really be brother. I fail when I would like to take care. I only pretend I could do it. And then, you see, Barbara, I run far, I run halfway around the world.

X

Camilla did take in some last-minute cousins so all her kids had to double up. Lucius kept saying he'd sleep at Grandma's but I think Camilla knows she's got to watch him now and she might even have some idea what's going on because I catch her looking at him funny.

Going over with her to see rehearsals I never seen such a crazy bunch of people. Dom was taking a fit because they had to find some new baritone since the cousin that was supposed to be Renato turned out to sing terrible so instead they put him in the chorus. Mr. Allison from Stinted Common High was in there being conductor but he sure couldn't use too much of his marching band because even the good ones sounded a little off compared to the cassette Paul bought. The Ippolitos are coming through with money though and making headlines in the Commoner about their generous gifts so they're hiring music students from colleges to fill in. Then Wilba Suggs said she had a friend she knows in New York who was Renato once so they fly him up in time for the dress rehearsal and he's a little short Puerto Rican named Tranquilino something. It fits because Renato's supposed to be a Creole in the story. But he sure looked small for Marianna Antonelli's husband when I finally saw him rehearsing that desolate plain scene.

Julia was my helper for setting up refreshments. She was going to bring a whole bunch of her bottle birds for decoration but Dom told her they'd look too cheap. Instead he's got bouquets for all over the lobby. Before the dress rehearsal Julia was crabbing around about Dom and I heard her say a few bad words but just to herself. Where'd you learn that talk, Julia? I asked. Well excuse my language, she says fussing with the plastic cups she's organizing on trays. It's a good thing it's just her with me back there, anybody bigger wouldn't give us much room.

We can hear them doing the witch scene in there and I'm humming to the parts I know best. I'm wishing Paul would get over from the library soon. Colonial-type people keep running around the lobby looking like when the Stinted Common Historical Society turns out to see Paul Revere's Ride up Milk Street on Patriot's Day. But we stick to our organizing so as to be able to go in soon and watch the dress rehearsal. Do you think Ryan's cute? Julia wants to know. He's cute enough, I say. Did you see him in his costume in there? she says. I didn't but she says he looks real sexy and he knows it too. So now you're showing interest in boys, I say. Not boys my age please, Barbara, Julia says like she's disgusted. You know how one of them'd look in those tights? Like toothpicks! she says. So I tell her I definitely like a little meat on the bones too and she goes to grab behind my knees but it's too cramped in behind there for us to wrestle our usual way so I try holding her tight till she says let go.

It's Act Two by the time we get up to the balcony and Marianna Antonelli is floating around on the stage like a lost balloon. Too much mist! More moon! Dom is yelling and Mr. Allison's yelling all the time at the instrument players so I don't know how Marianna keeps on singing. Just after Procopio pops his head up over the fake Autumn Hill I see Paul standing back under the exit light looking for us. When I wave he sneaks down in the dark to us and Julia hops to my other side so he doesn't land on her. You got here for our favorite part, I tell Paul which of course is the love song. It's not like in Utopia Limited where they sing that Sweet and Low song. These Italian operas they blast it out like there's nobody around for miles. Imagine being on the old clay flats in seventeen whatever at midnight when you're governor of Massachusetts and you're singing away about being so radiant with love there's no need for the dawn to ever come!

Old Procopio really gives it a go and of course Marianna Antonelli is her usual fabulous. I'm thinking, holding onto Paul, how there's nothing like this, hearing these two fat people up there singing at the same time as each other. I don't really notice they're fat now. I don't notice it's crazy they're standing supposably right where my own sister lives now in the project. All I think is how sometimes love really is radiant like that, like in their singing.

Then her husband gets there, that little Tranquilino friend of Wilba Suggs, but he sings with a macho low voice. Renato doesn't know it's his wife there yet, he thinks he just caught his friend the governor messing around, but he's warning him about these conspirators hiding out up there. And even though I know what's going to happen next I get excited all over again. It isn't like when I heard Marianna Antonelli singing in her concert. I might've liked those Willow Songs more if she was in some long cape out in the mist and something big was going to happen any minute.

So then the governor escapes and Renato's taking this woman back to Boston but then the conspirators pull her hood off and it's his wife Renato finds out! She's practically going crazy singing Pietà! Pietà! but now we know who's joining up for the assassination plot, namely Renato—and that was when I started thinking somehow about Stephen.

Suddenly Dom's running down the aisle yelling how they have to do the whole last part over and he's screaming: Lights! Lights! I can see where Lucius is jumping around back in the booth they showed the movies out of when it was the old Atherton but somebody's telling him what to do in there luckily, he's just the apprentice still. By now Julia's had it with too much opera so Paul gives her money to go across for ice cream. All she could figure from that last scene was that the little guy was supposed to be the fat lady's son and she was taking him home because he got lost in all that fog.

Then I told Paul what I just thought, that maybe Stephen might get an idea from all this conspiracy stuff. Paul doesn't get what I'm talking about. But it was in the Commoner today how the governor's coming for opening night, I tell Paul, I mean our governor now, you know, that offered me my job back? I assure you, Barbara, Paul said, Stephen's not likely to pay attention to the plot even if they manage to coax him in here. But Camilla made Catherine buy three tickets off her so that's her and William and Stephen, I say. Well but what are you imagining, sweet one? says Paul.

I didn't know what exactly. I started thinking of what Stephen wrote on his hand and how Paul said he stood there like my private guard when that jerk of a governor talked to me in the box. I can't explain it though, I told Paul. Barbara, he said, sometimes you have such an operatic imagination. I thought Paul was sounding a little too snooty saying that. What did he mean I wanted to know. Well but it's only an opera, Barbara, he said. But Paul, you were in Utopia Limited being the Public Exploder and was that only an opera? I mean it was anti-imperialist and anticapitalist and all what you said. And so maybe The Masked Ball is not so serious as a story but I just think it's stupid the governor's coming to see how the very same governor back then as he is right now gets stabbed to death in some opera. I mean there really are terrorists and like you said they're not cowards, how else can they fight for themselves when people take their land away or whatever? Just because Horst was pretending doesn't mean Mikey isn't really one of them.

Barbara, Barbara, Paul says, I only said no one, least of all Stephen, is likely to get ideas from this opera about, well about what, assassinating the governor? Maybe Paul was chuckling but I still felt mad at him like that time in the car back from Concord. That's not how I mean it, Paul, I say. Then he looks at me like he shouldn't be laughing because he sees I'm aggravated and so he tries to stop. Well what then? he says more serious.

So I say, I mean if it was me that was the governor I'd be afraid there's people out there that are pretty mad at me lately. But Barbara, Paul says, I'm beginning to think you'd actually like to see the poor man stabbed! Poor man! I say. What kind of poor man is that! He probably thinks if you start off being some poor immigrant like him from somewhere you should end up governor! But that's hardly the point, says Paul and I can tell now he's getting aggravated at me. Somebody downstairs yells: Quiet in the house! Dom's jumping all over the stage telling people what to do and Mr. Allison's making the orchestra players play this same part over and over and over.

So I whisper to Paul how he shouldn't keep telling me about these political things like they happen somewhere else in the world and I'm getting tired of him acting like it's only some game he's studying up on. I never said it's a game, he whispers back. Well you and that governor, you're all getting along just fine and smiling too, I say. You think you're so smart, Paul. Well what if someone isn't so smart and never got a fellowship at a fancy college and their father wasn't a minister and what if someone's let's say always getting sick a lot or maybe got hit when they were a kid or they're some poor immigrant who doesn't speak English? Sweet one, sweet one, Paul's saying, let's go get some ice cream with Julia, we're arguing about nothing, I'm in complete agreement with you, it's just that we're not about to be planning a private plot against the governor of Massachusetts and you know Stephen isn't either and neither is Mikey or anyone else I fear. Well maybe I'd like to, I say, sometimes I really would, like when all I saw was that back of his walking off like I really got him a little scared. And he thinks he can just walk in here!

I don't feel like budging but Paul's getting up and then leaning over to me and saying come on. Looking up at him, he's losing patience I can see. Just after we were holding onto each other for that whole love song! Mr. Allison starts yelling down there and Dom yells again once and off go the lights. So I decide I'll get up and follow Paul but I don't say anything to him going down the stairs from the balcony. What I'm thinking is I didn't realize I wanted to see somebody get hurt, I mean killed even, not someone I loved of course but still someone, someone who thought he was such a big cheese. Maybe it was really the opera like Paul said getting me so excited with all that music but still I felt it.

Out under the marquee there's the posters from the high school poster contest. Stinted Common Grand Opera Gala Opening, they say, A Masked Ball by Verdi starring Marianna Antonelli in her American Stage Debut. I like best the poster that shows the page boy reaching out to you with the invitation to the ball but he looks more like it's Ryan in his costume than that fresh little Giuseppina with her hips. I catch Paul looking off across the street. Ah the real world, he says.

XI

When Paul came back from his teaching to our dark little place under the stairs that now we're squeezed into I was studying through the words for The Masked Ball that came with the cassette. You could almost learn some Italian that way looking at the two sides. I showed Paul what line I liked best which came right at the start where Riccardo the governor says on the English side of the page: That power has no beauty which cannot dry its subjects' tears. I would never understand words like that before I knew Paul. It's like the kind of sentences he talks too but when you hear them enough you get to understanding them easier. When I think of all the vocabulary I learned when we were studying Utopia Limited it was an education in itself. I think sometimes if I could understand every word in one book that would be enough to live on for a while.

Read it in Italian to me, says Paul. You'd have to get Gregory to, I say but I try anyways even though it comes out sounding more like it's English: Bello il poter non è che de' soggetti le lacrime non terge. You can tell it goes in a different order in Italian, like you can tell bello means beauty and poter means power probably, so it goes: Beauty that power has no or whatever. If I was still writing my sayings that would be the first one I wrote, I tell Paul, I'd memorize it or copy it down so I'd get it right.

But why don't you? Paul says. For one thing I don't wait at bus stops too often with no job now, I say. Ah but when you start at the doughnut shop, he says, then I shall expect a fresh set of Barbarisms. Now what is he getting on me about I'd like to know. He's acting so pleased with himself because he thought up something clever. You've heard of

Barbarians, he says. Yeah and I heard of Barbarism too so don't think you're so smart. We were back to being friendly after our fight at the rehearsal.

There we were, sitting like when we had our first dinner together and Paul had his legs crossed and I was looking at that patch of his skin above his black sock. Now I know the patches of all his skin. I know them like they were mine. Sometimes I don't even have to notice if he's wearing anything at all or if I am either. Back when all I thought was of Clint Eastwood I would never think there could be a naked man around I wouldn't be looking at. And what else is how I never did think you don't have to be making love each night, that maybe you didn't even want to sometimes. But then other times you don't know why but you really suddenly do. And so what if it isn't always the greatest. It's different being with each other all the time for months now. We're getting used to our ways. If Ma and Pa found out how there's only one place me and Paul are living in now and my old phone number goes to this place instead I'd just tell them they don't know how it was for me all alone for those years even living home with them. And sure maybe Paul and me would get married someday but I'm not even listening if Ma starts in on what the Church thinks. And why should they be so worried about me anyways like I couldn't take care of myself. Can't they see me taking good care of myself lately? And maybe I don't know if we'll go to Paul's island ever but that's for me to worry about and I'm not worrying really somehow, I'm changing too and who knows?

Then Paul leans back and says, I told you once about Communism, now perhaps you'll tell me about Barbarism in return. Only if we get to climb in under our blankets though and just go by the light of the All-Night, I say. So we're laying there with that soft red light going on and off around us and I decide to just go ahead and tell Paul what I really think about sometimes.

There's an island, I say. Oh? he says. Somewhere, I say. Then I go on: Maybe it's an island up in the wilderness. It's where Barbarians live. They only have tall trees and moss grows over everything to make it soft. You can be naked there, it doesn't matter. Anyways, Paul, it's not like here or your island either. It's a place where you couldn't see why anyone would ever want to aggravate you. I don't know why it's like that up there but they have other things to think about. Like they love to put on operas and there's Centers to go to when you want to talk to someone who doesn't know you and you need some good advice. Everyone has accents, I tell Paul, some are like his even and the people come from all over but they don't mind. At night there's always a red glow flashing in the woods which is like the blood going through everything.

I'm really into this. And the neighborhoods aren't different, I tell Paul. They're like it is around here but without popsicle wrappers on the sidewalk or the slush cups. You wouldn't have to move somewhere else to go to a better school because who would want to have better chances than anyone else? And there's no chains buying up the companies and no one even actually owns the companies to make money off of. They're more sort of like just trees. No one has their tax deductions or their real estate. You can't hear yourself walking on moss, it's more like being in bed. And you have a box you can go into with your own secret sayings inside for you to read by yourself. And it's divided by the rangeways—

The stinted common, says Paul.

Sometimes you can read about what's happened in the

real world, I say. Oh yes, says Paul, we were there just yesterday. We're having a good time thinking about this Barbarism idea. I see Paul's eyes looking through the red flashes at me and his head's all black on the white pillows and then he opens his lips and I see the flash of red on his teeth too. He's staring. What do I look like to him? I wonder.

Who is this person I'm holding so close and loving so? says Paul. I'm not even thinking. Is it me? You, says Paul. There's some old lady over us going up the stairs slowly. I'm in some dream now. You, I say, me. It's only Paul's voice. I think I was saying some words. Bello was one. And good night. I love you. Tomorrow.

XII

Dom started by having to get up and announce it wasn't his cousin but this Tranquilino being Renato tonight. Somebody in the balcony booed but that got a laugh and then they all applauded. Julia and I were peeking in the doors but Camilla came by and said as soon as the music started we had to go get the refreshments set up for intermission. It's not going to take us an hour, Mom, says Julia but I tell her if we get it done now we can sneak in the balcony for most of the witch scene then.

Earlier it was really something with everyone all dressed up coming in. The mayor and George Ippolito and Joan too who stopped to say hi to me like somehow she thought she remembered me from somewhere, they all went by. Dom made us stand there to look official even though we weren't serving till later. Gregory goes by with Gwen and her sister Ellis that I didn't see since Gregory's wedding but she's down living with them for a while now because of marital difficulties, says Gwen, and then comes Tommy and Tessa. Hi Bronto, I said but he wasn't into that right now, he was dressed up with his collar tight making him look more pink but he looked excited about the opera even though Tessa looked like she could go to sleep and not miss a thing. How come Quintus didn't have to come? she's complaining. Oh shut up, says Celia who's head usherette.

This time Ma and Pa had just Catherine and Stephen over for dinner first. They were supposed also to have William but he was off drinking, said Catherine when she called me in a fit in the afternoon looking for where Stephen was. But I guess Stephen turned up at Ma's like he was supposed to. He had to take a night off from Veracini's for this. Catherine gives him his ticket separate and she goes in with Ma and Pa and then Stephen comes over to see me and Julia a minute. Paul's already inside saving my seat for later, I tell him. So how'd you get roped into this refreshment thing? he asks. You ever had a sister-in-law? I say. No but I had a mother, he says, otherwise you couldn't drag me here for nothing. Then he wonders if maybe Horst isn't there because he tried calling him since there was William's extra ticket he could use. I didn't think Horst was coming though. Yeah he wouldn't probably come to a thing like this, Stephen says.

Then I can't help myself telling him he might like the opera better if he just knew what it was about. A bunch of fat people spitting on each other from all I hear, he says then he realizes he said fat people to me and I can see he wishes he didn't say it. But that's just when some kid from the high school marching band lets fly in the lobby with his trumpet. It's the governor coming in.

A friend of yours? I say to Stephen but when he sees who

it is he opens his mouth and looks almost sick over at me. Who's he think he is coming here? Stephen says. There's his limo out front and reporters and cameras and the mayor's coming over to shake the governor's hand. His wife's coming in with him too, she's the one with all the good causes on TV. I'm thinking she wouldn't know a good cause from the looks of her dress and that coat she's got on probably from some fancy downtown store.

After all those cameras flashing it got even more crazy with people craning around to see the big cheeses. I couldn't really say hello to anyone I knew. Alice McKeever went by with some new guy I never saw, he was a bit graying and had on one of those beepers that went off just when he walked by. Alice, Alice, I'm saying. So you recognized me despite the new hair, she says. She's wearing it more bouffant now. Alice and me never really got to know each other outside work, I'm thinking, and I can almost tell I won't see her much from now on. Then it's Gregory's neighbors the Bartlettes going by looking duded up.

First intermission was just us putting out the trays for the champagne waiters from Dom's VFW post to come around and pass but everybody was so excited after that witch scene you'd think it was Pavarotti in there. I hate to say it but I think maybe Wilba Suggs is even better than Marianna but what do I know. It's too bad they couldn't put in another witch scene again later for her.

We couldn't see Act Two at all because for the second intermission not only was it the champagne trays but we had to get all those canapés out with the cheese spread squirted on each one fresh before the scene of Autumn Hill in the mist is over but it's almost more exciting just to hear them singing their hearts out in there like it was from far away in the night. Julia and me get Celia in on our preparing. We're going crazy with those little squirt cans of different cheese flavors. These refreshments are pretty paltry but Dom said the only way they didn't need a license for food and drink was to give it out like as part of the ticket price. It's to make it more gala, he said. Well it's better than nothing but since when did George Ippolito have trouble getting around a license?

Then after the second intermission when we get the trays put away and all the little napkins in the trash under our counter we're free. Celia and Julia figure they'll hang out with the usherettes down there in the lobby. But don't you want to see your big sister dancing? I say. Are you kidding, says Celia, that's all we see around home anyways is her flabby legs. So I go slowly alone up those stairs where I used to go when I was little and I quickly slip through the exit door so not too much light gets in.

That little Puerto Rican is singing the song Nonno used to sing. Gregory must be loving this bit. I don't think he's studied the opera though except for this one part. When it ends with that speranze d'amor line I'm thinking how long a way I came since I first heard that one. The audience is going nuts so I figure I'm not disturbing anyone when I sneak down to find Paul. I don't have to climb over anyone because he saved me a place on the aisle. I missed you, he says holding me to him like he really did miss me for two whole acts with all that music floating around in there when we should've been together.

I'm not too wild about this particular next part though. It's just where Giuseppina comes in supposably looking like a boy. It's those hips which is the part of her outfit I bet Dom likes best actually. She, I mean he, is inviting that Puerto Rican Renato to the masked ball. Paul said they never would've really had masked balls in Boston back then because they were all Puritans but what did Verdi know and who cares anyway. Like Gregory said it's the drama that counts.

Then comes Procopio's song and I can tell his voice is just about going to make it and luckily the other performance isn't till Sunday so he can rest up. But of course everyone loves him around here from him singing at their weddings and in the old days at some nightclub that burned down in Pollard Square so they're whistling and stomping as usual when he's done.

Then right away comes all the dancing. It's just a bunch of kids from the high school dance class but there's Ursula hopping around and I think that's Ryan but I can't really tell. Everyone's crashing around all over the stage because all the chorus is hopping too and singing at the same time. I keep looking for Annie Randall but you can't tell who anyone is because they all have their masks on. I'm sure Annie's having fun, I whisper to Paul. And in this part you can tell Giuseppina really knows how cute she's being. She's singing her little song about how she's not going to tell Renato which one's the governor. I can't really figure out why they have her in this opera, for sort of a little cuteness I guess. This is Lucius's big part though. He was explaining how he uses the follow spot on her and they had to practice it over and over together to get it perfect. I bet you practiced over and over, I said and I think he got what I meant because he looked at me like he didn't dare say anything more. Why should I be mad at him for being with that little Giuseppina? I'm wondering.

Then it gets totally confused. Dom said they planned all the moves out but it just looked like a bunch of people smashing around the stage. There's dancers and there's the assassins and Marianna Antonelli is bulldozing around and flinging herself at Procopio singing Addio, addio because he wants her to go back to England where she came from. Well here's my good-bye! is what her husband sings when he jumps out of all those people to stab the governor. That Tranquilino at first couldn't find where to jump out from but you could hardly miss Marianna Antonelli so pretty soon he finds the governor and then they all just sing awhile when he gets stabbed till he finally dies after he goes: Addio, America!

What's the real governor thinking right now? I'd like to know. He's right down there and it's like he just saw himself get killed. Knowing him he's probably grinning.

Paul and me clap along like crazy even though somehow it was all better when you just saw them practicing and you could imagine how it would finally be. Maybe the big-time opera over in Boston would give you a better idea because a lot of times it didn't really sound half as good as on the tinny cassette. But there was times like at the dress rehearsal when they sang about love being so radiant when I didn't mind anything that went wrong, it was all as beautiful as I could have ever imagined at least for a few minutes.

The curtain keeps going up and down and they keep waltzing out on the stage holding hands and bowing and Mr. Allison pops up there with them hugging everyone and they're bringing flowers to Marianna. And there's Annie Randall with her mask off in the chorus, I finally see her. She's going hysterical, I'm thinking, she looks so happy down there with her eyes almost popping out. I'm glad I don't have to hear about it from her over and over at the Center though. She'd never shut up about it.

Paul wants to stay and keep clapping but I think we

should maybe get out before it's too jammed. I don't really like being in crowds. And I'm feeling strange. All that dancing and singing and hopping around made me dizzy, I feel like I might tip over. So we get down to the lobby where people are just starting to come out from the downstairs and the usherettes are holding open the doors. Stephen left before it was over, Celia whispers at me. Paul puts his hand on my elbow and says, Now don't imagine he went to assassinate the governor, sweet one, so I give him my aggravated look.

But when we step out under the marquee and pass the governor's limo sitting there I grabbed Paul's elbow back and pointed to the rear window. It said: SWAPO GONNA GETCHA written with that cheese spread squirted out of a can. Stephen must've found one behind our counter on his way out.

And there's my old high school pal Larry Walsh running back from down the street. I almost caught that little punk, he says. Let's get some wet paper towels from the ice cream place and get it off before someone important comes out. What is it anyways? he asks me. I act like I wouldn't have any idea what SWAPO meant.

XIII

Yesterday I felt relieved when we woke up and it was all over. I think I went a little crazy during that opera myself too. Paul and me even were laughing during our breakfast but then it wasn't funny when Stephen got there. He was first peeking in at our window at us there in his old room. Paul went to let him in. Stephen had an empty peppermint schnapps bottle in his hand with the glove Horst told us about and he walks in like he's almost asleep or frozen and goes over to the window right away and closes the shade again. Don't want DiNapoli seeing me, he says. I go to touch him and his cheek feels very cold. Were you out all night? I ask.

I was down the project with my friends, he says. How could you stand something like that stupid opera, Barbara? he says looking at me in a tired way. Well at least I could sleep in there, he says. We enjoyed your message to the governor, Paul says trying to keep Stephen from acting worse. You mean the cheese? he says. He bet the governor loved it too so we didn't tell him Larry got it wiped off before the governor came out. Larry was assigned for duty outside the theater and it's not the kind of event he needed for his promotion.

How about some breakfast, Stephen? says Paul. That usually gets him but not then. He didn't feel like eating, he said. Well then let's sit and talk, says Paul. Stephen looks at him like he thinks Paul's kidding. But Paul says it again in a way I never hear Paul sound, low and slow, and he gets Stephen to take off his Members Only jacket and to sit on the edge of the bed under the stairs. Paul pulls the wooden chair up and I settle into the Danish-style one. We're both still in our bathrobes looking like the Saturday morning lazies the way we like to.

Your Aunt Barbara was talking about you in her sleep last night, says Paul. I look at Paul wondering what he's talking about. I couldn't sleep yet myself so I lay awake under these stairs, he says, listening carefully for late footsteps. Remember those footsteps you'd sometimes hear, Stephen? Paul asks him. Stephen's looking at Paul like he hypnotized him or else he's just falling asleep anyway, sitting up and staring. And then Stephen, says Paul, my dear Barbara here started saying things from her sleep. You didn't tell me that, I say. You often say things at night, he tells me. Now you tell me! I say. Well he never told me because they're my secret sleep words to him, he says, that only he gets to hear, that I don't even know about. That's why I treasure them so, he says. But so what did I say, Paul? I say all curious but Paul puts out his hand to make me be quieter and let Stephen keep going to sleep or whatever he's doing.

Then Paul keeps going on in this way I never heard before, like almost a deep singing voice but not to any song. She said first: I want to be his mother, Paul says. Whose mother? I asked her quietly not to wake her up. Mothers don't hurt children, she said next. What children? I asked her, Paul says. Stephen, she said. And I said to her that fathers don't hurt children either, Stephen, Paul says. What is a father? your Aunt Barbara said to me then. I was thinking of what to say but then she said: You are a father. I would like to be, I said to her. I love you, Stephen, is the last thing she said, says Paul.

Now I get up and lay Stephen back on the pillows because he's sound asleep not hearing anything after all that peppermint schnapps. Was that all true? I asked Paul. Oh yes, he says. I really talked all that in my sleep? And you talked back to me like in a conversation? And I don't even remember anything? You've done it before too, Paul says, I love it when you do it.

It was funny our getting dressed together knowing Stephen was right there sleeping but we did it quick and went out for a walk. It's getting too cold for our usual long one so we just went for doughnuts and coffee then come back in and Stephen's already sitting up awake. We brought doughnuts back for him too. He's looking better except he needs a shower and shave, he looks so furry.

Me and my friends had a great time last night, he says. They didn't believe about me doing that to the governor's limo though. Oh well, you know what I'd like? Stephen asks us. A car, he says, just some car so I could go some other places sometimes. Me and my friends got a car last night, this Cutlass parked over Walnut Hill. One of my friends he's always stealing cars like just for the ride, you know? So we went to New Hampshire and knocked it into a couple trees. He was so drunk, Stephen says, and I'm just sitting laughing in the back of that Cutlass there. Then we come blasting back down here before it gets morning. We dumped it on some corner. It's easy doing something like that. The fag that owns it's sleeping right on through so what's he care till he wakes up and he's like hey, where's my car! Stephen starts laughing but we're looking at him not saying a thing. I know you don't think it's such a good idea, he says, but so? You're sure talking a lot, I say to him. When did you ever get talking so much, Stephen? You know what I want? he says next. A Trinitron TV and a VCR.

Paul is thinking very hard listening to this. Then he says, Why do you try to appall us so, Stephen? I'm not trying to appall you, he says. But you do, says Paul. What do you mean anyways? Stephen says, look, I'm just telling you about me and my friends. But we're not interested, says Paul getting up and going to open the shade again.

You could tell it to somebody who wouldn't ever tell anyone else, I decide to say. I could call Alice on Monday and make you an appointment at the East Common Center. I'm not going to see no Alice, says Stephen. You know I got your mother to go, I say. Yeah and look at her, he says. Well she thought everything was getting better so she stopped going is all, I say, but things don't get better so easy. They sure don't, says Stephen.

Paul stayed looking out the window. He was feeling too confused, he told me after. He doesn't understand how all this keeps coming back out of Stephen still. He thought Stephen was changing. What I told Paul is I seen enough people at the Center to know they don't change that much, sometimes they don't change at all except get worse.

You got today's paper yet? Stephen was asking us because he wanted to see if it had a picture of his cheese on the limo so I'm about to say we wiped it off when Paul says from the window: Your father's here. I thought he meant Pa but Stephen is getting up and looking for where he put his jacket. Then he's looking over to the window and we can see William coming up the walk. Soon as he gets in I'm going out that window, says Stephen. No you're not, says Paul. Let him, Paul, I say, we don't know what's happening. William's ringing our bell ten times in a row. I'm not letting Stephen out, we're all talking to William about this, says Paul. But not about the car ride, Paul, I say. Of course not, says Paul going to open the door now. Stephen doesn't go anywhere but he's got his jacket on and he's snapping on that glove back over his fading SWAPO that I could see when he was eating the doughnuts.

In comes William laughing. I knew I'd be finding him over here, he's saying. But when William's laughing I know it's when you have to look out most. Get over here, he says to Stephen. I'm here, Stephen says. Your mother wants you, William says like he's teasing. So? says Stephen. Actually she doesn't, William says. Paul has the door closed and stands in front of it looking soft and black to me with William there in his green work shirt with the red William above the pocket.

You weren't home last night either, Dad, Stephen says.
Well I sure wasn't at some opera, says William still in his
teasing voice. Hey Barbara, he says like he didn't see me
till now, what do you think of this kid here anyway? I hear
he's still a waiter. William rolls up his sleeves like he was
readying to fight someone. He wouldn't hit Stephen now
in front of us though, I'm thinking.

So I hear you're still a waiter, he says again. So? says
Stephen. So what're you waiting for? William says like he's
making a great joke and he starts laughing louder. When
did you ever think past tomorrow, kid? he says. Now he's
walking around our room with Stephen keeping along the
other wall from him. I go stand next to Paul by the door. I
ask William if he would maybe want some coffee but he
doesn't even really hear.

Let me tell you something, William says, you got a long
wait. He gets up close to Stephen now so he could touch
the collar of his white jacket but he just makes like he's
going to. Stephen's knuckles really do have silver studs
shining on them. Get off me, Stephen says. You know
what, William says, your mother kicked me out again
yesterday, and he's laughing but I say suddenly: She did
not, William, she was waiting for you to come go to dinner
at Ma's, she was calling me about it. She gets on that phone
and she makes up lies about me, says William, you believe
her because she's your sister is all, maybe she really had it
all figured out herself, did you ever think of that, Barbara?
I knew William and me weren't back to friends again, I'm
thinking, despite the box and us talking at Pa's birthday.
Well you think you can trust that sister of yours, Barbara?
he says. Yeah I trust her, I say. Well I don't trust her, I didn't
trust her for a long time. Stephen, do you trust her?
William says. I don't trust you, Stephen says. Do you trust

her I'm asking you! says William. Dad, Stephen says with his lips tight.

You think I don't know you been out joyriding in some stolen car? says William then. You got a great bunch of friends, Stephen, a bunch of car thieves. They're better than you, says Stephen. Oh yeah they're great, William says edging up on him again, I'm coming in this morning to get my tools I left and they're sitting out between the buildings like it wasn't even early morning yet yelling at each other.

After last summer, William, you better not talk to Stephen like that, I say holding Paul's hand and we're both shaking. After last summer what? William says but he keeps looking at Stephen and all I see is his big green back and Stephen's mussed-up hair on the other side of him. All you know is what your lying sister told you, he says. I seen Stephen's cut-up face! I yell at him. Then he says real low do I want to see Stephen's face again? I don't even know how Ma let you back in the family, William, I say to him. Maybe she knows something you don't know, Barbara, you better watch it, William says. Our family's loyal to each other, I say, we're trying to help Catherine. Yeah I notice, William says back. It's only because Catherine wanted us to be nice to you, I say.

Hey Stephen, he says, your mother messing around with anybody when I'm gone, huh? What would I know, says Stephen. You'd know! You do know! Don't you know! William shouts. Do you know? Stephen says. There's nothing I don't know, there's nothing I don't know, don't you know that? and that's when William's got himself all worked up so as he swings back and slams Stephen's cheek and suddenly Paul can't stop jumping at him from behind and trying to wrestle him off but William doesn't really feel him there because Paul's too soft and not strong.

Stephen's lip is cut. Get off me, Dad, he's saying. William twists around and yells at Paul to get off, you fat black pig! He shoves him back toward where the bed is and Paul lands on his bottom and then I started beating on William's chest but he's got Stephen with one big fist around his skinny wrist where the black glove snaps. Stephen's trying to kick at him and William's saying, You're coming with me now up to the Heights like we said, I'm getting you out of that project and away from your mother and all that, I'm going to teach you something about working for a living, Stephen, I'm going to get you straight, you understand me! That's what I went and told your mother just now. I'm not waiting anymore. You know what she says? She says, All right let me see you do any better with him. That's what your own mother says, Stephen. What's she want you hanging around there for when she's got, well let's say it's a neighbor coming around maybe, huh? What do you know anyway, Barbara! William says turning quick on me. Now he's calming down more and I think he's feeling like he was losing something. I don't believe a thing he's saying about Catherine though, I never believe a thing he ever said. I got to get him out of there, Barbara, William says like somehow I'd maybe be on his side. Then what about Stephen's lip? I say.

William leads him over to our sink next to where Paul's standing now and he washes the blood off the cheek for Stephen. It isn't a bad cut, more like a scrape is all. We're going to go stay with my aunt, says William. I got all Stephen's things out there in the truck. You mean Catherine's really letting you take him? I ask. Paul looks all scared still just looking at William like he's a crazy person.

I told you what Catherine said, says William, she said see if you can do any better with him.

William, I say, do you remember when I used to come baby-sit Stephen in that first place you had? Then I try describing how it was for me being still just a little girl coming to see my tiny nephew over there all the time and even when William and Catherine used to fight then they always went back to hugging each other right in front of me and I thought always I should be leaving then. Well we used to really love each other, says William, we been together twenty years now. Maybe she thinks it's good getting Stephen out of the project, he says, maybe she's going to move back in with your ma. No, I say like I can't believe it could happen but that's what's happening, William says, they worked it all out. Maybe we'll even get together again when I get more money and she saved up some too, he says.

But I want to know when did all this happen. Even Stephen knew about it, it turns out, because Catherine talked it over with Ma at dinner before going to the opera, Stephen told us then. And then he got in that theater sitting with his mom and grandma and each time he kept trying to sleep Catherine was poking at him, Stephen said. And then there was all that screaming on the stage and he couldn't stand two hours of that junk, he said. But you didn't want to go off with your dad either, I say, you were hiding out. No, I want to, Stephen says, it's better living up the Heights, it really is, Barbara. And I'm not hitting him anymore, says William.

Paul says but he just did. Yeah, says William, putting his big hairy arm around Stephen's collar, but that was the last one, wasn't it, Stephen? If you say so, says Stephen. When they go it takes Paul a long time to get me calmed down and us both stopped crying for him.

XIV

I don't understand my family like I used to. Ursula and Ryan are planning on getting married after they graduate high school next spring. They're telling everyone like it's a sure thing so that makes Ma happy to have that to talk about instead of just Catherine's being so depressed around the house. What Peter and Gregory's kids think is that William's living up where he works to save money and Stephen's getting a job there too and that's why Catherine's getting finally out of the damn project and back on our street. Tommy and Tessa are used to it from Gwen's family, like her sister Ellis still visiting, so it's no big deal to them. Celia knows and Lucius knows that it's something really wrong but they're not asking and Camilla's not telling them. And Ursula's not really thinking about anything else now. Julia was asking me about it though. I wish it was you living back at Grandma's like you used to not Aunt Catherine, she says. What's the matter it being Aunt Catherine? I asked her. What fun is she? says Julia. Well it's true she's got too skinny knees to grab, I say. Yeah but also she's too sad all the time, you know, Julia said.

We were sitting on Peter's front steps in the sun. Pretty soon it was going to be winter again and you couldn't sit out long even if you get out of the wind. Are you going to like your new brother-in-law Ryan? I decide to ask her. I mean I already know you like his legs, I say. Aw shut up, Barbara, says Julia.

Quintus popped out the door then with my shoe box. I just went with Camilla and them to get winter shoes and got myself this new pair of nice boots I was wearing and they put my smelly old sneakers in that box. You want these anymore? Quintus says. He wants to try looping them. That's what the kids love doing, tying the laces together and trying to get them up over the phone wires. Any street where there's kids in Stinted Common you probably can find some sneakers looped up there.

All right, I'll donate them, I say, they're too pinchy anyways. So Julia and me sit watching Quintus after he ties the laces trying to heave them up over the phone wires. Catherine's not going to like looking out her window at my old sneakers, I say. She doesn't care, Quintus tells me. I can see the old man on the second floor over there watching out at Quintus too. He'll be looking at those sneakers of mine till he dies, I'm thinking. It takes a long time to throw them just right but Quintus finally makes it and he's cheering and whistling and stomping like it's some great accomplishment. You're lucky you didn't have a little brother, Barbara, Julia tells me.

I guess Peter's kids are turning out all right. There's not much to Ryan as far as I can tell but he was up at the Trade taking the upholstery course so that's a pretty steady thing, better than auto body because you don't have to always breathe in that paint, he said, and Ryan's sort of a clean type. There's some program they have at the Trade for getting him working for some big furniture company. It's Celia who's almost my favorite right now, I mean not more than Julia but I'm so glad seeing Celia be nice again, trying to be friends to people and help her mom even, that it feels like she's my favorite. Some guy's going to come along for her I'm sure.

Lucius has been in a crummy mood just like Peter ever since they had the second performance of the opera which did go better than the opening night really so too bad not that many people came to it. That one they didn't have refreshments for so Paul and me got to watch it all the way through together in our complimentary seats and we never stopped holding hands. I knew it so well by then it was almost like I understood Italian. Now it's over Dom's just got to deal with what they're saying in the Commoner about some misuse of city funds. One of the aldermen's on their case and Joan Ippolito's been on TV denying everything. Anyways the Boston paper said it was a production that gave a rare glimpse into a lost and more innocent operatic past, meaning I suppose the simpler way things were back in colonial times.

But after they took Giuseppina to the airport in the van, Peter and Lucius came back both looking real down. What Peter said to me that day was: It's like there was this artistic feeling in our lives for those months, you see what I mean, Barbara, but what are we going to do now, you can't keep always putting on an opera. And then he leaned in close to me and pointed after Lucius who was slumping off into the house. Or falling for twenty-year-old sopranos, Peter whispered. I look at him like I don't know how much he knows about that but then I can't help smiling to let him know I know everything.

Thank God it's over, whispers Peter, I was taking a fit that Camilla'd find out. You mean you didn't tell her? I say. Are you kidding! Peter says. Barbara, there's one thing I learned and that's you can't tell everything to the person you love. Don't you know that?

I don't know that yet, I say. And I think it depends more on who you are but I wouldn't tell Peter that. He likes being the wise big brother sometimes. How's it having Catherine next door? I asked him then. Hey come on,

Stuffs, let's go up to Totney's and talk this one over, he says.

So we lock up his van and walk up to Pa's favorite place. It's getting to be my favorite place lately too, says Peter, you got to have somewhere to get out of the house to.

I never been in there in all my years on that street except to look in the door a couple times. No one's in here usually on Saturday afternoons much till later, Peter says. Then when we get our beers he starts telling me how it was true about Catherine messing around with somebody else for a while, he doesn't know who, some out-of-work guy, but who could blame her considering how William is anyway? It wasn't that she actually told Peter. But William told Ma and Pa last summer to get them off his back and put all the blame over on Catherine. All that time without me even knowing it there was all this going on. So who told you? I ask Peter and it turns out first Ma had to tell Camilla about it because they always end up talking after the kids get off to school and Ma needed some woman she could really cry to. Then Camilla let Peter know and he let Gregory know. But why didn't anyone let me know? I'm saying. Because you're our little sister, says Peter and he didn't want me to have to know that sort of thing.

So why are you telling me now then? I say. And he says because he can tell I'm really serious with Paul. It ain't easy to say this, he says, but maybe you're getting married sooner than even you think. There you go still pushing me into it, I say. No, says Peter, believe me, I'm not pushing it, I'm trying to somehow deal with it. It's not I'm dead against it. I don't care he's black like Ma and Pa. But things can happen fast, Stuffs, and there you are, stuck with it and he's not even American.

It's funny Paul and me don't ever really talk about that

whole idea still. I mean we did a couple times but that was all. I don't know why it doesn't bother me though. I'm not afraid I'd lose him the way Ursula acts that if she doesn't get Ryan now it may be her last chance. I don't think about a last chance because I didn't have much chances anyways back when I was her age so to be with Paul seems more like the thing I didn't ever expect. I'm happy enough from it already. I think Paul thinks that too because he was a lonely overweight kid and his father was out being in the government always and he didn't even come from a large family like me. The only time he ever did something to stand out was when he was the Public Exploder. He mostly liked just to study, he says. So what's he see in someone like me that never even studied much? That's what I bet Peter was worrying over. And Paul going back to his island and taking me with him where I wouldn't know anybody. Or maybe Paul not taking me with him. I'm not rushing into getting married, I told Peter then. We'll see is all he said. Then after we finished our beers he says, Look what happened to Catherine. But I'm thinking about the opera last Sunday, about me and Paul, me and Paul.

After that performance I said let's call Horst to come meet us across the street for ice cream. I knew Horst wouldn't care about the opera but we had to tell him what happened with Stephen because he'd want to know, not just what Stephen wrote on the limo but how William came and got him. But is he unharmed? Horst said in his English-style voice because he just won't use his real accent to us anymore. We said we didn't hear anything yet and Horst kept looking now like he was a worried kid much younger than us, the way he never looked when I figured he was a terrorist, when he seemed so sweaty and always joking. I remembered then how he said Stephen was a beautiful sad boy. Americans wouldn't say it that way but it's how I feel too.

Maybe he'll be all right for a while anyways, I say but I don't believe it really. People don't change that way, at least not William. But please, Barbara, Horst says then, you must tell that nephew of yours the next time his father starts beating him that he must call for the old SWAPO Volkswagen and it will come fetch him, I promise. We will, Paul says before I have the chance. But the thing is I'm afraid Stephen would never call. He wouldn't believe in something that much.

X V

Gregory was responsible for getting Nonna into his Buick and driving her over to Ma's for the birthday. We're all there beforehand, not Stephen and of course not William, but everyone else. Something's going on next door too in the other half of the house. There was a whole bunch of little brownish kids playing on their side of the steps in the sun when Paul and me got there.

Luckily for Nonna it was one of those last days that suddenly feels like it's never going to be winter after all. But it's my last free day, I'm thinking, I'm off to Quarry Hill tomorrow early to start selling doughnuts again. At least I can go back to writing my sayings on a whole new bus stop shelter. I got the one about power has no beauty all practiced in Italian and ready to go.

Tommy and Tessa meet us at Ma's door being dinosaurs. We wouldn't know that's what they're being unless Gregory told me. It's funny the way Tommy likes playing with his little sister more and not going out back with Quintus and Lucius to throw the ball at Peter's back wall.

Gwen's sister Ellis got dragged along for the party too. She's like a not-so-talking version of Gwen but the same TV-shape glasses. All I can think of is that now our family turns out to have been just like Gwen's when it comes to who you can tell things to.

Earlier Gregory brought up Nonno's old phonograph from down the cellar and all his old records. It was his idea for a birthday surprise but I don't know if Nonna's going to go for hearing all that from the old days. Maybe she'll think it's Nonno singing not some record. I wouldn't want to do that to her but Gregory thought it was a great idea. And Ma was just telling him before he went to get Nonna that he's got to be sure and cart that thing back down after the party.

Somehow Gregory likes running parties. He made the cake and a whole thing of lasagna too even though Ma told him not to. Gwen just sits there at the table yapping at Ellis and not doing a thing to help but it's Camilla and Celia out helping Ma in the kitchen the whole time and Peter playing dinosaur with Gwen's kids. He's the Tyrannosaurus he says and he's got Julia in on it too, running away from him screaming.

Paul and I decide the best thing is to sit on the sofa with Catherine. She was flipping through the Sunday magazine looking at pictures of how to renovate your house with carpeting and paneling and whatever. Pa's got a library book he's reading in his recliner but it's on his lap now and he's just watching everybody. What's it you're reading, Mr. Orsini? Paul asks him. Oh you know me, says Pa, I have to keep reading up on what you probably know already from high school. What's that, more of your geography, Pa? I ask. Then he shows us the book which is about Southeast Asia. I'm reading up on Portuguese Timor, Pa says, when I was talking to that Armindo about the aluminum siding he said that was where they came from. I could've told you that already, I tell Pa. Then he shows us a big map in the front of the book that even has where that little chip called Ocussi is.

There's Nonna! yells Julia running in. Go out and get Lucius and Quintus in, Camilla yells to her. They're out there in back, with those new neighbor kids, Ma's saying like she's worried for them. Where's Ursula? Camilla's yelling. Paul knows when it's the whole family there the only thing really to do is stay quiet. So we're standing at the door smiling and waiting for Gregory and Peter to carry Nonna up the steps in her folding wheelchair they brought along for her. It's like a queen coming in. They get her to the front door and then roll her right in. Everyone's yelling Happy Birthday but she doesn't really know what it's about I don't think.

I was nervous mainly because this is when she would see Paul the first time. Ursula and Ryan were sitting up the top of the stairs so they come down and mostly Ma is making a big deal of introducing Ryan to Nonna so she'll know who the new member of the family's going to be. He didn't wear his earring today for once because Ursula said it was better if he didn't. My children! is about all Nonna says to them but she keeps nodding with what Ma's saying about how they're planning the wedding for next July even though it's so hot then but they're waiting to graduate first and on and on.

Gregory went right to put on an old record which no one's noticing the way he wanted so he keeps turning it up. It's not the one he played me down the cellar either but some scratchy Willow Song probably. Where's Stephen? says Nonna which I'm amazed at. Ma says he had to work.

No, his father, says Nonna. Stephen's father, Nonna? Peter says, he's working too, the rest of us are all here. When's supper? Nonna says next which gets a laugh from all the kids. They don't usually see her so they think she's being funny on purpose. Tommy starts telling her about his dinosaur project which I know he put into a notebook for her birthday present but he can't wait till he gives her the actual thing. Tessa's just leaning her little elbows on the wheelchair arm and staring up at all Nonna's wrinkles and twisting her head like she wanted to look up Nonna's nose.

Nonna can't even see Paul from where she is. Pa is coming over to kiss her and he introduces first Ellis but then he's looking around for Paul. There's someone else here you have to meet, Mamma, Pa says. Paul doesn't know if he should come over or what but Pa grabs over to his hand and makes him come up to the wheelchair. I never saw Pa touching Paul's skin except for just a quick handshake before.

Mamma, this is Paul who's Barbara's friend. He's come here to graduate school, says Pa. Who? says Nonna. Paul, Pa says. Nonna puts her shaky hands up to her face like she would suddenly cry and she says, Paolo. Paul has his hand out bowing to her and he says, Mrs. Orsini. Paolo, she just says looking at him like she knows he's not her Paolo at all but she keeps saying Paolo and shaking her hands in front of her face till Paul touches them to stop them shaking and she grabs on almost as if she was going to pull herself up for a moment. It's how sometimes the attendant gets her rearranged in her chair I think. Luckily the kids start yapping at her and Tommy's already organizing bringing the presents so we got through that one.

Lucius made Gregory turn off the record when he started playing the Masked Ball song because Lucius didn't want to be reminded I bet. After presents from all the kids, mostly decorations for her room at the home like another of Julia's bottle birds and a witch drawing Tessa made of Wilba Suggs then comes all the food laid out in the dining room and finally for dessert there was Gregory's cake that he wrote her name, Caterina, on in red icing. Hey how come there's not eighty-eight candles, Dad? says Tommy who eats about three pieces one after another. It's angel food not chocolate unfortunately.

Later Quintus says to Lucius: Hey we could go play some ball. Use them Cussi kids for fielders. Hey yeah, says Lucius. Take them up the vacant lot then, Pa says because last time Lucius and Quintus were playing catch on the street they broke Armindo's rear window of his car. His insurance covered it but that's why Peter's been telling them to be real nice to that bunch to make up for it.

The last thing Nonna did before they wheeled her out was when Ursula was kissing her cheek good-bye she touched over on Ursula's stomach like there was something in there. She probably thinks you're married already, she thinks you're already pregnant! Gwen's saying. Mom! says Tessa like she's too embarrassed. But Nonna rubs away on Ursula's stomach and I think I know why, not because she's confused but as her kind of blessing to say that's where the next of her children is coming from even if maybe she'll never see it.

Then Peter and Pa go with Gregory to take Nonna back and Lucius gets all the kids to clear out and go play ball too. Even Ryan and Ursula go and I send Paul along because he loves to be with all those kids. I say I'll be right out after I help clean up and there they go up the street with those kids from East Timor.

Well, Barbara, Gwen says sitting down in Pa's recliner, if

you don't get on the ball it looks like Ursula's going to beat you to it. Gwen always kids me about supposably being next in line for having the babies. Oh and I forgot Stephen, she says, he's older than Ursula too.

I can hear Ma and Camilla stopping the dishwater running so they don't miss this one. Let's lay off on Stephen, says Catherine on the sofa flipping through the Sunday magazine again. He's doing better up there, he's doing a lot better, she says and she puts the magazine down beside her. He's getting along with William now, when they get along I feel even almost left out around them, it's that good, believe me, Catherine says. But all I can think is when did she ever once learn something? She's not really like my big sister anymore, I'm thinking, I'm feeling older than her.

Anyways, she says, you think I could ever get Stephen to stop hanging out with those friends he has? And what am I supposed to say when he's coming home with that weird glove of his? But then Catherine looks over at me where I'm standing by the front door and she says like she planned it out to say it: Well maybe it was even better though when he had his own place.

You mean staying with Barbara, Gwen puts in from Pa's chair. She knows Ma isn't supposed to know and she's got practice keeping things like that straight in her family. No, Stephen's own place, says Catherine, you knew about that, Gwen, when he lived downstairs from Barbara and Paul. What, Catherine? Ma says coming through the dining room where Ellis is sitting at the table looking bored. Stephen was staying with Barbara then, says Ma. He had his own place downstairs, Ma, says Catherine, he had Paul's old room.

Ma's looking at me like I'm supposed to say something

now. Instead I just let myself down onto the furry brown rug. I'm keeping it in. I could almost go punch Catherine. I sit with my knees up the way I did when I was in my box and I put my elbows out on my round knees. I know why she's doing this, I'm thinking, I know, I know. Because William told Ma about her. Because she doesn't want to feel she's the only bad person. How many times am I going to have to keep making friends all over again with my own sister?

Ma was still looking at me. She knows about Paul and me anyways, I'm sure she does, she likes Paul so much now too. Last year she would've let me have it for being with him but not now. It's probably only the way she thinks she has to act, like she's full of so much worry and full of disappointment. But why should she ever have to act that way? Who's here to make her act that way? I look around. Camilla's coming in now from Ma's kitchen with her dish towel and now Ellis is turned around watching us all. Ma's leaning in the doorway to the living room with the back of her hand on her forehead and now she's not looking at me or at anything. Then Gwen gets going with: It doesn't matter these days who lives where, Ma, really it doesn't matter. It does matter, says Ma behind her hand. She's right, it does matter who lives where, I'm thinking.

It's just us women here, isn't it? I say finally. As usual cleaning up, says Camilla. And I'm still the youngest, I say. You're all mothers and I'm not. And you're my mother, I say to Ma to get her to look at me. They're all quiet and listening. And I'm not a mother now, I tell them, but maybe I'll be one and maybe not. Paul's mother died when he was little, I sometimes feel now I'm his mother, I say. But also I feel he's my father or I feel he's my brother too sometimes and I'm his sister. I'm only saying how I really

love him even if we're not from the same place, he's
everything I care about, I say. How it is for us there in our
room when we fall asleep against each other— Don't say
this to me, Barbara, Ma's saying like she's going to cry, I
can't listen to this. But I'm saying it: —when we fall asleep
against each other under the stairs, it's like a long road is
above us and old footsteps are climbing up in the darkness.
Our walls are the soft kind of red with the All-Night sign
flashing. I don't even know if I'm awake sometimes, I tell
Ma, but I feel like in our bed no one ever has the power to
hurt us there.

> *Bello il poter non è*
> *che de' soggetti*
> *le lacrime non terge.*